Memorial Day

Memorial Day

A Mick Callahan Novel

Harry Shannon

Five Star • Waterville, Maine

This novel is a work of fiction. Names, characters, places and incidents are either the product of the author's imagination, or, if real, used fictitiously.

First Edition
First Printing: May 2004

Published in 2004 in conjunction with Tekno Books and Ed Gorman.

Set in 11 pt. Plantin by Ramona Watson.

Printed in the United States on permanent paper.

Library of Congress Cataloging-in-Publication Data

Shannon, Harry.
    Memorial Day : a Mick Callahan novel / Harry Shannon.
        p. cm.
    ISBN 1-59414-199-1 (hc : alk. paper)
    1. Radio broadcasters—Fiction.   2. Children of
the rich—Fiction.   3. Psychologists—Fiction.
4. Nevada—Fiction.   I. Title.
PS3619.H355M46 2004
    813′.6—dc22   2004040394

This is for my wife Wendy,
and my daughter Paige Emerson

"All that is necessary for evil to triumph is for a good man to do nothing."

—Sir Edmund Burke

Prologue

Beverly Hills, California

"He doesn't mean to hurt me," Bonnie said. She fingered the blue swelling near her eye. "He's always sorry afterwards. He starts crying like a baby and tells me how much he loves me." Downcast eyes and flushed cheeks indicated the presence of healthy shame. Bonnie clearly knew she was rationalizing.

The young therapist didn't respond. He seemed exhausted and preoccupied. He needed a shave, and his gray Armani suit was wrinkled. Bonnie thought him better looking in person; on television his face seemed thicker, the broken nose less attractive. She blushed again, but he didn't seem to notice.

"Walt is a good man, really. He had a terrible childhood. His mother had a bunch of affairs. Could that have really messed him up?"

"It's possible," the therapist said. He spoke with a slight twang.

It was a beautiful office: thick carpeting, rows of books stacked high on polished wooden shelves, an amazing view of the city. You'd have to work long hours to afford a place like this, Bonnie thought. She'd noticed alcohol on his breath when they met at the door, but this was an emergency session and he wasn't her regular therapist. Hell, he'd probably come straight from a cocktail party. "I feel better just having talked about it," she said, brightly. "I'm okay, now. I can wait for Dr. Dorio to get back."

The therapist frowned. "I'd rather you didn't."

"Huh?"

"I said I'd rather you didn't. In fact, I think you should check into a domestic violence shelter."

"Well, if it happens again . . ."

"I mean tonight."

Bonnie sat up straight. She laughed, but the tone was a bit too shrill. "That's ridiculous," she said. "Walt has a temper, but . . ."

He cut her off with a wave of his hand. "I'm going by the book, Bonnie. The violence has been escalating recently, and you've given me no reason to think that won't continue."

"But . . ."

"But nothing. Now, let me give you some phone numbers." He scribbled on an embossed business card, slid it across the antique coffee table.

It came to rest at her fingertips. Bonnie wanted to argue. There had to be some other answer. "Hey, I probably just made it sound worse than it is. Walt says I get melodramatic."

"Put that card in your purse, Bonnie." Something feral flashed behind those dark eyes; his tone had an edge like cold, blue steel.

Bonnie obeyed instantly.

The therapist sat back in his chair as if nothing had happened. "The first number is for a shelter, and the second is an attorney. She will take you on for next to nothing. You need to get a restraining order against your boyfriend."

"That will just piss him off even more, won't it?"

"It's the only other weapon we have at our disposal. That bottom number is my private line. I'll be taping my show tonight. If you need me, the service will track me down."

"I don't know . . ."

"I'm sorry," he said. "Our time is up. I have to get to the studio."

"Oh. I love your show, by the way. You're funny."

"Thank you." His mind was already elsewhere. He stared down at the multi-colored lights of the city, then rose, took Bonnie by the elbow, and walked her to the door. He put his hand on her shoulder. *"Don't go home,"* he said, softly. *"Call the shelter."*

She smelled his breath. He had definitely been drinking. *"But I have to feed my dog!"*

"Send a friend."

"Look, you're scaring me."

"I mean to. Remember, call if you need me. I'll get right back to you."

"You promise?"

"You have my word." He glanced at the clock on the bookshelf as if growing impatient, but now she didn't want to leave.

"So I should just never speak to him again?"

"You don't have any obligation to take my advice." He led her to the hallway. *"But I hope you do. Nice meeting you."*

"You too," she said, but the solid oak door was already closing. Bonnie walked down the hall and entered the elevator thinking: *He doesn't know Walt! Screw him and his fancy fucking office building.* An old Disney song was playing on the Muzak. Bonnie punched P1.

And who was he to tell her she couldn't go home? He was half smashed, for Chrissakes. He wasn't her regular therapist. He didn't know her whole life story. Jesus, he's really just some kind of a glorified television celebrity . . .

The lobby, then the stairs. As Bonnie left the building, a light rain began to tap dance on the awning. It was dark. Icy cobwebs of fear tightened along her skin as she crossed the nearly empty parking lot, heading for her car. *But what if he's right?* she thought. *The last time Walt went crazy, he broke your jaw and sent you to the hospital.*

Maybe you do need to run, Bonnie.

9

But what if Walt agreed to try and work things out, finally go to therapy? She pulled over, opened her little red cell phone, and called the shrink. He wasn't there. She assumed he was in make-up or already rehearsing. She left a message.

Bonnie drove aimlessly for a couple of hours, then stopped at a filthy gas station, dialed the shelter, and arranged to meet someone who would take her to a safe house. She called the shrink again. She didn't feel comfortable leaving personal stuff with an answering service, so she gave just her name and cell number. She said it was important.

There was one last thing to do and she'd be free.

The tiny Maltese terrier started yipping the second he heard her pull into the driveway. Macho knew the sound of her engine. Bonnie looked carefully in every direction; got out of her car. She moved briskly up to the side door, peered inside. The living room was empty, exactly as she had left it. She stepped in, closed and latched the screen door. She gave Macho some food.

Bonnie turned the television on and began packing. The therapist's show started. He stood on a small black stage, in front of a live studio audience. He was wearing a dark jacket that complimented his hair, a silk shirt with an open collar, and cowboy boots. He opened with a brief monologue about the evening's subject: "Make no attempt to adjust your television set," he said with that slight drawl. "We now control what you will see and hear." The audience laughed. He grinned. "Seriously, ladies and gentlemen. That is the message the members of this cult received."

They cut to some footage made with a hidden camera. It showed the therapist, disguised as cult member, sitting in a state of meditation. Now Bonnie had a major crush on him. He was cute, in a rough sort of way. She watched the set out of the corner of her eye until she had a small bag and a bathroom kit packed.

Was that the back gate?

Something was outside in the night, moving.

Her heart jumped into her throat. She grabbed the regular phone but the line was dead. Bonnie fumbled through her purse for the therapist's card; dialed him again on her cell phone. She started pacing. Macho sensed something, whined.

"Did he get my messages? It's been hours, now. I really need to speak with him."

Bonnie dropped the phone in her purse. She grabbed the bags and put the dog under her arm and started for the front door. But something made another rustling noise, out in the yard. Jesus, I'm scared, she thought. Bonnie decided to call 911. She ran into the kitchen, put her purse down, and reached inside for the cell phone.

WHAAAM!

The screen door folded into a V and fell off its hinges. Walt blew through it like it wasn't there. He slapped the cell phone out of her hand and punched her in the stomach. Bonnie fell to her knees, gagging, while Macho barked and nipped at Walt's ankle. Walt kicked him across the room. He shuddered and lay still.

"Please don't hurt the dog," she mumbled.

Walt was shrieking he was fed up with her fooling around. He'd been smoking crack. He was punching the wall, throwing things, really out of his mind. When he brought his clenched fist down on the top of her skull, Bonnie saw clear, crystal fireworks. She collapsed and curled up on the kitchen floor, waiting him out. After a minute or two, she dissociated, watched from a distance; saw her flesh cringing and coloring as if this were happening somewhere else, to someone else. The pain wasn't bad; she was past all that. She was just numb, exhausted, and so in shock she found the yellow checkered pattern in the filthy linoleum fascinating.

"Bitch!"

The toe of his boot broke something deep in her chest, near her spine. Her breathing became ragged and it HURT. What if he went through with it this time? She focused on the little red cell phone lying a few inches away. She wished she had followed directions, or tried a little sooner to reach out for help. She prayed for one last chance, grabbed for the phone. She had the correct number all dialed in. She just didn't have enough strength to push "send."

Forensics said the blow that fractured her skull was the one that killed her. From all accounts, it was a mercy.

One

Three Years Later
Friday Night, 11:42 p.m.

From high on the bony ridge above it, the tiny town of Dry Wells looked like a scattered set of building blocks draped in faded khaki. During the day, harsh Nevada sunshine splintered on the corrugated tin roofs and vanished into black tar shingles. Several of the cracked, dusty windows had been taped over with tinfoil to deflect the smothering heat. It was closing in on midnight. I had been on the air live for hours and was fast approaching burnout.

Here I was, broadcasting my hard-earned wisdom to the fringes of society for chump change, loitering around booted Neanderthals with maybe twenty teeth between them and trying not to relapse on watery beer.

It was good to be home.

At the far end of town, where the high metal tower sprouted, I sat hunched over the aging console of the little radio station. I'd spent most of the night staring at a small fish tank and praying for another caller. The multi-line telephone remained silent: six hollow dice, discolored and lifeless. I leaned over the microphone, voice oozing sarcasm, playing it FM to the max.

"People of the high desert, how many chances do you get to talk to a real, live media shrink?" I repeated the telephone number for the station, stifled a yawn. "Call me, just call me. We are live this Memorial Day weekend on KNVD, the Loner McDowell show, from right here in Dry Wells, Nevada, second only to Roswell, New Mexico in purported UFO sightings. Old Loner will be back tomorrow, promising to take you seriously, whereas I know we're all nuts. I'm your guest host tonight. My name is Mick Callahan, I'm a professional therapist, and I will be right back after this brief message."

My fingers pushed the cassette in, killed the mike, and hit play before the chair squeaked backwards. So far, two redneck morons who thought lust was a sin, one housewife with a weight problem, and some couple thinking about divorce for the fourteenth time. Yuck. The commercial, a badly recorded song praising a used car dealer down Elko way, ran for over sixty seconds. Line four lit up.

"Mick Callahan."

"Hello. Is Judy there?"

"What? This is Mick Callahan, and you're on the air live."

Pause. "Who? Hey, I'm sorry. Wrong number."

Dial tone. I lowered my head to my hands and sighed. "Oh come on, folks. Stick your neck out."

Another call came. I grabbed it in a millisecond.

"You're on the air live with Mick Callahan. Please remember to keep your radio turned down."

"I think I know who you are," the man said in a reedy, western tenor.

"That's good."

"Didn't you used to be somebody?"

I rubbed my eyes. "You could say that."

"You're that black Irish kid, face like a boxer. Maybe six two, going about two-twenty and change. Navy Seals, right?"

"I washed out."

14

"That there fist fight you had on television in Denver," the caller cackled. "That was really something to see."

"I got my nose broke."

"It was great entertainment."

"It got my butt fired."

"Goddamn it," the man said, ignoring me, "you got some *quick*. You can *move* when you're pissed off."

"I appreciate your interest in my storied career, but would you mind getting to the point? Did you have a question?"

"Not really. I just enjoyed that one show, is all. Called in to say so. Most of the crap you get on the tube these days ain't up to snuff, but that was worthy of Jerry Springer."

"Thanks for sharing."

I hung up, fought back a groan. "We have a few minutes left, people," I said. "Last chance to get some sage advice from a real professional."

Seconds ticking by. "I'm patient. I can wait."

I made snoring sounds. Eventually two lines lit up; I played piano in the air above the phone, chose one, and pressed down. The other caller bailed out.

"Mick Callahan," I said. "How can I help you?" My words repeated themselves: *how can I help you?* "Please turn your radio down or there will be a time delay. Thanks."

"Hi! Hi! Am I on the air? Really? How cool!" She sounded slightly stoned. The "h" came out all round with air and wonderment. She was young and had a flat, slightly nasal accent.

"Hi back," I said. "And yes, you are on the air with Mick Callahan. What's up in your life this balmy desert evening?"

"Wow. I'm on the radio."

The sounds of a party going on behind her: heavy metal rock and drunken rebel yells. I heard cowboy boots on a

15

wooden floor, a door slamming nearby as someone else entered the room. "Can I talk about some friends of mine?" Something electronic went wrong; she kept drifting in and out as if she was using a portable phone.

"Of course."

"Me? Nothing," the girl said. She wasn't addressing me. She sounded uncomfortable.

A male voice, indecipherable.

"Ma'am?"

"Sure, honey. I'll be right there."

The stoned-sounding girl abruptly hung up the phone and left me listening to a series of clicks. *Damn!* I had to fill sixteen more minutes. "You know what, people? I feel about as popular as a Baptist preacher at a rave!"

The air conditioning *whooshed* on behind me. I played a long Chicago blues rendition of "I Heard It Through the Grapevine" to kill time. The world ground to a halt. I went live, did the station ID again.

"We have time for a few more callers," I said, and then lied: "They tell me some of you have had trouble getting through. Please excuse us, we've been having some problems with the phone system again."

Silence. I eyed the five striped fish in Loner's decorative tank, wondering idly why the one downstairs was so much larger. Wondering why the station's owner had tropical fish at all, especially in the middle of the goddamned desert.

"I have patience, I can wait. But unless you want me to break into a tap dance or some old Irish ballad, you'd better call this station soon." I gave the number again. "Hop to it."

I typed a brief command into the old computer keyboard and a recorded news summary kicked in. The digital timer announced that it was five minutes, four seconds long. I still needed nine more minutes. I began searching through CD jackets, looking for something else to play. I was starting to feel pretty desperate when I spotted a classic George Jones. All of a sudden, line one blinked. The news was still running, so I grabbed it.

"Hello, this is Mick Callahan. Can you hold on? We'll be back on the air in a minute or so."

"Not if you know what's good for you. How's it going, my man?"

"Jerry? What the hell are you doing?"

"Busting your balls," Jerry Jover said. Laughter: Was that a woman with him? Jerry sounded five beers into a six-pack. "Man, you are not exactly kicking ass tonight, are you?"

"I start out slowly, but then I tend to taper off."

"An original approach," Jerry said. "I think I'd best hold off on building that website for your fan club."

"Appears like it."

Jerry, the local computer geek, was generally alone, but another giggle definitively announced the presence of a woman. *Good for you*, I thought, miserably. *Somebody should be getting it on.* "Have a drink on my behalf."

"I'll do that."

"Maybe I'll stop by later on."

"Only if the light's on," Jerry said. "Hang in there, man. It's almost over." He cut the connection.

I watched the digital display. I'd need seven more minutes. But as the news short ran out, line one started to blink again. The caller had flawless timing. I turned in the chair. Suddenly the room seemed to grow colder and smaller and when I reached for the phone I was startled to see my hand trembling.

"You're on the air live with Mick Callahan."

17

Light static and then some ragged, feathery breathing. "Thank you," she said. It was another voice, not the hippie girl. She had the vague twang of a local; her cadence and tone were familiar. She was disguising herself, pitching her voice too high and thin. The effect was artificial.

"Thank me for what?"

"For taking my call," she said. "I didn't think I'd get through again."

Get through again? If you only knew, girl. "I remember you from last night," I said. "How can I help you?"

"I'd still rather not give my name, Mr. Callahan."

"That's okay. I'll just make up a name."

The breathing again. She seemed anxious. I heard background noise, some music and voices. If this was the same party, she was further away from it than the other caller.

She started slowly. "The truth is that I have something important to ask you about. You see, I'm in love with this guy, but he can't ever make his mind up about me."

"He can't make up his mind? Okay, I'll call you Ophelia."

"Huh?"

"Never mind," I said. "It's a pretty name. It'll do."

"Okay." She was still disguising her voice. "This man, he can be so sweet and wonderful to me, you know? Really. But then sometimes . . ."

"He can be mean?"

Shy. "Yeah. Sometimes he really scares me."

"Is he violent, Ophelia?"

"Not too often," she said, carefully. Heavy denial, then more of the same: "Nothing bad has ever happened unless he's had too much to drink or use. You know that kind of guy?"

"Trust me," I said, "I do. Has he ever hit you?"

"A little, only when I set him off, though. I can get out of hand now and then. Hey, but that's not even what bothers me."

"Oh? Then what *does* bother you?"

"He's always scamming people to get money. You know how it is."

"Just out of curiosity, how often do *you* drink or use drugs, Ophelia?"

"Me? Just once in a while, to unwind a little. I don't like to feel all out of control, not like he does."

"He likes to party?"

"Oh yeah. Too much."

"This sounds like a bad situation," I said. "I'm not going to kid you. But since we have a few minutes to go, tell me a little more about yourself. Did you grow up out here in high desert country?"

She pitched her voice even higher, as if terrified. "Yeah. On my Daddy's spread."

"He's dead, then?"

"Can we talk about something else?"

"And he used to hit you too, sometimes. Didn't he?"

Did I move too fast? Damn it. Dial tone. I clenched my teeth, then saw a light blinking and grabbed the line.

"Hello."

A man, slurring his words: "Is this the Loner McDowell show?"

"Loner will be back tomorrow. You're on the air with Mick Callahan."

"Oh. Never mind, then." He broke the connection.

I chuckled ruefully. Now the wheels were *really* coming off. A few seconds of dead air later, there was another caller. "It's me again," she said.

"Ophelia?"

"Sorry. I guess I freaked out," she said. "You're good at this."

I winced; glanced at the clock and saw three minutes remaining. I had to stretch. "Would you be comfortable talking about any other things from your childhood?" I found myself curious. Something in her tone made me sad. Then she surprised me.

"Mr. Callahan, I can't talk about myself too much. I'm putting my life in danger by calling you."

My pulse quickened, I sat forward. "Do you really mean that, Ophelia?"

"Look, I'd rather talk about this guy who can't make up his mind," she said. If we had been working together in therapy, her eyes would have begun to spill over with tears. It was time to back away.

"Okay," I said. "What about him?"

"He's just so hard to figure. I'm starting to be really afraid of him. Sometimes I think he loves me, and sometimes he acts like he hates me instead. I don't know what to think."

"Have you talked to him about it?"

"Yeah." She was sounding very childlike. "But he says it's all in my head."

"Could it be your imagination?"

"I don't think so. It's the drugs. I think I have a right to be scared. But damn, I don't like how this feels, talking to a voice on the telephone with maybe everybody listening."

"I wouldn't worry about too many people listening," I said, and pinched the bridge of my nose.

"I'm sorry?"

Two minutes to go. "Ophelia, the truth is I'm starting to wonder if we have much to talk about," I said. "If this man parties his bootie off, beats you like your Daddy did, and

20

apparently can't commit to you, then what the hell are you doing there? This is your life, not a dress rehearsal." I had one of those moments of clarity, where you can see yourself a little too clearly, and knew it was a cheap shot.

"It's not that simple," she said. Her voice trembled. "I'm really scared. Oh, I don't know why I called, because I can't really go into it. Not like this. I guess I just wanted . . . to talk to somebody."

Back down, be soothing. "We all need to talk to somebody."

The background noises were getting louder. She was walking towards a large group now. I heard voices, some distorted music, more static ebbing and flowing. Probably not a lot of Friday night parties in the Dry Wells area, so the same one as the first caller? She was on a cell phone and moving around outside, in the night.

"You seem like a smart man," Ophelia said. "I wish we could talk in person."

"I don't do private therapy any more," I said, speaking rapidly. *And you sound like you need someone a whole lot better than me.* I started to prepare another taped commercial, and the show's closing theme.

"Mr. Callahan, please . . ."

I forced myself to sound cheerful. "Well, ladies and gentlemen, it seems we're out of time. Ophelia, I would advise you to find some private therapy, perhaps a good domestic violence group, even if you have to drive all the way to Elko. As for the rest of you folks, thank you for being such a kind audience. Loner McDowell will be back tomorrow night, interviewing aliens with anal probes, psychics, astrologers, and all of those eerie men from the black helicopters. Again, my name is Mick Callahan. Good night."

I popped in the next station CD, a Loner McDowell

21

promo; dialed down the volume, and went back to line one. "Look, I owe you an apology." But Ophelia was gone. I shrugged and tried to let it go. Ignoring the uneasy feeling in my stomach, I tossed the doodles and reminders I'd scribbled to help in the event of dead air. When the promo finished, I shut down the electronics and began to lock up.

It was good to be working again. That on-the-air brawl in Denver had pretty much trashed my career, so when Loner McDowell first tried to find me I'd all but vanished. Fortunately, Jerry had run a cyber-search on Loner's behalf. He'd tracked me down and relayed the offer to return to the Dry Wells area. So now I'd finished three days of non-union work and I was still sober. That's about all I had going for me at the moment.

I trotted down the rickety stairs, past the giant fish tank in the lobby, and turned out the lights. Something about the sudden darkness made my gut clench. I fumbled for the doorknob, trying to shake an uncomfortable mixture of anxiety and remorse, and left the station.

Two

Saturday Morning, 12:16 a.m.

Outside the radio station, stars speckled the black velvet sky and the temperature began to fall. I love the desert at night, always have, so the gloomy feeling lifted a bit. I stretched and moaned. My muscles felt stiff. I had worn my old Reeboks instead of boots, hoping a long run would help me shake the blues.

I checked the laces on my shoes, rolled my shoulders, and broke into an easy jog, breathing deeply and slowly. The long road ahead unrolled like ribbon in the darkness. I calculated four miles or so to circumnavigate the town; then I'd check-in with my sponsor, grab a shower, and some sleep. I let my mind go blank for a few minutes and picked up the pace.

Falling into a steady rhythm now, regular breathing and the sound of shoes on the blacktop, the town silent and shadowy as I passed by. My thoughts began to turn bleak. *A few hundred bucks and a bed for a crappy job like this and worse yet, I need the money.* I was a cliché. I'd succumbed to all the usual temptations: manipulative women, expensive drugs, and booze. Two houses had gone up my nose; an investment property in the mountains was confiscated for back taxes. And then the riches, the syndicated television show, and the slick Hollywood friends all vanished. I'd blown it.

Behind Sheriff Bass's office, up on the sidewalk. I looped around and added on two lengths of Main Street for good

23

measure, thinking I may as well shoot for five miles. I was starting to feel it now; erratic slapping of worn out shoes, hot stitch in the side. *Hurts. Getting thirsty . . .*

So now I was just another arrogant and talented guy who ended up bankrupt, friendless, and humiliated. No one returned the plaintive "let's grab a coffee sometime" telephone calls. Show business is like that when you're yesterday's news.

Run. Faster, faster . . .

I was at the bottom, back where I came from. Doing funky little towns and odd, quirky radio programs for a couple of hundred a night. After one remaining obligation in Dry Wells, to speak briefly at the holiday picnic on Monday, I'd be heading back to L.A. to try again.

On impulse, I doubled back towards the radio station. I slowed down to an easy jog, started boxing the air. The endorphins were flowing now and I was starting to feel optimistic. I trotted past the grocery and went into the alley. A motion detector kicked on one puny Halogen floodlight. I saw something odd near a large, dented trash container but only half registered what it was. I stopped, looked again. A man's naked buttocks, pointing up at the moon.

I almost laughed, thinking it was some kind of joke. Then I looked more closely. There was a lot of blood by the man's shattered head. His hands had been tied behind his back; they were swollen and dripping something thick and dark. His fingertips had been sliced away. I looked down at my feet and realized that I had almost stepped in a slowly widening, crimson pool. I swallowed and silently cursed myself for leaving footprints. I smeared them with the side of my tennis shoe and started to back away.

"Freeze."

Something cold and hard pressed the back of my head

Memorial Day

where the spine joins the brain. The gun was placed dead solid perfect for a "kill shot," in fact exactly where the dead man's skull had been penetrated. My gut clenched. I slowly put my hands up.

"Easy." My voice was hoarse and strained, understandable considering the circumstances. "Don't shoot."

"On your knees."

I was gathering information as rapidly as possible. It was a big man, pretty close to my size. He armed the gun and I recognized the shifting click of a 9-millimeter automatic. I dropped to my knees and also locked my fingers behind my head without being asked. "Sheriff Bass? It's me, Mick Callahan."

The pressure lessened. "The fuck you doing out here, boy?"

I stared at an oil stain in the dirt near my knees. I suddenly had a nasty twitch just under my right eye. "I just finished at the radio station, decided to go for a run. I was on my way back to the motel."

Another small click brought relief as Bass put the safety on. I unlocked my fingers. "Can I get up?" Bass grunted. I got slowly to my feet. I had to lean on the wall of the grocery to hide a bad case of the shakes. "What happened?"

The sheriff stayed just out of sight in the shadows, as if deep in thought. Then he put his weapon away. "I'm not sure what happened, not yet," he said. "I just found the body a minute ago."

"Who is it?"

"Don't know that either."

I looked at the body. Hands tied behind the back, fingertips sliced away; the wound to the back of the head, execution-style. "Was this a mob hit?"

"Maybe."

25

I blew out some breath. "Well, I think you can rule out suicide."

Bass chuckled without humor. The light went out, so we stood there in the dark. I couldn't see to read his face. "Callahan, we're not exactly friends, but we both know you owe me. You agree with that?"

I spoke cautiously. "Sure."

"There's no easy way to say this, so I'll come right out with it. I need a favor, and it's big. Give me some time."

"What do you mean, Sheriff?"

"I'm not asking you to lie. I just want you to keep your mouth shut for a few days. Forget what you saw here tonight. Think you can do that?"

"Sure, but . . ."

"I don't need your testimony. You didn't see anything. I'm fixing to take pictures and measure that blood splatter on the cement. I'd say the shooter took the shell with him, so ballistics will likely come up zero. Doc Langdon is on his way over to check things out. I plan on notifying the state police right after the holiday, but I need these next three days."

"I don't understand."

Bass moved and the light came back on. His face looked gaunt. "Look, I got reasons for not wanting everybody around here upset tomorrow, *good* reasons. You'll have to take my word. I need you to forget about seeing me, finding this body. Will you do that?"

I thought about having to stay around Dry Wells indefinitely, or maybe having to return to testify at a trial. I thought about the possibility of losing an interview I had scheduled for Tuesday, back in L.A. I didn't like either idea. I probably should have found the sheriff's request morally repugnant, but the truth was I didn't want any part of this mess. Besides, he had a gun and I didn't.

"What body?" I asked blandly. "I didn't see anything."

Bass patted his thick belt, and the leather squeaked. "Much obliged." He nodded. "You best go finish your run, then."

"Yes, sir." I was reluctant to turn my back, so I jogged sideways for a bit. "You sure you won't need me for anything?"

"Not a thing," Bass said. "Not a thing."

"Fine with me," I said as cheerfully as possible. "Night." I turned at the mouth of the alley and raced away. For one long block, I felt like I had a target painted right between my shoulder blades. That little spot at the back of my neck where the gun had pressed my flesh felt ice cold.

I ran faster. Finally exhausted, I rounded the last building, an abandoned service station. I crossed the rusty, unused railroad tracks and started towards the antiquated motel. I slowed to a brisk walk, bringing the pulse rate back down. My light sweat was cooler in the midnight air.

The Saddleback Motel was a horseshoe-shaped dump, the kind that labeled rooms in the hundreds when there were only eight. The wood was ragged at the edges, and the ancient paint had been pounded by sandstorms and bleached by the sun. Jerry's two-room office was up front. All the windows were dark.

I stood there in the darkness, feeling jumpy as hell, and toyed with the idea of pounding on the door to wake the kid. I felt like I needed to talk. But then I remembered he had company and decided to be kind.

Jerry had given me a so-called "suite" in the back, number 500. It consisted of a one-room kitchenette with a couch, a table, a bed, and a small bathroom. I was grateful to have it. There was a scruffy-looking old gray alley cat loitering on the porch. I pushed the vagrant away with one tennis shoe. "You picked the wrong house this time, fella," I said. "No mercy."

I entered the room, stripped off my clothing, and tried to open the back window. Stuck, as always. Irritated, I banged it open with my fist. It was still hot, but the air conditioner was too loud. I wouldn't have been able to sleep if I left it running. After a quick shower, I opened my well-worn IBM laptop, slipped in the phone cord, and booted up to check my e-mail. There were two messages. The first came from an e-mail address I didn't recognize.

Dear Mick Callahan@starlightlink.net;

A friend of yours has given us your name because he or she genuinely cares about your self-esteem. That is why you have received this FREE TEN-DAY TRIAL of our MIRACULOUS PENIS ENLARGER for only $29.95. It comes with a rock-solid (pun intended) MONEY-BACK GUARANTEE!

Jerry, you idiot. I shook my head and deleted the message. The second e-mail was from Hal Solomon. "Callahan," it read, "call me in London." A phone number followed. I grabbed a cold soda from the kitchen, used his phone card, waited out the scratchy bongs and pings. *Beep. Beep.* "Excelsior Hotel. May I help you?"

"Mr. Solomon, please. America calling."

Beep. Beep.

Hal was my AA sponsor and my rock. He was a colorful guy who had been many things in his time, including a shady investment banker, the foreign affairs advisor to a senator, and an incarcerated white-collar criminal. He had also been a serious alcoholic. Hal was now in his sixties and semi-retired, although he still owned a stake in the media conglomerate that had once employed me. Hal loved food and he loved to travel.

Beep.

"Good morning. Is that you?"

"Last time I looked."

"Just wanted to check in on you, son. What transpires in the high desert? You have completed your engagement?"

"The on-air portion."

"And it went swimmingly?"

"It went. And Jesus, Hal, you're not going to believe this." I told him about seeing the body, nearly getting shot by Sheriff Bass, and then what had been asked of me. "If I had to guess, I'd say it was some kind of a mob hit."

"Strange how the sheriff waved you off," Hal said. "He didn't want you to sign anything?"

"No, he didn't. Like I said, he wants me to keep my mouth shut for at least the next few days. Look, Bass kept me out of jail back when I was a teenager, so I'd best take him at his word. Besides, the last thing I need is to get stuck up here for another couple of weeks."

"True enough. My word, what a frightening experience."

"Funny, nothing concentrates the mind as wonderfully as the business end of a pistol. Hey, how is your trip going?"

Hal sighed dramatically. "I am a vibrant and eccentric gentleman not well-suited for retirement. In truth, I find the lack of activity soul numbing. I have also come to the sorrowful conclusion that at least one well-worn cliché is, in fact, still accurate. The English cannot cook. In fact, the local cuisine often tastes suspiciously of what you westerners mordantly refer to as road kill."

"An epicurean such as yourself must be distraught."

"I am. The dark ale in the tavern below is probably world-class, but since I've been sober since the Jurassic period, that knowledge avails me nothing. And how are your lodgings, young stallion?"

I looked around the room and forced a grin. "Hal, I will remember this night always."

"And other than the dead body in the alley, you are feeling . . . ?"

"Sober, Hal. It's good to be working."

"Repeat after me. I never had it so good."

"I never had it so good."

"You are a joy to sponsor. Seriously, how are you holding up? It must be difficult being back in that area, after so long away."

"It is. Hell, after living in cities it's downright strange to see all this open land with nothing on it. Everything is blue jeans, sweat-stains, and shit-kicker radio."

"Are you going home?"

I chewed my lip. "I'm not sure. I'd kind of like to see my mother's grave. But my uncle's ranch has been abandoned for a lot of years, now. It might be more disturbing than healing."

"I think you should go."

I changed the subject. "You know what gets to me?"

"What?"

"The smell of the sage, Hal. When I was a kid I *loved* that smell and riding bareback in the dry heat, swatting the horseflies away. Part of me always meant to come back here. You know that. I just meant to do it as a conquering hero, not as a washed-up drunk."

"You are far from washed up, Callahan. In fact, you and I can resume our drinking careers at any moment. Has your young hacker friend been behaving himself?"

I laughed. "Jerry's incorrigible, as usual. He just sent me an ad for penis enlargement. Metaphorically, he might have a point."

"Nonsense."

"I need to get back into the game, suit up and show up. The truth is I'm *scared*. I can't seem to re-engage."

"That's probably because you never were engaged in the first place," Hal said dryly. He plays rough. "You made a living exposing other people's dirty laundry, without once looking at yourself in the mirror. Sober was bound to be more difficult."

"Yeah, I know. I'm just having a rough night."

"*Oy*," Hal sobbed. "This may be the saddest story I have ever heard."

I laughed. "Screw you, old man." Then I allowed myself a moment of self-pity. "Hell, I've just screwed it all up so badly. I feel like saying . . . why me?"

"Why *not* you, Counselor?" Hal said. "What the hell is so special about you? Stop whining. You are ready. Get back into the game and resume your life."

"Okay."

"Until tomorrow, then."

"Wait a second," I said, still feeling needy. "Don't go yet, Hal. Are you off for Vienna, as planned?"

"Maybe. I may take a train to Zurich instead. You return to Los Angeles . . . when?"

"After the three-day weekend," I said. "I have two interviews next week. One job is radio, and one is at a fair-sized television station."

"Investigations again?"

"No, another talk show. But it's a good one."

"Who's the honcho?"

31

I sighed. "Unfortunately, it's that little prick Darin Young."

"Zounds."

"Yeah, but he's got clout. This may be comeback time, so cross your fingers."

"I could make a telephone call or two. Bring a bit of pressure to bear on our Mr. Young."

"Don't. Like you said, it's high time I faced up to the mess I've made."

"As you wish. Dead bodies or no, try to get some rest. Sleep well, stay sober, and be sure to meditate. Check in with me again tomorrow. Have I told you lately that you are valued?"

"You have."

"*Shalom.*"

When I sat down to meditate, my mind raced, so I read some passages from *Disorders of Personality* by Theodore Milan. It's incredibly dry and boring stuff. Then I tossed and turned for hours, trying not to think about Ophelia.

I slept poorly.

Three

Saturday Morning, 7:48 a.m.

"Seven come eleven, damn it! *Oh yeah!*"

I jumped and the mattress squeaked noisily. Loner McDowell was howling his way down Main Street. I'd heard mediocre marching band music in the distance for several minutes; the dress rehearsal for the Dry Wells Memorial Day show had begun. I'd overslept by more than an hour.

Dry Wells, now on life support, had at various times been a mining town, a railroad hub, and a trailer park for whores serving the local cattlemen. In the early twentieth century, it had boasted a population of nearly one thousand. Post World War Two, it had gradually become a wizened shell of a town with a gas station, a motel, a grocery, and a casino for drive-through traffic coming down from Utah. Now Dry Wells sported a population of 278, counting those on the nearby spreads. Most folks had moved lower down in the state, towards Elko or the Irish area of Carson City.

These days, tourists barely remembered passing through. Yet whenever an occasion warranted it, and honoring veterans on Memorial Day certainly qualified, people came back, often after several years away, to participate in the ceremonies. I remember standing in front of the grocery store with the other kids, watching the stately Memorial Day parade.

"Luck has smiled on me, I am a rich man! I have been to Sodom and Gomorrah. *Gomorrah* I see it, *Gomorrah I like it!*"

The voice was moving away, towards the park. That would definitely have to be Loner. With McDowell, everything was larger than life.

"Don't dare wager with me, fool, for I am on a hot streak and burning up. *I am the King!* Elvis *has not* left the fucking building!"

I sat up, rubbed my eyes, and prepared a speech. First, something about the joys of having been gainfully employed here; maybe a word or two about having grown up a few miles south, near Starr Valley. Then I'd take a question or two and hold forth on the wonders of modern psychology and how I got my degree and license at such a young age.

Oh, bullshit.

I did several alternating one-arm pushups and 200 stomach crunches and jumped to my feet. Cold shower: tall, howling dervish under icy needles. Then I opened the peeling, fake wood-grain kitchen cupboards to retrieve the spoon, a chipped cup festooned with Disney characters, and one small jar of generic instant coffee. I groaned. Maybe a dozen fossilized, dried brown flakes remained in half-moon clumps near the bottom. I dressed in a flash: the local uniform of a T-shirt, comfortable blue jeans, and plain cowboy boots. My short black hair would dry on its own. When I was a kid, I had fried an egg on the sidewalk on a morning just like this.

The office at the far northern end of the Saddleback Motel was open. I saw a little red scooter parked in front, heard rap music. Jerry looked after the motel, did odd jobs all over town, and had a collection of used electronics big enough to open a repair shop. As I approached the motel office, a thin girl with long, dark hair appeared in the doorway. She had a sweet face, wore blue jeans and a white blouse and a long string of red beads. She glanced my way, seemed to recognize me, and ducked her head. She walked away, arms folded and eyes on the sidewalk.

"Yo, Callahan!"

Jerry was a skinny twenty-something, with shaggy brown hair and a seemingly endless supply of dark glasses. He had taken to wearing a baseball cap backwards, a cultural trend I despise. He was playing with what appeared to be a graphic equalizer now attached to an old desktop computer. Music wailed from quad speakers. "Jerry?"

"*What?*"

"Turn it down. Who was the babe with the beads?"

"I can't hear you."

"Okay. It's none of my business or she has a boyfriend."

Jerry smiled. He sat up and turned towards me, trusting me with the bad side of his head. Jerry had a nasty, triangular burn scar that ran from the corner of his jaw and spread ever wider as it crawled to his temple. The scorched area had no hair; it ended in a straight line high on his scalp. I had never mentioned it. I think Jerry appreciated that. I crossed my arms, shook my head. "Now, please turn down that damned noise."

"Hey, I just got this thing fixed." Jerry grinned, although he complied. "And it's not noise, it's music."

"That most emphatically is not music," I said. "Randy Travis, Dixie Chicks, George Jones . . . they play *music*. That is a recording of a twelve-ton oil rig, pounding in the middle of a sorority house while an angry teenager argues with his parole officer."

"*Good morning,* Mr. Callahan. That's why everybody used to watch you on the tube." Jerry also wriggled his eyebrows a lot. It was the telltale facial twitch of an obsessive-compulsive. I wondered if he had a counting ritual.

For just a moment, I considered telling him about Sheriff Bass and the dead body, but I decided to keep my word. "By the way, thanks for that stupid e-mail."

"I thought you'd need a chuckle. I caught the entire show last night. Man, enough dead air for a prayer service."

"Then you should have called in while I was on the air, instead of during a damned news break."

"I did call," Jerry said. "You took somebody else. Some chick who blew you off after a minute or two." He adjusted his baseball cap, pushing the bill backwards. "Man, you really sucked."

"Gee, thanks."

"Well, you did. I burned a CD of the show, just in case you want to hear for yourself."

"Pass. Jerry, I need coffee. Can you help me out?"

"Sure thing." Jerry went to work with packets of synthesized creamer, pre-packaged sugar, and powdered coffee. He produced something potent and handed over a tall Styrofoam cup, the kind that doesn't decompose until entire civilizations have risen and fallen. I checked out the back room, where Jerry slept. It was packed with old computers, monitors, TV sets, and miscellaneous pieces of electronic gear. There was an open pack of condoms by the dusty futon.

"Jerry, what were you going to ask me?"

"Aw, I pulled a dirty letter out of an old *Penthouse* magazine. I was going to call you up and read it. Man, you sounded desperate. I felt guilty for helping Loner drag you back up here."

I snorted. "Maybe you should."

"I do." He whined for effect. "Fact is, I can't hardly

sleep at night. I figured I would try to spark things up for the audience. You were really awful."

"Jerry," I said, "don't start this early."

"But you're so cute when you're mad."

I went stern. "Listen, can I tell you something personal? I mean, we've become such good friends and all. So I can kind of step out of line and speak my mind to you, right?" I took a sip, waiting.

He flushed a bit. The increased blood flow darkened his burned cheek and forehead. "I . . . guess so."

"Jerry, I know this will come as a shock to you, so you'd better sit down."

The kid sat back, eyes wide. "Go ahead."

"Jerry, this is Nevada, not South Central. Put the fucking hat on forward and people will think it looks fine."

He snorted in relief. "Give me my coffee back."

"Not a chance."

"Should I tell you what's in it?"

"No. Listen, are you going to the picnic on Monday?"

His eyebrows did a jig. "Probably." He opened a drawer and pulled out a well-worn video cassette. "Hey, I got something to show you." Jerry popped the tape into the mouth of a small television set with a built-in VCR. He leaned back, swung his legs up, and slapped his booted feet on the empty metal desk.

"Don't tell me."

"I've got satellite. This ran on some pissant cable channel last night. You'll probably get a two-buck residual check next spring."

I sipped coffee. A younger me addressed the camera from somewhere along a dilapidated Sepulveda Boulevard in Panorama City, California. This Mick Callahan was wearing a cheap blue suit and sported a fake moustache. He was wearing a hidden camera and wired for sound. He walked into a crowded office of clinical psychiatry. The program switched to a tape of my experience as I filled out forms and suffered through the charade of an intake session where a mental health history was taken.

Jerry broke the spell. "This was maybe five years ago, right?"

"Six," I said. It felt like fifty.

"And you got an Emmy."

"A nomination."

We watched in silence. Within a few minutes I had coerced the portly, balding psychiatrist into suggesting an unwarranted prescription for potentially addicting anxiety medication. He also offered to file an insurance claim padded with a kickback. I pretended to agree to the terms, but then opened the office door and invited my camera crew in. And then I absolutely ripped the psychiatrist apart.

The man perspired heavily and tried to hide his features, but I produced copies of previously forged insurance documents, files we would now be turning over to the police. The papers were guaranteed to cost the man his license. The segment was theatrical, brisk, and brutal. It was dynamite television journalism. It was also ruthless and insensitive. Jerry leaned over and stopped the tape.

"That must be amazing."

"What, humiliating people?"

"Figuring out the scam, following up on leads, asking questions, and finally busting the bad guys like that. I envy you, man."

"Those were the days," I said, looking out the window. Watching the clip had made me feel empty and sad.

Jerry swung his feet back up on the desk. "You know something," he said, "some day I plan to get the hell out of here and make a name for myself. I'm going to be just like you, man, a celebrity. You believe me?"

I sipped some coffee, tore a few bits of Styrofoam away from the upper lip of the cup. "Sure, I believe you," I said. "If you can dream it, you can do it." I launched the crumpled cup through the air and into the trash basket. "Check it out," I said, "nothing but net."

"If you can dream it, you can do it. Cool. Did you just make that up?"

"I doubt it. Anyway, thanks for the caffeine."

"*De nada.* Want to grab a bite to eat after the rehearsal?"

"Sure, let's do it, but give me a couple of hours. See you, kid."

I walked the maybe quarter-mile stretch up Main Street. I saw Glen Bass, the tall, weathered sheriff. He was on the upstairs porch of his two-story office, faded boots up on the railing. We exchanged nods. I strolled by as if I'd never seen a body and last night had never happened. It was already hot, and growing hotter by the moment.

As I passed Margie's Diner, a young woman with short, dark hair peered out through a dusty pane of glass that was spider-webbed with cracks. She used one hand to shade her face as she followed me with her eyes. She pulled the curtains when I stared back.

The ragged band music from the little park grew louder and climaxed: Sousa honked by elderly amateurs. The band finished rehearsing. I stepped over the narrowest part of the shallow creek that rimmed the park, and out onto the surprisingly green grass. All around me townspeople were picnicking, roughhousing, and enjoying the sunny morning. I strolled around the half-empty, rectangular grounds past picnic tables with fading paint near small clumps of stubborn trees.

I saw two cardboard targets pinned to tall bales of hay, large concentric circles with numbers. Someone had placed signs warning people to stay clear of the contest area. Nearby sat a collection of bows; two were large aluminum Caribou Reflex, forty-six inches in length. Someone else had a dark crossbow of unfamiliar design, fully camouflaged. The last bow was an Oneida Stealth Eagle four-pounder with one hellacious pull. I stopped to watch.

The first archer was a big blonde kid who looked like he might have played defensive lineman. He was tall, beefy and handsome in a country-hick way. Two slightly scraggly-looking young groupies gave him rapt attention. One was the thin girl wearing long beads who had walked out of Jerry's motel office.

The kid took the Oneida and let fly three arrows, tipped blunt for target practice. He scored big.

"Go, Bobby, go," the girls squealed.

The next kid, a Latino, had a silly goatee, jet-black hair and eyes. Real macho, empty-faced, probably antisocial. He swept up the crossbow; squinted, and stuck out his tongue. Two out, one in. Jerry's friend, the thin, dark-haired girl in blue jeans and beads, called the boy "Mex" and giggled. He blew a raspberry.

"Oh boy, oh boy!" The last shooter was tall, about my size, lean as a pro wide receiver. He was jumping up and down and screaming obscenities, oblivious to the scowling families nearby. He had dyed blonde hair all spiked up, some body piercing, a gold earring, and a little wisp of dark chin fuzz intended to make him look dangerous. He grabbed the other Caribou bow and three arrows, saw me.

"You got a problem?"

I smiled and shook my head. "Nope." I allowed the smile

to widen, seem genuine. "No problem, just watching."

This kid had an extraordinary body, a dim intellect, and something to prove. His eyes made me think of an old Emily Dickinson poem about a man who made her feel "zero at the bone." In a blur of motion, the kid loaded the bow and aimed it right between my eyes. My vision slammed into close-up and I couldn't see anything but the wicked, barbed tip of a real hunting arrow. My stomach dropped to China and my heart stopped beating. The crowd of kids immediately fell silent and time slowed, stuttered, and ground to a complete halt. I didn't dare blink.

"Donny Boy, cool it." The big blonde jock.

Donny Boy cocked his head and looked at me the way a vulture looks at a dying animal: no animosity or emotion, just hunger. He was breathing rapidly. After a moment I came to my senses and looked away, conceding the turf.

He chuckled, turned, and fired at the target.

Donny Boy was a hell of a shot, almost as good as Bobby. He put all three in, and the wickedly barbed tips blew the target to pieces. They all began to razz the kid who lost. I walked off, head down and hands in my pockets, heading for the small makeshift stage. My pulse was thumping like an oil rig. I needed to get my mind on something else, like what I would be scheduled to do at Monday's event.

Loner McDowell, dark and muscular with a three-day stubble, was chatting with an elderly cowboy, the town vet. Doc Langdon wore a red, white, and blue striped shirt, string tie, and a big hat. He had a giant belly to match his outfit. Loner towered over him.

"Howdy, Callahan," Doc said.

"You remember me, Doc?"

"I saw you fight a few rounds when you were a kid," Doc

41

said. "Hell, even bet on you a time or two."

"You know what, old buddy?" Loner slapped my back hard enough to loosen some fillings. "I don't think we'll need you. We got a lot of ground to cover, what with the music and those fireworks out to Starr Valley Ranch that evening. Besides, our main speaker is Lowell Palmer, and he has a way of running on. You remember Palmer, right?"

I felt the blood leave my face. "Yeah, I remember him."

"Anyhow, I think we'll try and keep the show short and sweet." He peeled five hundreds from the roll he kept in his custom-fit black jeans. "Here you go, boy. Take Monday off. And thanks again." A huge laugh, another slap on the back, a sideways bear hug. "Hey, you're flush now. You want to cut some cards, double or nothing?"

"I'll just take the something I have."

"Well, I got to pay my respects to the man. I'll see you, Callahan. Good luck over to L.A." He strode away. Loner was so large and overbearing, the air seemed to be sucked out of that area of the park.

"Man," Doc drawled, without a trace of rancor. "You must feel poorly this morning. I heard you liked to up and died on the air last night."

"Thanks."

The outlaw kids, Bobby, Mex, and Donny Boy, started whooping like Apaches in some tacky western, chasing one another around with water pistols. The coterie of girls looked on, fascinated.

Loner was now kneeling by Lowell Palmer. I remembered him as a middle-aged man. Palmer was ancient now, all jowls and a shock of white hair; he looked like King Lear in a wheelchair. His son Will, standing immediately behind, was now a handsome, slender young man in a tailored suit. The two appeared to have just arrived in the brand new blue Mercedes that was parked under some trees near the creek. The car seemed out of place.

After a few moments, Loner rolled the old man over to the wooden stage, where a ramp had been provided for his benefit. He handed the microphone to Palmer, who began to rehearse a brief speech. His gravelly voice had a wheeze to it, and he popped his P sounds when he spoke.

"Welcome," Palmer intoned, to no one. "Some people say these are hard times. Right off, let me tell you I'm no pessimist. In fact, it is my considered opinion that Dry Wells is entering the dawn of an exciting new era. Despite indications to the contrary, this is a time of new economic promise and true growth for our community. We are strong, and we will survive. Why? Because we are a town with heart, founded on the fear of God and with a sincere respect for traditional family values."

Doc made a farting sound with his lips. "What a bunch of horseshit," he muttered. "Sounds like he's running for something."

"I haven't seen the Palmers in years."

"And you're as concerned about their happiness as the rest of us?"

Lowell Palmer droned on, more purple rhetoric about his deep respect for American values, Mom, and home-baked apple pie. Meanwhile, Doc said: "Way I hear it, old Will fakes things okay, but he don't exactly worship the ground his father rolls on these days."

I was not certain if that was a clever turn of phrase or a slip of the tongue. "What do you mean?"

"Just heard it said," Doc replied. "Shitfire, the old man is a tyrant, right? Still owns everything around here ain't nailed down, some things that are."

"What's Will's story?"

"Went off to college and came back worse. Been hell with the local ladies, including some of them what's married. You remember old Toby Galloway? He come home from Reno one time and found Will banging his fifteen-year-old daughter in the back of a flatbed truck, her knees all up and her toes curled. Cost Lowell an arm and a leg to keep it quiet."

"Small town. What happens when he runs out of women?"

"Oh, he'll probably move on to the livestock." Doc grinned. "You know us country bumpkins. We screw a lot, eat moon pie, and drink Nehi orange. We're not all that bright."

I was starting to like the man. "Truth is, the only Palmer I actually knew to speak of was Will's little sister. She used to follow me around. Cute little blonde girl."

Doc gave me an odd look. Lowell Palmer had finished running through his speech, so Loner McDowell rolled him back down the ramp. "See, I'm no fan of the Palmer family," I said. "The old man had a lot to do with my step-father losing his ranch a long time ago. He sprang a nasty surprise on Danny, called in a high-interest note he'd promised to hold."

"That's the way Lowell operates." Doc leaned closer. "Picture two nuns riding bicycles in Rome, on their way back to the convent. The lead one, she goes on a short cut up and down the side streets. They get to bouncing and almost fall off the bikes. Finally they get home and the other one says, 'I've never come that way.' The first one says, 'It's the cobblestones.' *Har. Har.* It's the cobblestones, see? Get it?"

"I get it." Suddenly Doc didn't seem as likeable.

"Say, Callahan, I watched you brawl when you were

44

younger. You were one ruthless fighter, especially for such a little kid. You ever do any pro fighting later on?"

I could feel my throat tighten up. "No."

"What's the matter?"

"That's not something I like to talk about, Doc. I'd rather put those days behind me."

"I guess I can understand that," Doc said, but he didn't mean a word of it. "After you left town, you were in the service, right?"

I never know how to answer that question. "For a little while. It didn't much agree with me."

"Mr. Callahan?"

I shaded my eyes, saw a young woman approaching. "Doc, please excuse me."

Doc spat on the ground. He seemed amused. "Sure, son."

One of the girls who'd been standing near the archers was approaching eagerly, almost skipping in the grass. She looked to be in her early twenties, a very pretty face shining through blonde, tousled hair. She had straight, white teeth, striking blue eyes, and a smattering of freckles on her arms. She was barefoot, and wore a white summer dress with a yellow sunflower pattern.

I walked towards her, feeling like I was being watched every step of the way. We met in the middle of the cleared area, near an empty picnic bench. Somewhere behind us, Loner was now using the microphone, pretending to welcome a non-existent crowd.

The vision said: "Hello. I wanted to meet you."

"Hello back. I'm Mick." *Idiot, the girl already called you by name.* "Do I know you?"

"Yes and no." She grinned flirtatiously. She touched my arm and whispered in that artificially high and airy voice, "I'm Ophelia."

45

Four

Her squinting eyes were full of mischief. Her pupils dilated involuntarily, as if she were attracted to me. There was a strong sense of seduction in her posture and tone, yet the behavior seemed reflexive, rather than personal. Ophelia wore a bit too much makeup, and her clothes seemed to have been carefully arranged to bare a great deal of tanned young flesh.

"I just wanted to talk face to face. I need your help."

"I was serious when I said that I don't do individual therapy any more," I said, more regretfully than I had intended. She made me feel like a dirty old man. "I'm sure you can find some help down in Elko."

She shrugged. "Elko? I live here. I'm not going anywhere." We shook hands. I enjoyed the touch of her skin. "I was kind of young the last time you saw me, Mr. Callahan. I used to follow the boys around. My name is Sandy Palmer."

I blinked and slowly inclined my head towards the long, blue Mercedes.

Sandy smiled. "That's right. I used to hang around the grocery store and be a bother. Truth be told, you're the one I had the crush on."

"*Little* Sandy?"

"Will is my half-brother, and Lowell is my Daddy. I still live on their ranch, maybe three miles out to the south."

46

"I remember you, Sandy," I said. "But what I recall is a cute little tomboy."

"I suppose I was then," she said, "not any more."

Sandy spun in a circle, flaring her skirt. She held her head at an angle and kept her eyes fixed on mine. The long blonde hair caught slivers of sunlight and stroked her cheek. I felt my heart kick and thought: *Turn your goddamned libido off, Callahan.* I kept my tone neutral and my expression kind: Shrink 101. "I'll help if I can, but don't you have anyone else to talk to, Sandy? What about your family?"

The light vanished from her eyes. "I can't trust my family," she said.

I debated, decided. "Okay, but let's keep this nice and light," I said. "It's not a good idea to do intense psychotherapy in the middle of a park with your whole damn family watching from the trees."

Sandy giggled. As we walked, she squeezed my hand. I got another physical rush. Damn, she was really something. I discreetly slipped my hand from hers, tucked in my shirt, and cleared my throat. "Tell me about yourself. I know a bit about your father and brother, but catch me up on the rest. Is your mother still alive?"

She shook her head. "She's been gone over ten years, now."

"I'm sorry. Were you close?"

"No, I guess you could say I was Daddy's girl." We sat on opposite sides of an empty picnic table. I observed her quietly. She blushed and played with her hair. An old Police lyric ran through my mind; it was a teacher pleading to a young girl: "Don't stand so close to me."

After a moment, I asked, "Sandy, do you have many girl-friends?"

"Not really, no. Mostly boys." She seemed defensive, so

I smiled to reassure her. She lowered her eyes. "I don't really know where to start."

Will Palmer had noticed his half-sister's absence. He leaned down over the wheelchair, whispered something to his father. They started waving to townspeople with frozen smiles, staring at the grass, looking everywhere but at our picnic table. Sandy Palmer continued to stare down at her folded hands.

I resisted the urge to speak. Sometimes you have to wait. I kept my face blank, but pleasant.

She looked up again. "You know much about the law?"

I hadn't visibly responded to the seductive quality, so it vanished. Now she was just a little girl. I answered carefully. "The law? Not much, actually. Just what I have to know."

"Oh."

Too much space followed. I was losing her, so I risked a probe. "Which law did you have in mind, Sandy? And who broke it?"

Pause. "I can't answer that," she sighed. "I wish I could."

"Okay. If you could answer, what would your answer be?"

A Frisbee sailed behind her and landed near the bench. Two boys tussled for it and then ran off again. Sandy became a bit less regressed, more like a teenager. I thought for a moment and then rephrased the intervention. "What kind of question *can* you answer, then?"

"I'm not sure."

"Let's play a game. Can you finish a sentence for me?"

"I guess."

"What's got me upset is . . . ?"

"What's got me upset is my boyfriend and his drug

problem. I want to do something about it."

"I see. I can certainly understand how that is upsetting."

"I have to make him stop."

"*You* have to make him stop?"

"Yes."

"I see," I said, gently. "Well, let me ask you something. What makes you think you're that powerful?"

I knew instantly that her observing ego wasn't strong enough. She had no answer. My technique was confusing; it had closed her down. "I apologize, Sandy," I said, meaning it. "That didn't come out right."

"Hey," she said after a time, "maybe this was all a mistake."

"How can I help you if you can't trust me?"

"Maybe you *can't* help me."

"Maybe I can't," I said, honestly. "Believe me, it wouldn't be the first time."

Sensing my compassion, her face drained of light. She regressed again; became someone very young. "Secrets hurt," she said in a small, forlorn voice.

"I know." I took a calculated risk and touched her hand. "That's why we all need to talk to somebody. Sandy, on the air last night you said you thought your life was in danger. Were you serious?"

"Yes," Sandy sighed. My touch seemed to melt her resistance. "He'll probably kill me, but I really need to tell somebody. And I do trust you, Mr. Callahan."

Suddenly I wasn't sure I really wanted to hear this. "I'm listening."

"Here it is," she said, the words rushing out: "I just found out that he's been doing something bad. More than partying, I mean *really* bad."

"Doing what?"

"He's . . ."

49

A male voice, scratchy baritone: "You're like a case of the crabs, aren't you, dude? You just won't go away."

I turned. The big, blonde football jock stood behind us. Mr. Spiked Hair and Chin Fuzz, who'd pointed the bow at me, had come along for the ride.

"Damn you, Bobby Sewell," Sandy said. "You and Donny Boy leave me alone, okay? Stop bothering me."

"Sure, Sandy." The big one grinned. Said: "I'm gonna bother this here big shot, instead."

"Yeah," said Donny. "Big shot." He giggled.

They had left their weapons behind, but there were two of them, both younger than me. Bobby Sewell might give me some real problems if he got in close. Donny Boy looked lean and slippery, and his eyes were slits. He was amped up, really soaring. This was a bad situation.

"Let it go, boys," I said.

"I would," Bobby said, "but seeing as how you're talking to my girlfriend, and seeing that Donny Boy has taken an active dislike to you . . ."

I slid my legs around, outside the bench. My lower stomach went cold with adrenaline. I rose to my feet and Donny Boy got more excited, like a big, angry dog. He started saying, *oh boy, oh boy* under his breath. Sandy tried to get between us, but Bobby swept her aside.

"Damn you, Bobby. He's just an old friend who used to live here."

Bobby: "Come on. Let's take a walk."

"I don't want any trouble," I said.

"Buddy, you've got you some."

I would take Sewell first, because Donny Boy was a real nightmare. I thought, *you'd best break his nose to blind him, maybe punch him hard in the throat,* without even recognizing the voice of my stepfather, Danny Bell. *Stay calm and just take them one at a time.* I didn't want to fight; *I don't want to, Daddy Danny.* I breathed in and out a couple of times, slow and easy. I smiled, nodded pleasantly, my eyes locked on Bobby's. The eyes always tell you what's coming.

"You sure we can't talk this over?"

"Not a prayer." His eyes were roaming over me and seemed to settle on my midsection. He would try to work my body first.

"Okay, then." I let my knees go loose.

Suddenly, way off behind Bobby, I saw Sheriff Bass spot the problem. He started to jog our way. There was a way out, so I took it. I eased back on the throttle and tried to stall. It was difficult, but I made myself shrug and appear to relax. "Wait one, Bobby. Your girl and I, we were just making conversation."

"He's not my boyfriend any more," Sandy sounded like a different person now, more like the girl I'd first heard call in on the show. "He's my *ex*-fucking-boyfriend."

Bobby squinted at me, eyes cool and taking measure. "Actually, we're still negotiating on that."

"We are not."

"Goodbye, Sandy," I said, evenly. "It was good seeing you again. Please do whatever you have to do to take care of yourself."

"Who the fuck do you think you are?" Bobby Sewell snarled. He edged closer, his hands up and balled into fists.

Donny Boy said, "Watch out, Bobby."

Sheriff Bass arrived, broad thumbs hooked in his Sam Browne belt to emphasize that 9mm Glock. "Y'all having a good time?"

"Absolutely," I said. "Time of my life, Sheriff."

"I can see that from the big, country grin on your face,"

Bass said pleasantly. "Nothing like two-to-one odds to focus a man's mind."

Donny Boy. "Why are you busting our balls?"

"Shut up, Donny," Sewell sighed. "He's the man."

"That's right," Bass said, "I am the man. Now run along." He stared at Sandy Palmer for a long count, and his eyes visibly softened. "Honey, maybe you ought to go over there, give your Daddy a hand. He's getting back into the car. Let's move it."

They scattered. I sagged, shivering from the effects of adrenaline and some long-buried memories. I felt both guilty and relieved. I didn't want any trouble. Dry Wells was already making me remember—and *feel*—far too much. I watched Sandy trot back towards the copse of trees. She turned, waved, and disappeared.

"You going to be okay?" Bass asked kindly, as if in honor of our secret. "You look like you're about to cry."

"And here I thought I was so scary looking," I said, blandly. "I'll be fine."

"Good," Bass said. "Loner told me you're done here. You remember our agreement?"

"Yeah. What body?"

"Have a nice trip, Callahan. I'd suggest you commence leaving."

"Goodbye, Sheriff."

Bass strolled back across the grass, lean frame and long shadow shimmering in the heat. The immediate surroundings, so recently claustrophobic, seemed to expand again. I found myself back in a peaceful park on a bright green Saturday morning.

There had been something uncomfortably familiar about the conversation with Sandy Palmer. Talking with her had made me feel the pain of old, unhealed wounds. *I'm sorry, sweetie,* I thought. *I'm fresh out of hero. Maybe I don't even remember how to let myself give a damn.* I glanced towards the stage. Loner had vanished; so had the Palmer clan. The lame band was now limping through the national anthem. The two vets with the flag had worn their full-dress blues for the rehearsal; their chests were covered with multicolored medals.

I turned back towards the motel. I suddenly felt pressured to go, pushed from behind as if by an arctic wind. I crossed the creek bed in one hop, walked down the railway tracks and across the parking lot, moving fast.

Five

The low-end car-rental company in Elko had given me a Ford Mustang hatchback that was metallic green, out-of-date and cranky about it. The heap looked like it belonged to some housewife high on mescaline. I tossed my suitcase and the laptop computer into the back and slammed it shut. I juggled for the keys and opened the side door, then heard a crunching sound, footsteps, and something rolling down the driveway.

"Got room for me?" Jerry, scarred scalp reddened by effort, pushing his red motor scooter along the gravel. "I could just tie my wheels up on the top."

"Where the hell are *you* going?"

"Someplace else," Jerry said.

"This seems pretty sudden."

Jerry looked over his shoulder. "It is," he said. He sounded upset. "Truth is, I'd really rather stick around."

"Then what's up?"

"That nice little lady you saw me with this morning?"

"Yeah?"

"Well, she came over to listen to some music last night. We had a couple of beers and one thing led to another. We fell asleep. She didn't leave until this morning. I didn't plan on anything like that happening, you know?"

"I believe you," I lied. "So?"

"So she hangs out with a Cro-Magnon named Bobby

54

Sewell and some other unfriendly locals."

"I just made their acquaintance."

"They seem to think that she's their property. Now, I really like her a lot, but I found out that Bobby plans on knocking the taste right out of my mouth."

"Hence the urgency."

"Yo, I'm overdue for a vacation from this dump anyway." False bravado, forced smile. "Nothing interesting ever happens around here."

"What about that space-age junkyard you have in the back room?"

"I locked it up. I decide to move permanently, I'll rent me a truck and come back." Jerry looked back like a man pursued by a posse. "When I can see her again."

"I get it."

"Come on, Mick," he said nervously. "I'm kind of in a hurry."

He was a likeable kid. "Hop in," I said. "I can take you as far as Elko, but then I have to turn the car in and catch a puddle jumper."

"Not inviting me to come along to Hollywood?"

"You serious, kid? Well, if I get lucky, I guess I could poke around a bit. Maybe find you a gig."

"Never mind. I'll settle for a couple of weeks in Elko, so I can come back for the girl. Besides, I got a couple of friends there who are already earning a living."

I laughed. "You're relentless, you know that?"

"It's probably in my genes."

"Genes, or jeans?"

We strapped the red scooter onto the top of the Ford, secured it with bicycle cords and twine. My smile was too thin by half, and I found myself making dumb little whistling noises and drumming my fingers on the dusty roof.

"What up, dude?" Jerry asked. "You in a hurry, too?"

"Maybe. Let's move."

I spun the car around in the gravel and headed back down Main. Impulsively, I overshot to Station Street for one last look at the park. I was only half-aware of my motive. When I turned at the parking lot, I stared across the old railroad tracks at the cool, green grass. I couldn't help myself. I looked for her.

Two seconds later, I hit the brakes. Jerry grabbed the dash to steady himself. I stared at the park. Something was wrong. The picnic tables seemed empty: food baskets, soft drinks, and miniature flags, but no people. Distant voices were muttering, like a mob in a grainy old film. I heard a high-pitched scream from far away and felt my heart twist and sink. I knew I should drive on, told myself to leave, but that vital moment passed. I sighed and put the car into park.

"Let's check this out."

Jerry was gone, passenger door standing open. I don't know how I knew, but somehow I *knew*. I understood in a flash what I had only sensed moments earlier, why I'd been in a rush to leave town. I rested my head on the wheel for a moment, then undid the seat belt and got out of the car like a man facing a firing squad.

Up north, about a half a block, a raggedy-assed wooden fence made a lazy V at one end of the park. The people were all gathered at that spot, milling around, some taking pictures with disposable cameras. Crowds change mood on a dime. The situation had gone from a boring rehearsal to true event. At first I didn't see anyone I knew except for Glen Bass. Then I saw a garish, tri-colored shirt and white hat: Doc Langdon. Jerry was already at the edge of the group when I arrived, peering down at the creek bed with the rest of them. I stayed back a ways.

"Some drinking going on here?" Bass asked. Doc Langdon shrugged and wrinkled his nose.

"They'll find out with an autopsy," Doc said. "What a goddamned shame."

She was on her back in the shallow water; pretty dress pattern mixing well with the assorted twigs and flower petals. Her arms were floating gently with the current, those striking blue eyes wide open and staring up at the sun. There was a wide pink swirl near the back of her head, so delicately placed it might have been a Zen painting.

Someone had done real violence to her face.

The left eye was spider-webbed with blood veins, bruised into blackness. Her pretty lower lip was split and smeared with blood. Flies were arriving. Sandy Palmer seemed surprised and excruciatingly young. She didn't look sexy anymore.

A plump woman I didn't know began to cry. "Oh, the poor thing . . ."

I felt my eyes sting with rage and grief. Something deep inside burst into flame and then blackened. I turned away, unnoticed by the others, and strode rapidly back towards the rental car. I started the engine.

Jerry slid into the car, panting. He was pale. "What the hell are you doing?"

"I'm leaving town."

Jerry touched the wheel. "Not now! Goddamn it, man, did you see that? Did you see that poor girl lying there?"

"I saw her."

"What's the matter with you? You got ice in your veins or something? That girl was *dead*." He grabbed my arm.

I took my foot off the gas. "Jerry, you'd best back the fuck down." My voice was low and hoarse. Jerry tried to make his body smaller against the car door. His hat tipped up, revealing angry scar tissue. His large sunglasses slipped off and fell into his lap. He was terrified.

I turned the engine off. "Sorry."

"We can't just leave," Jerry said. "Sandy called you on the air last night, remember? You called her Ophra, or something."

Another long, slow breath. "Ophelia. I called her Ophelia."

"She had a problem she didn't want to talk about over the radio. It was something bad about her boyfriend. Mick, somebody murdered her for that."

"She's dead, Jerry. Who knows why?" I tried not to remember the man in the alley, naked with his hands tied behind his back. I pictured him anyway.

Jerry clenched his fists. He fingered his scalp, came to a conclusion. "We could do the kind of thing you used to do. I can help you out. Let's investigate."

"Jerry, don't be ridiculous."

"I liked that girl, Mick. She was a nice person."

"The answer is no," I said, a bit too forcefully. "Now, drop it. The law should handle things like this."

"What law? Dry Wells has one burned-out cop. Give me a *good* reason we shouldn't poke around."

"Okay, how about I'm pretty fucking rusty. You ought to know. You're the one who had to track my ass down and drag me out of hiding."

"You used to go at people for a living, man. It'll come back."

"Forget it, Jerry. Why the hell are *you* so hot to do this?"

"Dude," Jerry pleaded, ignoring the question. "Please help me out."

I weakened a bit, allowed myself to consider his idea. It seemed dumb. We'd be in way over our heads. Maybe if I hadn't seen that first body, trussed up like a turkey . . . but I had. And right now Dry Wells was looking like a very dangerous town. "No, Jerry. Let Bass and the Palmer family handle things."

"It might be therapeutic, dude. And it would be just like the old days, when you were at the top of your game."

"The old days? Back then I was too drunk to be cautious."

"Help me," Jerry said. "I even know *who* killed her. There's not a doubt in my mind."

"Oh?"

"It was that prick Bobby Sewell," Jerry said, triumphantly.

I whistled with mock admiration. "Oh, now I get it. And he just happens to be the same guy who wants to kick your ass over a girl. Hey, with that kind of impartial evidence you can't miss."

"Then who did it, and why?"

"Beats me," I sighed. "Oh come on, Jerry. How the hell should I know?" I didn't want to care, but now the anger was coming back; low and urgent like a sexual heat. "Listen, proving who did it won't be easy."

"I want to try."

"I'd like to help, but if I don't leave right now, I may not get that job in L.A."

"So fuck it."

I stared at him evenly. "This wouldn't be Jerry thinking he finally has his big chance to be a celebrity, would it?"

Jerry shook his head. "Whoa. That was a cheap shot."

"Level with me here. There's no better reason for wanting to stick your neck out like this? Come on, kid. I want to hear you say it."

Jerry studied his tennis shoes. He blushed and his scar darkened. "Skanky."

"The girl. The one I saw you with this morning."

Jerry, urgently: "Look, if I'm right and Bobby Sewell killed Sandy Palmer, then Skanky is in a world of hurt. I don't want to leave her behind. Hell, I didn't really want to leave town in the first place, man. I need to see her again." He looked up with wet eyes. "Mick, you got to help me out here. Please."

"Okay. Let me think for a minute." I lowered my head, massaged my temples. *This is stupid, really stupid. Bass is going to lose it if you stick around.* But when I examined my motives for refusing to help, I did not like them either. A few moments passed.

"Can I ask you something, Mick?"

"Sure."

"What the hell happened to you?"

It took me a long time to answer him. "Life happened."

Maybe I could help him out. Maybe there was still time to make something good from a whole lot of bad mistakes. But the wild card was that dead man in the alley. How did his murder factor into this, if at all? My head was spinning.

"So you won't help me. Wow, I looked up to you, dude." Fussing with the baseball cap again, wriggling the eyebrows. "You were my hero."

"Jerry?"

The kid unlocked the car door and got out. "I'm going to find out what happened on my own, then. If I can prove Bobby Sewell killed Sandy, I'll be able to help Skanky and all my problems will go to jail along with his hillbilly ass."

"You're crazy, you know that."

"I'll handle it." He began to walk away, but then froze when he heard me start the engine.

"Jerry? Wait." He turned with a widening grin. I sighed and patted the seat. "Get in. Let's go somewhere and talk."

Six

Madge Wynn's parents opened the tiny diner before the Second World War, when Dry Wells was still thriving. They called it Margie's, after Madge Wynn's mother, now long deceased. Madge herself was in her late sixties. Her customers were drive-through tourists or aging friends who skipped meals at home to keep Margie's in business. Strong coffee, eggs, home fries, and gigantic pancakes were her specialty. The food was plain, but always good.

Old Madge was back in the kitchen, her silver hair bobbing above the stove beyond the pass-through. Three empty cardboard boxes cluttered the hallway. A dry mop sat near a tipped-over, empty bucket. The lone waitress was a slender, pretty lady a few years shy of forty. She was the same woman who had studied me through the front window earlier. She had short brown hair, wide eyes, and the tanned face of someone accustomed to high desert sunshine. I think she may have tried to catch my eye as we ordered, but I was too preoccupied to notice.

Jerry and I sat in a corner booth. The cheap wall clock flagged the passing seconds like a woodpecker. We ate our sandwiches in relative silence. Jerry ordered a bottle of beer. I drank cola.

"This is so sad. I can't stop thinking about it."

"Me neither." My anger was muted, more manageable, the rage channeled.

61

"She was special, Mick."

"They all are."

"Huh?"

"Jerry, I want you to do me a favor. Let's change the topic. I want to talk about something else."

"Talk about what?" Jerry was puzzled.

"In one of your e-mails, a few weeks ago, you told me about being a kid on the streets back in Arizona. It was funny stuff, and I found it interesting."

"Mick," Jerry sighed, "what the fuck?"

"I want to change the subject, clear our heads. It's a technique. You're from somewhere in Arizona, right? You ended up in a foster home?"

"Yeah, a few of them. The last was a pissant burg called Rock Ridge," Jerry said. "It really sucked."

"Go on." It was getting hot. I wiped my face with a forearm.

Jerry slowly warmed to the subject. "Dude, it's ugly. People who need a few extra bucks sign up, take some dumb shit course, and figure they've got themselves a house slave."

"What happened to your real parents?"

"I don't know. I become successful, famous for something, then maybe they'll find *me* . . . if they're still alive." Jerry spilled some salt on the table and moved it around with his fingertips. "Or I guess I could go looking for them online."

"You found me fast enough," I said.

Jerry laughed. "I used to run away all the time, dude. The very last time, I got away from this old drunken fart named Boone and his fat wife. I hot-wired two of his cars, sold them off, and bought myself the scooter. I was sixteen years old, and I left and never looked back."

"Revenge is sweet."

"So is hot-wiring cars, but I cut it out. Hey, pirating electronics is a step up for somebody like me."

I stared out the window for a moment, then back. "Jerry, what happened to your face? Do you mind talking about it?"

An enormous chasm opened and filled itself with a thick, syrupy silence. Jerry's left hand began to rise as if to touch the scar tissue, but he stopped himself. Eventually he answered me with the scratchy, broken voice of a little boy.

"Mrs. Boone was ironing," he said. "I was doing the dishes. I accidentally broke a glass. When I turned around to say I was sorry, she grabbed my hair. Then she held the hot iron against my face."

"Jesus Christ."

"Jesus was nowhere to be found, my man."

"How old are you now, Jerry, twenty-five?"

"Twenty-three." He looked up as if something had just occurred to him. "You know what, Mick? You ask a lot of questions, but you don't answer many."

I squirmed. "Force of habit."

"Is that why you became a shrink?"

"My stepfather used to make me fight other kids for money, Jerry."

"Whoa. Damn."

"My real father was a drunk. I guess I wanted to understand people like that, and why my mother married those men. I wanted to understand myself, because I kept drinking even though I knew better. I washed out of the Seals with a bad attitude, but then became a straight A student and licensed shrink. The shrink got radio and television work that made him rich and famous, then he lost it all. Same old story."

The pretty waitress was cleaning up. Her pink blouse

and the knees of her torn jeans were damp. She started wiping down the table of the next booth. She caught my eye and winked. Something tickled my memory. I smiled back at her, puzzled. Her smile grew wider. She said: "You boys need anything else?"

"Not now, thanks." I still couldn't place her. The woman frowned and wandered away. "Now Jerry, look at me. Why would someone murder Sandy Palmer?"

Jerry was caught off-guard. "Jesus, dude. She called you saying she had a serious problem with her boyfriend. That he was into something and she was scared. Now she's dead. Doesn't all that strike you as a little too coincidental?"

"Of course. But we're not cops, and we don't have anything to go on, or real evidence suggesting who would have wanted her dead."

"No? Let me enlighten you," Jerry said. "Take that big bastard of an ex-boyfriend Bobby Sewell. He's got to be the meanest redneck in four counties. Sandy dumped him a couple of weeks ago, and Sewell ain't used to losing. I say it was him, or maybe one of his asshole buddies did it so he'd have an alibi."

"Maybe."

"Mick, work with me. I liked Sandy, but never had the balls to ask her out. I hardly ever do stuff like that. I just got lucky with that girl Skanky last night. Look, nothing like that ever happens to me. *Nada*. You know that sign some people stick on their cars that says, 'Just Married?' Well, mine is gonna say, 'Just Friends.' "

I laughed out loud, but Jerry looked dead serious. His eyes turned wet and shiny. "I really *like* this girl, Mick. Can you understand that?"

"Sure," I said. "I understand."

The moment vanished. "Anyway, back to Sandy Palmer.

She was always cool. It made her stand out. I'd crack a joke and she would giggle. I might say good morning, she'd say it back. Pretty girls aren't usually that nice to geeks, especially with a face that's . . . anyway, Sandy was different."

"Okay. Who else besides Bobby do we consider a suspect?"

"Well then, there are the Palmers themselves," Jerry said, "or their enemies. The old man is really hated. Rumor has it he's terminally ill, but some say he fakes being in a wheelchair so folks will be nice to him."

"What about the brother?"

"Will? He's loco."

I leaned forward on the table. Silverware clinked. Flies buzzed on the window. "Okay, let me feed this back. Her ex-boyfriend doesn't like you, so he's a suspect. So are all of his strange friends. Will Palmer and his father are garden-variety rich pricks so we add them, and likewise anyone who works for or with them. Also enemies of the family, which means half the county, and don't forget any strangers passing through, and every horny male that was unaccounted for. Have I left anything out?"

"Well damn, if you put it *that* way."

"If I put it that way, damned near everyone in or around Dry Wells could have killed Sandy. Jerry, let's take off for Elko. I can still catch a late plane."

The waitress approached our booth. She was drying her hands and rubbing her clothes with a towel. "Sorry, I lost control of a hose there for a minute." She tried a little more eye contact. She was very pretty, so I smiled back. She let me know she liked it. "You boys done here?"

"I guess so," I said. "What's the damage?"

She handed me the check, still trying to hold my gaze. She chuckled uneasily, a bit surprised and perhaps hurt.

"You really don't remember me, do you?"

"I'm sorry," I said. "I know I should." Then my jaw dropped. "Sonofabitch! You're Annie?"

She nodded and blushed, her jaw tight, as if she were upset that it had taken me so long.

"Of course I remember you, sweetheart," I said. And some of what I was remembering embarrassed me. "No glasses?"

"I wear contacts. My hair is a different color now, too. And it's shorter."

"Hot damn, Annie." I stuck out my hand, and she shook it.

"Hot damn is right," she said. She surprised me with a bear hug.

Flustered, I turned to Jerry. "Have you met? This is Madge Wynn's niece."

Jerry snorted. "Met? Hell, I only eat the food here every damned day so I can look at her." Then he shrank back as if he had revealed too much.

To her credit, Annie just smiled. She kissed him on the cheek, right next to the lower end of his burn scar. "Why, Jerry, what a sweet thing to say!"

Jerry swallowed. "S-So you two know each other too, huh?"

Annie slid closer to me. "Mick here was a couple of years behind me in middle school. We knew each other real well."

My mind visited a lot of old places and hot memories. I smiled, determined to keep things light. "I seem to recall you had a pet turtle when we were in elementary."

"That I did, Callahan. And you gave me a pretty miserable time about it, as I recollect. From there on, and all the way through." She smiled brightly again, but bitterness

66

crouched between the lines. Jerry wriggled his eyebrows at me.

"I hurt you some. Especially by up and leaving for the Seals like that," I said, softly. "I'm sorry."

She shrugged, but it was clear the apology meant something. Annie let the tips of her fingers brush my arm. She moved a few inches closer. Startled, I stepped back and cleared my throat. "You haven't been living here the whole time, have you Annie?"

She shook her head. "I moved to Ely for a while. Right after I lost a baby."

"Oh, I'm sorry."

Tone chipper, smile forced: "It was a while ago. Then I tried Reno. I had a couple of marriages bust up, still no kids. Now Mom's getting on in years and needs help . . . so, here I am. Hey, I caught your show on the radio."

"I'm afraid it wasn't very good."

"I don't know about that. Probably better than you think," Annie said. She licked her lips. "You remember me now, right?" She meant sexually, not socially.

"Oh, I surely do, ma'am."

Annie gathered confidence from my discomfort. She looked me over as if I was up for auction, taunted me. "You're all grown up and filled out, boy. Television don't do you justice."

Jerry looked envious. I blushed. "You look great too, Annie."

Satisfied she'd made her point, Annie turned and walked away. She seemed to put a little extra energy into swinging her hips.

"Lord God," Jerry whispered. "I just *got* to be famous someday. You gonna tell me about her? I'm all ears."

"You're all hormones," I said. I dropped the check on

the table and searched my pockets for money. "Let's stick to the point. Look, Jerry, I promised myself I'd get another job right away. I vote we hit the road for Elko, and I mean ten minutes ago, and send the girl a bus ticket. You with me?"

Jerry dug for change. "You go on, then," he said, sadly. His body sagged. "I'll stay here."

My mind flashed on that dark alley and the dead man's bloody fingertips. "Jerry, I'm telling you this as a friend. Best let the law handle it."

"Mick, you know it's not just about Sandy Palmer's death. I told you, that girl matters to me." He seemed surprised by his own intensity. His scar pulsed. "I'm staying."

"Okay, okay."

"*But* Sandy Palmer shouldn't get swept under the rug, either. She was a nice girl."

I covered the check, left a good tip. "You pick up the next one."

"Thanks. Mick?" Jerry made a show of studying the horizon. "If you need a job, if this is about money, I have five hundred saved up. I could pay you to help me out."

Emotions flickered by: shame, irritation, an urge to laugh out loud. I started to walk away, even covered a yard or two of dusty pavement, but then my well-oiled mercenary streak kicked in. Solving a murder could mean the kind of publicity that generated high-profile employment. I stopped, turned. *I may live to regret this.* Against my better judgment, I said: "Give me five."

"I don't have the whole five hundred on me, I meant . . ."

"Give me five, Jerry."

He saw I didn't mean a handshake. Jerry moved from dim-bulb to genius, found five ones, and passed them to me. I stuck the money in my pocket. "Okay," I said, "I'm hired. I'll hang in here for the night. Unless there's a Lions' convention coming to town and my room is rented out."

"Fat fucking chance."

"That's what I figured."

We headed for the door. I felt a female gaze boring into my back. I turned in the doorway. Annie Wynn was grinning with frank appreciation and a hint of fire in her eyes. Meanwhile, her mother glared daggers from the kitchen.

"By the way," I called, a bit louder than necessary, "did you hear what happened in the park?"

Annie shook her head.

"They found Lowell Palmer's daughter in the creek. She was murdered."

Old Madge froze and looked up. Annie frowned. "Sandy? Why, that's terrible. What happened?"

"Oh, I have an idea or two about that. I'm going to hang around and see what I can prove."

"Wow," Annie said. "Be careful, Mick. See you again soon, I hope."

We waved goodbye and walked out. "Why the hell did you do that, Mick? I thought you said we don't know shit."

"It's a small town," I said, "and Madge has a big mouth. Word will get around fast. Somebody around here is a murderer. What I said is bound to make them nervous as a long-tailed cat in a room full of rocking chairs."

"Oh."

In the car, Jerry said: "Some day you got to teach me that bit you do with your face, that bright red 'I'm so modest' thing. I've always wanted to know how to fake sincerity."

"Jerry, shut up. Look, I'm just going to stir things up and poke around a little. If we find anything solid, we turn it over to Sheriff Bass. He can drag in the state police. And I am out of here by Memorial Day, one way or the other. Any part of this you don't understand?"

"You're a good friend. Thanks."

"I'm doing this for a few different reasons. I'm no fan of the Palmer clan, but Sandy was a good kid. I spoke to her at the rehearsal. She reminded me of someone I owe. But I am hard core about staying out of any serious trouble. No hero stuff."

"No hero stuff. Right."

"And you're not getting the five bucks back."

Back at the Saddleback, it seemed to take forever to loosen the knots holding the red scooter to the top of the Mustang. I lost patience, used a pocketknife to cut the motorbike free. "Give me a couple of hours to figure out how to approach this."

"You got it." Without another word, Jerry rolled his scooter back to the office.

I guess I expect the heroic sound of trumpets and a swelling chorus of violins. Instead, I felt irritable and apprehensive. I went back to the little motel room to think things over. It seemed even more stuffy and oppressive than before.

The scruffy gray cat was by the door again. This time I knelt down and petted him for a moment. His breath was pretty gnarly.

"Aren't we a pair?"

I went inside, set up the laptop, checked for messages. There were none. I composed a quick e-mail.

Dear Hal,

Someone nice died today. I have been unofficially asked to find out why. A question for the Oracle: How do you know for sure when it's time to get back in the game?

Pls. advise.

Mick

I grabbed the phone; sat quietly, composing myself, and then punched in the cell number of a Hollywood producer. As the phone beeped, I reluctantly envisioned the arrogant little prick: tanned, sneering features, with a trendy haircut. I shuddered.

"Who is this?"

I instantly reacted to the man's voice, but swallowed my comeback. "It's Mick Callahan."

"It's a fucking holiday weekend, Callahan," Darin Young said. "I am here floating in my pool because it's a fucking holiday weekend."

"I know. I'm sorry."

"And you had better not be calling to disappoint me about the meeting next Tuesday."

"I just thought I'd ask if that date is absolutely firm."

"Firm? The date is very fucking *firm*, Callahan. Are you fucking drinking again?"

"No."

"Good, because I have put my ass on the line for you, Callahan. You fuck this one up, you can forget about working again. Do you read me?"

"Look, Darin, I'm not screwing around," I said. "I have a real problem. I may need to push us back. A friend of mine just died, so I really may not be able to make it to L.A. by Tuesday afternoon. This can't be helped."

Young was silent.

"Hello?"

"That response does not please me, Mick," Young said, finally. "It doesn't please me at all. Okay, I am going to see if it is possible to postpone the meeting. It may not *be* possible. Do you understand?"

"Perfectly."

"If it is *not* possible to postpone that meeting, then I

71

want you to think very carefully about what will happen to your life if you don't show. Are you reading me?"

"Can you call and let me know?"

"Like I said, I am floating in my fucking pool. I do not have a pencil to take down the number. So I want you to call me back tomorrow night, you pain in the ass. Are we clear?"

"Perfectly," I said. *Shut up, don't say it, don't rock the boat. You need this job.*

"Good. Now go away again."

"I'll call you back tomorrow night."

"Fine."

I closed the cell phone and sat hunched forward on the bed, head in my hands. *Somebody murdered Sandy, and if it wasn't Bobby Sewell, then who? Why? And how the hell am I supposed to find out in a couple of days?*

I needed to clear my mind. I turned out the light and listened to some country songs on the bedside radio. One golden oldie made me remember Annie Wynn: *Those honky tonk angels, they light up the night.* I closed my eyes and heard the sexy little crooning sound Annie made during sex. I pictured her young and naked, and felt myself stir . . . until Sandy Palmer's corpse intruded, her vacant blue eyes shimmering under an inch of clear creek water.

I jumped and sat up again, heart stuttering and stammering in my chest. After a time, I put the air conditioning unit on high. This time the racket it made seemed comforting.

Seven

Afternoon shadows were lengthening in the park and litter blew lightly in a warm, welcome breeze. Most of the crowd had gone home. The area around the dilapidated fence was nearly deserted, except for Glen Bass and Doc Langdon. Someone had driven small posts into the dirt and draped yellow police ribbons all around the bank of the creek. The ribbons looped across the water, back and forth. The water was clear. Her body was gone.

"Mr. Callahan," Bass said. "You promised to leave."

"I need to talk to you first."

"About what?"

I looked at Doc, who shrugged. "You don't got to pussy-foot around. I know you saw that body."

"Where is it now?"

"Callahan," Bass said pointedly, "we had a deal for you to get your ass out of town. No offense."

I smiled brightly. "None taken."

"You believe this?" Doc grimaced. "Two bodies in two days. You remember Dry Wells, Callahan. Hell, nobody around here dies of anything but old age."

"That guy last night? That looked like a mob hit, maybe. But what the hell happened here?"

Doc looked at Bass. "Somebody knocked Sandy around some, a man, judging by the upper body strength. She fell or was shoved backwards at the end, landed on a rock. The

73

back of her head was a mess."

"Does all this tie together, Sheriff?"

Bass grunted. "Don't get carried away. As of now, I don't think this incident is connected with last night. Can you give me a reason to?"

"Maybe."

Doc turned slowly; eyes widening, face washed out like a man startled by a flash bulb. He shook his head slightly, as if to signal a warning.

Bass said: "I'm all ears. This had better be good."

I looked down at the creek. The sheriff seemed to swell in size and I could see him growing dark with anger.

"There's this young gunslinger," Doc said, softly. "He asks an old pro for advice. Old guy says to draw and shoot the bow tie off the piano player. Kid does it. Old guy says, now cover your gun with grease. Kid says, why cover my gun with grease? Will that help my shooting? Old guy says, no, but that's Wyatt Earp playin' the piano, so it won't hurt as bad when he shoves it up your ass! *Har har har.*"

I ignored the warning buried in the joke and let some more silence feed the fire. I remembered Sandy Palmer's bright smile and waited for Bass to erupt.

"Mr. Callahan?" Bass barked impatiently. "You were saying?"

"Where's her body?" I had intended to sound detached. I was surprised to hear my voice break.

"Over to my office, in a big old fridge," Doc said. "So is that stranger. I'll keep them both cold until the state can set up an autopsy."

"You won't be doing it yourself?"

"*Hell* no, boy. I'm a vet, not a coroner. But a body is a body. They're just dead meat."

Bass was really steaming. "I'm all ears, Callahan. What

was it were you saying there before?"

I faced him. "A young lady called my show last night. She said she had a serious problem with her boyfriend. She sounded terrified, said her life was in danger. I didn't want to get into it on the air, so I ended the show. Then when I tried to get back to her, she'd hung up. Today, Sandy comes over to talk to me. She uses the name I gave that girl on the radio, Ophelia."

Puzzled looks. Bass frowned. A brief gust of warm wind ruffled our hair and swirled around a row of dry, multi-colored leaves near my feet. There was a faint sound like bacon frying in a pan.

"Ophelia was a character in Shakespeare's play about Hamlet. Sandy reminded me of Ophelia when she said her boyfriend was acting crazy. But it sounded like there was a lot going on . . . drugs, for example."

Bass seemed intrigued. "So that's why you were sitting with her when those boys came over?"

"Yes. And by 'boyfriend,' she likely meant the kid who was in my face, Bobby Sewell, although she never gave a name. Look, I remember Sandy Palmer as a little girl. I liked her, Sheriff. I want to see the body."

Bass frowned. "No."

Doc squinted and spat. "Why would you want to, Callahan? That's a bit morbid, ain't it?"

"I'm not looking forward to it," I said, truthfully, "but I talked to her last night and again this morning. She asked for help, in fact she was almost a client. What's the problem?"

"Look, I said no," Bass said. He glanced at Doc Langdon. "This is a police matter."

Doc sighed. "The judge may end up wanting to talk to him anyway, Glen. And he's bound to ask for a statement as to how she called the show."

"Doc is right. I can't stay out of this, not now. And Bass, you owe me."

"Like I said before, this is police business." Bass was clearly upset.

"Look, it would be almost impossible to get back here from Los Angeles if you needed a statement later. If we can get this over with now, I'd be much obliged."

After a long pause, Doc shrugged. "Why not let him look?" he said. "Won't take but a minute."

"All right," Bass said, reluctantly, "I suppose it won't do any harm. She's not a pretty sight, though. The back of her head got bashed in."

"I know."

Doc said: "Then let's go."

As we were walking, I asked, "Did you get any pictures?"

Bass smiled thinly. "I didn't have to. I just confiscated all the film those civilians shot. It's a long holiday weekend, Callahan. Things get busy in a one-horse town with one cop, especially when dead folks start popping up. That don't mean I can't do my job."

"No offense."

"None taken."

We walked. "Hey, Callahan," Doc said. "You know why the penis has a big head on top of it? That's so your fist won't slip off, hit you in the forehead, and knock you out cold. *Har har.* Get it?"

There were two entrances to Doc's vet hospital. The front of the building faced Main and the back door was on Station Street. The three of us crossed the railway tracks and the empty, littered parking lot. Doc fumbled for his keys and unlocked the back door. He slid open a large metal panel.

The interior of the lab was surprisingly spotless. Stainless steel sinks and tables; clean and gleaming surgical instruments. There was a large refrigerated area near the back, where pathology work could be performed on livestock that had died under suspicious circumstances. Doc slid another huge metal panel to one side. The sound rang and clanged like the door to a cellblock.

Two rolling carts stood isolated in the middle of the room, each covered with a white sheet. The man from the alley lay on his side because rigor mortis had locked his hands behind his back. He had black hair; his coarse features were distorted from the blow to the back of his head. His digits were like little swollen sausages, the amputated fingertips grotesque. I studied him for a moment, stalling, because I didn't want to look at Sandy.

Bass spoke. "You keeping your mouth shut, like I asked?"

"I haven't said a word to anyone in town," I said, truthfully. Hal didn't count. "Any luck identifying him?"

Bass shook his head. "Not yet."

"He was shot, right?" I asked. "You said you were looking for a cartridge but you couldn't find one."

"Wasn't a gunshot," Doc drawled. "Not in my opinion. Up close, that wound reads like penetration with a pointed object, maybe an iron pick or a spike, something like that."

I nodded. "Less sound that way."

"And then the perp tried to smash out all his teeth, but he missed a bunch. Maybe got startled before he was done. So the coroner might be able to ID this guy from dental records, once they have an idea who he was."

"Let's get this done," Bass said. He motioned to the other cart and the white sheet covering it. I saw small, vulgar reddish stains. A shock of long blonde hair emerged from one end of the sheet, tiny bare feet from the other. I shivered and had an absurd urge to rub her toes, thinking she must be cold.

Doc strolled over and pulled the sheet down with a flourish, baring her to the waist. Sandy Palmer's once-lovely features were now flat, bruised, and waxen. Her eyes were still open, the left one bulging and dark with blood. She was naked, her breasts exposed. It seemed obscene. "I thought you weren't going to do an autopsy?"

Doc smiled. "I ain't. Just want to make a point."

There was something strange about those eyes. I realized I'd stopped breathing, finally let some air out. "What point?"

Doc pulled the sheet down a bit further. He drummed his fingers on a slightly swollen abdomen, palpitated slightly. "I think she was pregnant," he said. "Maybe a couple of months along."

Bass seemed weary, beaten down. "So okay, just for the record, with Doc here, tell me Sandy Palmer is the girl from the park and the one that called you on the air. This is her, right?"

I nodded, sadly. "Yes. That's her." I realized Sandy and I were a lot alike, both raised on a lonely ranch in the middle of nowhere by an abusive father; lost kids who partied too hard, hoping to find a way out.

I got down lower, but coming close to that damaged face made me flinch. I crouched and looked around at the back of the head. I didn't know exactly what I was looking for, but I knew I had to see.

"Doc, it was the beating killed her, right?" Bass asked.

"Maybe not. We got us a subdural hematoma for sure," Doc said. "That much I can tell you. See, her left eye is a mess, but her right eye has a blown pupil, it's all engorged. Girl took a bad beating, that's for sure, but maybe not enough to do her in. But then she fell. Hard. When she hit her head, or somebody else hit it, the blow compressed her brain and damaged the lining. She had lots of internal bleeding that probably would have killed her eventually, but I'm willing to bet you dollars to doughnuts the pathologist will nail the actual cause of death as drowning."

"Bullshit. In less than a foot of water?" Bass asked. The question came out with a rasp, and there was a lot of emotion behind it. I made a mental note.

"Well, you got your two kinds of drowning," Doc said. I think he was enjoying himself. "In a wet drowning, and most cases are like this, the lungs are aspirated full of water. Person kept trying to breathe. In a dry one, kinda rare, there's a sudden laryngospasm when the first water hits the throat and then everything inside seizes up. No air, no water, no nothing. Lights out. I'd say she's a wet drowning."

"Hang on," I said. "That's absurd. You think her death was some kind of accident?"

Doc shrugged. "I'm just saying the beating alone would not have killed her, maybe not even the fall she took. We don't know why she drowned."

I held his eyes. "You're saying her death wasn't necessarily murder. It might have been some kind of freak accident?"

"Well, I'm not saying that a deliberate, murder one homicide is totally out of the question." Doc was becoming visibly uncomfortable. It was all he could do not to look to Bass for a cue.

Bass finally said: "Look, this poor sonofabitch over here got tied up and stuck in the back of the neck by something sharp. Not much doubt what happened. I think what Doc is saying is that with Sandy, what it seems like it is could turn out to be different. We're gonna have to wait for the autopsy in Elko to know for sure. Until then, it doesn't do us much good to speculate."

I wanted time to think. "I guess you're right."

"She sure was a pretty one," Doc said. "Damn shame I never got to . . ." Bass glared. Doc caught himself and backpedaled. "I'm just making conversation, didn't mean nothing by that."

I turned to the sheriff. "It's hard not to figure Sewell for this, whether it was deliberate or not. I assume you're going to grill him?"

Bass didn't answer, but I was stating the obvious. I pressed him anyway. "And maybe suggest to Bobby that he and his friends don't take any sudden vacation trips to Mexico until the report comes back?"

"Already done both," Bass said. "Not that it's any of your goddamned business. Why are you so interested in my procedure here, Callahan? What's on your mind?"

"She wanted my help. I guess it's as simple as that."

I drew the sheet back up over Sandy's face without asking for permission. Then I looked at Doc Langdon for a cool, steady moment. "She deserves respect," I said. "Everybody deserves respect."

"I'll see to it," Doc said. His upper lip was beaded with perspiration.

"You do that."

"And I'll be back in the morning, Doc," Bass said evenly. "Mr. Callahan, let's go for a stroll, just you and me."

We went out the front way, onto Main Street. The night was fast approaching, crouching on the boulders. The coming darkness felt more oppressive than liberating.

Long shadows slid along the desert floor. I licked two

fingers, held them up. "Bit of a breeze still. Seems somewhat cooler than last night."

For a few long moments, there was nothing but the sound of boots crunching in the dirt and the gravel. After a time, Bass grunted and replied, "Cooler? Yeah. Most likely it will be."

"Last night was pretty bad."

"It's not normally that hot this time of the year."

"I know. Could have fooled me, though."

Boots again, scooting along the cracked cement. Bass was tightly wound. His skin was tanned and dark, and seemed stretched as the leather in his holster. He stared off towards the sunset, squinting.

"So. How long you plan on staying around, Callahan?"

"Gosh, since we're getting so close again and all, you may as well start calling me Mick."

"I got enough information to make out two statements and type them up," Bass said, ignoring the jibe. "One for each incident. You come by my office tomorrow and sign the both of them. You can be on your merry way, just like before."

"Sounds okay."

"Good," Bass said. "I wouldn't want you to wear out your welcome."

"I get the feeling I already have."

"You have. I appreciate your keeping your mouth shut, like I asked. But this is a quiet little town, now. We like it that way. And you still have the smell of trouble about you, even after all these years."

"You've got to learn to speak your mind, Sheriff."

We arrived at his office and Bass started up the stairs. He turned a few feet up and looped his thumbs in his belt. "All right, here it is. I know you were some big shot on television and all, digging around in other people's private lives. You're likely used to getting your way. So listen up, I want to be sure and make this clear."

"I'm listening." I meant it, too. I was listening to what *wasn't* being said, and that made my instincts flutter. Bass was troubled, anxious, and felt defensive about something. I had him worried.

"Leave," Bass said. "I don't need any help, especially from an amateur."

"Okay." *Stay in neutral,* I thought. *Don't give him anything.*

"Callahan, all I want to see of you tomorrow is your ass and your elbows going the other way. You sign that statement and get the hell gone. Understood?"

"I think we understand each other," I said, with my best smart-ass smile. "You have yourself a nice evening."

Eight

Saturday Evening, 6:40 p.m.

The gray alley cat was nowhere to be found. I could have used the company. There was a note on the door to the room signed "J." It read: *Going to go get drunk.* I stood for a long moment in the cool evening air, debating my next move. I went inside, but instantly felt claustrophobic and isolated. I wracked my brain and came up with only one place where Jerry might be. I left the room; angled out of the driveway, crossed First Street, and entered the only bar I knew about, Tap's Place.

Originally a liquor store with some slot machines, Tap's was a makeshift local tavern. The cowboy who owned it had knocked down a wall to waist level, slapped down a varnished piece of cut plywood and created a bar. He'd set up card tables at night, open some folding chairs. People came these days because Tap had the only public satellite television around. The set, usually tuned to a sports network, was mounted on the wall above the window.

A boxing match was playing, the commentators jabbering away in Spanish. I looked around for Jerry, but the only occupants besides Tap were Loner McDowell and Annie Wynn. The slender, weathered brunette was perched on a stool, finishing a bottle of beer. Loner was at a table. I had wandered in at the end of some kind of confrontation.

"But I do believe you're my next ex-wife," Loner said.

"In your dreams," Annie said. "You got a little too much

of my *real* ex-husband in you." She turned her back, graceful as a cat, and took another sip of beer.

"Honey, don't be that way," Loner teased. "It would be a shame to see a pretty lady get all dried up and bitter. You don't get many chances for love in a pissant town like this. Strike while the iron is hot, if you get my drift."

Annie Wynn wasn't amused. "I get your drift, Loner. Anything with a heartbeat and panties looks pretty good right about now."

"The girls all get prettier come closing time."

"Well, that somehow fails to make a woman feel special." She dropped some money on the table and got to her feet.

"Stick around," Loner said. "You came in here to drink a beer or two, didn't you?"

Annie appraised him coldly. "Actually, I came in here selling health insurance. You keep undressing me with your eyes like that, cowboy, you're going to need you some."

McDowell roared with laughter and real appreciation. Annie was something special. She turned to leave, ran right into my chest, looked up at me, and cocked her head. My body responded immediately. The woman seemed to come alive at my touch. She smiled. Under her breath, she said, "Now you, on the other hand . . ."

"This man bothering you, lady?" I said, mostly for Loner's benefit. "Please excuse him. He hasn't been out of the institution all that long."

"Naw," she said. "He ain't even a half-pint of trouble to a gal like me."

"Yeah, yeah," Loner said, staring down. "I'm not listening." He shuffled a worn deck of cards.

Annie and I moved out into the darkness. "How you doing tonight?" she asked.

I shrugged. "I've been better."

"I can't believe this Sandy Palmer thing, Mick."

"I know. I can't either."

Annie moved closer. I didn't mind a bit. "Someone beat her to death in broad daylight. Christ, what a world."

She looked awfully pretty by moonlight. "Yeah, what a world."

"You figure things like that happen in the big cities," she said, sadly, "but not way out here."

I leaned back on the porch railing to ease away from her. "You are very sweet to Jerry," I said. "That really impresses me."

"Why? He's a wonderful kid."

"You don't take compliments any better than you used to."

She laughed and looked me up and down. "Neither do you. Mick, how have you been? Has the world been kind?"

I looked down and away. "The world was kind enough I guess, but I managed to fuck everything up anyway. You?"

"The same, I suppose."

"Great minds think alike."

Annie closed the distance and my blood pressure rose. "Callahan, does it bother you when a girl is a bit forward?" I didn't answer. She stroked the thigh of my jeans with her right hand. "Because I've been thinking about us again. All day long, in fact. You been thinking about me, too?"

"I have indeed," I said.

"When are you going to ask me out again?"

"I don't rightly know."

Annie touched my face with the tips of her fingers. My body sang opera. "Don't take too long," she said. "I might change my mind."

Loner called out. "Callahan?"

"Night, Annie," I said, as gently as possible. I gave her a hug. "I'll come by to see you."

"Night, cowboy. You'd better."

I released her, a bit reluctantly. Annie winked. I stepped back, clearing the sidewalk. She walked out into the night without another word.

"Callahan, you black Irish bastard. You come to drink with me?"

I walked closer, trying to gauge how many he'd put away. It was a sizeable amount, from the look of him. His pupils were saucers, his eyes more red than white. "You know better than that," I said.

"Then pull up a chair and die of envy," Loner cried. "It's all the same to me."

I sat down warily. I'm still uncomfortable in bars, particularly in nearly empty bars with someone who's drunk.

"Want to play a little blackjack?" Loner reached for the deck of cards he always carried. "How about you give me a chance to relieve you of some of that money I paid you."

"Nope, I can't stay. I was just looking for somebody."

"Heard you did okay last night," Loner said.

"Somebody lied to you," I said. "I stank."

Loner howled again. "I doubt it. You always were a slick bastard, Mick, fun as hell. That's why I called you. I know talent when I see it."

"I'm grateful for the job," I said. "I don't need you to blow smoke up my ass, too. I've lost my edge."

Loner shrugged. "Hey, it happens to everybody sometime or another. You're a smart man, Mick. You'll be back on track again in no time." Loner finished one beer. He screwed the top off another with his massive fingers. "What's this thing you got cooking over to L.A., a talk show?"

"A big audition. Maybe it will come to something, maybe not. I wish I had the setup you've got."

"Talking to astrologers? Numerologists? Crazy assholes who talk to aliens? Come on, Mick, get real. I may be making some heavy bread, but no one could accuse me of being a serious journalist. Or even a genuine cultural self-help guru like yourself."

Tap called out: "Mister Callahan, you want something to drink?"

"I won't be staying."

"You got to buy something, you start watching that boxing match."

"Okay, Tap."

Loner lowered his voice to a conspiratorial whisper. "You hear what happened today over to the park? They found Sandy Palmer in the creek. Somebody really slapped her around. She was dead, lying flat on her back. They say her eyes were wide open and she looked all surprised. Damn." He rubbed his eyes. Loner seemed genuinely upset.

"That's too bad," I said. "What a terrible thing."

Something urgent was crouching right behind his eyeballs. "Just goes to show you," Loner said. "You got to live all you can. A man can be dead before he knows it."

There was artificiality in the way Loner was expressing himself; perhaps it was real sorrow struggling with anger, but something seemed incongruent; the inside and the outside didn't match. I felt like he was acting a bit, and that piqued my interest. Loner McDowell was a big man and could be a very dangerous drunk, so I decided to move slowly. "What did they say happened?"

Loner shook his head. "They don't know. Somebody beat her to death, or maybe she fell down afterwards." He snapped his fingers, loud enough to startle me. "Just like that, such a pretty little thing."

"How well did you know her, Loner?" I pretended to watch the televised fight. "You seem pretty upset."

"Well who wouldn't be upset?" Loner sputtered. "She was a nice kid and now she's stone cold dead. Hell, everybody knows her family."

I eyed him, smiling. "I said how well did *you* know her?"

"You turning fucking *NYPD Blue* here all of a sudden, Callahan?" Loner snorted. "So I knew Sandy. It sucks that something happened to her, that's all."

"Okay."

"Okay what?"

"Nothing, just okay."

"Mick, I think you're trying to get under my skin."

I stood up and extended my hand. "I wouldn't want to do that, big guy. Just curious."

Loner grabbed my hand, squeezed, and forced me back into the chair. He began to arm wrestle with a big, bright grin on his face. I responded, squeezing and pushing back, and for a few moments nothing moved. Sweat beaded on our foreheads; muscles trembled. We were both grinning, macho pretension in full bloom. I was vaguely aware that Tap had stopped cleaning up to watch.

After a long while, Loner gave a little wheezing grunt and shifted in his chair, but that was about all. Finally, when my arm was killing me and my fingers started going numb, I surrendered. The back of my wrist hit the table and sent bottles flying. I shook my hand and bowed. McDowell puffed up with surprised pride.

"You didn't let me do that, did you?" Loner asked.

"You got me fair and square."

Loner finished his beer. "Thanks." He belched. "We should have bet."

I paused at the bar. "Tap, you seen that kid Jerry from the motel?"

Tap nodded. "He was in here a while back, but he left."

"Thanks."

Loner waited until I had almost left the bar and then called out. "Mick?"

"Yeah?"

"You'll be joining me for a drink one of these days. Sooner or later. You can't last forever."

I shrugged. "You could be right," I said, "but not tonight."

The evening air was cool. I strolled past several shuttered buildings, both business and residential. Only a few houses still had lights, their stubborn occupants still hoping something would change, perhaps waiting for death to take them. I heard a radio playing country music, then the baritone muttering of a television news anchor. A sudden silence would signal a long stretch of empty homes with storm-broken windows and boarded-up doorways. Many of the vacant lots still had FOR SALE signs, but the signs themselves were ancient now, fading letters on splintered boards hung from rusty chain. Most of the streetlights were dark, but there wasn't much left to see anyway.

Yeah, I had wanted to drink some beer. Seeing the intense, vapid expression on Loner McDowell's face, hearing that too-loud voice, I suddenly wanted to be caught up in the atmosphere of the tiny bar; rising to the silly challenge of the arm-wrestling. But when the urge came, I used a process Hal Solomon called "think through the drink."

I walked and remembered: Going out, heart thudding, to examine the bumper of my car to be certain I hadn't hit anyone in a blackout. Waking up to learn that I'd gotten into an argument with a good friend; in the meaningless brawl that followed, something about a girl, I had broken the friend's nose and chipped one of his front teeth. Then being arrested for propositioning an undercover police-woman. Shame boiled my blood. I recalled losing my home, career, so-called friends, and having calls to former colleagues rebuffed. And then I remembered a beautiful young woman who died all alone on a bloody kitchen floor.

Having a beer didn't seem like such a good idea anymore.

Think through the drink.

I stopped and looked up at the night sky. People who live in the cities are genuinely amazed to find out how much larger and brighter the stars seem out in the desert. Even I had almost forgotten. I inhaled the comforting scent of the sage and enjoyed the view. Hal was right, I'd never had it so good.

My drinking career lasted twelve years. I got sober after warrants for unpaid traffic tickets resulted in a "sentence" to twenty AA meetings. I sat in that room hating everyone and everything, but it didn't last. I began to identify with what I was hearing. In time, I came to accept that I had a disease.

I approached Hal Solomon for help after hearing him speak at a meeting in Beverly Hills. He agreed to walk me through my steps. Only later did I realize that Hal was a major stockholder in the media company that had just fired me. We both found the irony amusing.

A light breeze sang across the barren desert. It rolled a clenched fist of tumbleweed along the blacktop with a dry, scraping sound. I yawned and turned back toward the Saddleback Motel.

In my room, I booted up the computer and found another e-mail from Jerry. After a short loading period, the screen turned green and a drunken leprechaun started dancing around a pot of gold. It was an animated e-card, expressing friendship and gratitude, "even if I did have to pay you." I saved it.

Next was Hal Solomon's response to my query:

> Your question puts me in mind of a quotation from George Bernard Shaw, who wrote: "The true joy in life is to be used for a purpose recognized by yourself as a mighty one; the being a force of nature instead of a selfish, feverish little clod of ailments and grievances complaining that the world will not devote itself to making you happy."
>
> My answer is that you are ready.
>
> You should go forth into the world and identify another noble cause to which you can dedicate yourself, i.e., do a mitzvah. Extend yourself at your earliest convenience.
>
> As for myself, I must confess to a growing sense of boredom. I believe it is related directly to being retired and wealthy. Therefore, please inform me if and when my assistance (intellectual, financial, or otherwise) is required. You may count on me, as always . . .
>
> And remember that you are valued.
>
> Hal.

Nine

Sunday Morning, 7:37 a.m.

"You know what I need you to do, right?"

We were in the motel office. I stood and motioned Jerry into the rickety chair behind the metal desk. My old, reliable IBM ThinkPad chirped happily and played a musical chord. "I use this one if you want to borrow it."

Jerry was amused. "Callahan, I'm the one who tracked your country ass down, remember? Shit, we traded e-mails for weeks. You think I need to use this wimpy little piece of crap?"

"I just thought maybe . . ."

"Do you even know what the term 'hacker' means?"

"Hey, I know you're good with computers," I said defensively. "But I thought you could use mine too, maybe as an extra or something."

"I'll use my own," Jerry said firmly. "Check this out."

He stood up, went to the back room, and unlocked two deadbolts. The door swung open and Jerry waved at a gigantic collection of electronic apparatus. "Enter the twenty-first century. Your laptop is to this gear what a Model T Ford is to the space station."

For the first time, I looked closely. I assumed his stuff was mostly stereo equipment, but I had seriously underestimated my friend's capabilities. I whistled. "What *is* all this?"

"Took me years," Jerry said, proudly. "Every time I

fixed a computer I lifted a part or two and left used stuff in its place. Take this video card. I swiped it from a new Dell. I did the same thing with the memory, hard drives, and most of the peripherals." He touched a tall stack of electronics. "This is a state-of-the-art custom Wintel system; it's got a 3 gigahertz P4, 800 meg frontside bus with 2 gigs of RAM, the latest 128 meg video card, two 120 gig RAID-array drives, and this bitchin' 23 inch Viewsonic flat screen. Thus, the world is at our fingertips."

"I was afraid you would say that."

"Say what?"

"Whatever it was you said."

Jerry was getting excited. "These hick towns don't have DSL or a cable modem, right? So I have a two-way satellite that gives me 1.5 megs of bandwidth to upload and download. I use proxy servers routed from Puerto Rico, so I can't be traced if I go somewhere I shouldn't *be* going, you know? Since the U.S. basically owns Puerto Rico, I can gain access to all government, state, and local records."

"*All* of them?"

"It's not that hard, Mick. All DotGOV Websites are networked out of Norfolk, and they give access to their employees. Since the level of information accessed depends on status, status levels are traded like baseball cards by the really good hackers. You just need to know what newsgroups to look on."

I sat down behind the desk. "You're amazing," I said. "How the hell did you learn all of this?"

"They have desktop computers in coffee shops and bookstores all over. You can rent by the hour. I just never had the kind of money it takes to buy stuff for myself until I started fixing people's gear instead of lifting cars. Then I eventually got this cool stash together. Impressed?"

I shook my head in admiration. "Absolutely, and now I'm going to put you to work. A friend of mine named Hal has serious money and good contacts. He will be helping us out from Europe." I gave him the e-mail address.

"Way cool," Jerry said. "You sure you're up for this, then?"

"You paid me the five bucks."

"That I did." Jerry spread his arms wide to indicate his gear was warming up. "And now I'm set to kick some serious ass."

"Okay," I said. "Forget checking for alibis, because damned near everyone in Dry Wells was in that park and her death happened in broad daylight. I think we need to look for people who might have had a motive."

"What do you want me to do?"

"I want you to find out how Lowell Palmer got rich. Also, give me detailed bios on Glenn Bass, Loner McDowell, Doc Langdon, also Bobby Sewell and his gang. Go into old newspaper articles from the local and state papers, all the public records, law enforcement, and so on."

"I know the drill. Where are you going, Palmer's ranch?"

"Bingo. I'm going to grill Will Palmer and maybe see if I can stir up some trouble by acting like I know something." I turned in the doorway. "By the way, where the hell were you last night?"

Jerry looked sheepish. "I had a couple of beers and got lonesome, so I went out looking for Skanky. But I couldn't get her to sneak away with me."

"You're living dangerously."

"Yeah. That Mexican guy saw me, so I really had to haul ass. I came back, locked myself in, finished the beer, and fell asleep in the office. Sorry."

"I think we each need to know where the other guy is at

all times. And considering Bobby is one of our prime suspects, you'd best avoid Sewell and his gang from now on. Sorry, Jerry, but that includes Skanky."

"There's something really weird going on around here, isn't there?"

A dead man with his hands tied behind his back and his fingertips sliced away qualifies as weird, all right. I shoved the image aside. "I've just got a hunch, a gut feeling," I said, lying like a rug. "When I'm sure of something, you'll be the first to know. I'm taking my cell phone along so I can check in."

"Okay."

I paused in the doorway. "Hang in there, Jerry. You'll be able to see your girlfriend again. I should be back in a few hours."

I clipped the cell phone onto my belt, started up the Ford, and pulled out onto the highway. I headed south on Highway 93, towards the mountains and a little town called Currie. After a few moments, I opened the window and inhaled the perfume of the sage.

Nevada is a beautiful state in its own primitive way, despite the garish gaming establishments. It has long, open spaces and stunning high deserts with mountains that are dotted with single-leaf piñon trees and bristlecone pines. The state sprawls over 110,540 square miles and much of it is virtually uninhabited. Miners, among them the Irish who built Carson City, have pulled gold, silver, copper, zinc, and even uranium from the ground. Ranchers and farmers have successfully raised livestock and harvested alfalfa, wheat, vegetables, and even hardy fruits. It's rich land.

On the Bell ranch, slender deer would gather in the thick brush near a water supply, venturing out to drink only at dusk or in the cool of the dark. I had milked cows in the brisk cold just before sunrise, squirting precious streams to the feral cats crouched in the barn's open, wood-framed windows. There were bobcats and coyotes and badgers, a seemingly endless supply of gophers and jackrabbits, magpies that dotted the landscape with thin black and white feathers.

I dialed my cell phone. A woman answered the telephone on the third ring. "Palmer's residence," she said. She was young and seemed anxious.

"I'd like to speak to Wilson, please," I said.

"Hold on," she said. There was a moment of confusion and fumbling; the receiver was handed back and forth.

"This is Will Palmer."

"My name is Mick Callahan."

"I had heard you were in town. I remember catching your old television show a time or two. What can I do for you?"

"Will, I was very sorry to hear about your sister."

"It was a terrible shock. You knew my sister, then?"

"Many years ago."

No mention of watching Sandy and I conversing. If Will Palmer had no idea what I looked like, then he was lying about having seen the television show. Or perhaps he did know of me, but had something to hide. We hadn't even met yet, and he was already getting on my nerves.

"I was wondering if I might visit you for a few minutes. I'm not far away."

"I assume you have something significant to discuss since you have already expressed your grief at the passing of my half-sister?"

What a chilly personality, I thought. He sounded narcissistic and passive-aggressive. I decided to be cool, direct, and firm. "Will, I'd like to talk to you in person."

He bit. "Where are you?"

"Out on the 93."

"Take 93 past the 229 cutoff to Humboldt Forest. We're maybe a couple of miles north of Currie."

"I've got it. Is this a good time?"

"I'm not desperately busy, Mr. Callahan. Perhaps you can enliven my day."

Dial tone.

Sudden trauma can cause odd behavior; the larger the shock, the more bizarre the conduct. Grieving people have been known to break into giggles at the funeral of a beloved relative, for example. Gentle family members may suddenly have temper tantrums, drink excessively, and even find themselves in trouble with the law. But there was something far too cold, calculated, and deliberately insulting about Will Palmer's performance.

The Palmer spread was set back from the highway, right after the turnoff from the 93. The barbed wire fence and barred metal gate were nearly invisible. I hit the brakes and backed up, spraying dust. Thirty yards behind a smattering of small pines sat a cinderblock wall, about six feet tall. Huge twenty-foot gates, with a garish metal "Palmer Ranch" logo above them, were centered in that wall. The gates were open and I drove through.

On the left I saw a large half-sunken potato cellar, common to this part of the country; the door made of splintering wooden planks. To the right, more trees and a rocky slope that tapered out of sight. Straight ahead sat a blue one-story wooden house with a porch railing; beyond it a larger wood-and-brick two-story house, also with a wooden railing. The second house was painted red. A horse corral stood between these two dwellings and a full garden framed the back yard of the larger home. Further in the distance I could make out a grain silo, a large white wooden barn that seemed freshly painted, and some large animal pens.

Far to the rear of the property sat a cluster of dilapidated old mobile homes, three or more, located near a side gate. Past the gate lay a dirt road, likely something private that returned to highway 93 and curved south and east. I opted for the larger house, the red brick-and-wood two-story. I started along the left side of the two homes, but as I passed the empty horse corral realized that this was the back entrance. I turned around.

Wilson Palmer was seated comfortably on the wooden porch of the two-story, smoking and rocking in a chair. He had his booted feet up on the wooden railing and stared at me with studied insouciance. There was a blur of motion, the slamming of a screen door. I saw a scantily clad female with dark hair return to the darkness within the house. I parked and got out. A sickly-sweet smell struck my nostrils; Palmer was finishing a joint. He ground it out beneath his heel and got to his feet.

Close up, Will was as strikingly handsome as a movie star. His hair was dark and perfectly coiffed, black eyes cold and flat. He greeted me with a thin smile. "Mr. Callahan, I'm Will Palmer. Have a seat."

Ten

Sunday Morning, 8:46 a.m.

Will Palmer and I were natural enemies, cobra and mongoose. The tension was palpable and immediately filled the gaps between pleasantries. My counseling supervisor would have called it "counter-transference," and I suppose that's true enough. But the harsh fact is that I flat-out disliked the arrogant little bastard, and he returned the sentiment.

Palmer's aura of narcissism and smug superiority was a visceral presence. I needed to try to shake him up. I decided to be indirect, avoid activating his defenses. Otherwise things could very rapidly spiral out of control, because a man like Will Palmer actually had a very fragile ego. It would be difficult to get his mask of arrogance to slip, but I had come here to see what lay behind it.

"I was looking forward to meeting you, Mr. Callahan."

"The feeling is mutual. I heard a lot about the Palmer family growing up, but I never knew anyone but your sister when she was still a child."

"You never laid eyes on us?"

"Not up close." I found myself slipping into a drawl that matched Palmer's. *Maybe try for some kind of a narcissistic twin-ship? But then he'll know you're stroking him. He's a smart bastard.* Something about Will Palmer made my flesh writhe. It felt like a form of projective identification, so perhaps he had borderline-psychotic features, too. *Better tread lightly.*

His tone dripped sarcasm. "Why, how nice for you, then; I'll bet you're just thrilled to be here. Would you like a drink?"

"No, thanks," I said. My eyes wandered to the joint lying crushed on the porch.

"Too late to ask for a hit."

"I'd pass anyway."

"Have a seat. I trust this won't take long?"

I shrugged. "I'll stand." I meant to use height as an advantage.

It had no visible effect. Will Palmer yawned in a contrived show of disinterest. "So what can I do you for, Callahan?"

A female figure appeared, blurred by the screen door and hidden in the dark living room. "Honey? Do you need me to bring you anything?"

"What's the matter with you? Can't you see we're having a conversation?"

"I'm sorry." She turned on a dime and vanished. I felt frozen, at a loss for words. I couldn't recall meeting anyone quite as cruel as Will Palmer. He was Darin Young squared.

"Okay, I suppose you're just heartbroken about Sandy," Will said. "Got anything else on your mind?"

I felt myself losing ground already. "I just wanted to talk with you." Cattle started to moo somewhere to the south.

"Okay, where is it, Mr. Callahan?"

"Where is what?"

"Your hidden camera."

That explained part of the obnoxious attitude. He was paranoid that I was on the job. "No camera. I'm out of work again."

"I heard you had fallen on hard times. Otherwise, what would you be doing spending your holiday weekend in a dump like Dry Wells. Am I right?" We stared at one another and time crept by. I noticed that Will Palmer seldom blinked.

"Are you always so detached?"

"What do you mean by detached?" Palmer responded. He was not smiling.

"You just seem . . ."

"Bravo," Palmer said. He clapped his hands together. I jumped a bit. Palmer read my nervousness, enjoyed having startled me. "That was an absolutely dead-on impersonation of a sensitive therapist."

I'm losing this round. Instead of me getting to him, he is getting to me. What is it about him that throws me off?

"You seem angry." It was a weak, very textbook stalling tactic. I regretted it instantly.

"Reflection of feeling, Callahan? You can do better than that."

"Sorry, observation is an occupational hazard." I downshifted and forced myself to relax. *I've got to find a way to bond with him. Maybe if I opened up a little?*

At precisely that moment, as if reading my mind, Will Palmer leered and said: "Did you fuck her?"

My stomach went sour. "Excuse me?"

"Oh, come on, Mr. Callahan. We both know practically everyone in town fucked my sister. Did you?"

"I—I knew her as a child." *Christ, he's got me stammering . . .*

Palmer closed his eyes as if preparing to nap. "Then why bother, Callahan? You have no career left to speak of, you weren't fucking Sandy, and you're boring me. Go away."

My pilot light popped on; heat rose up from my rib cage to turn the world black and red. I almost kicked the legs of the chair out from under him. My voice sounded strange: low and tight: "You know, maybe I just remembered something I need to do."

"How about you go do it, then."

I started towards the car. *This is exactly what he wants. He thrives on it.* "You know something, Will?"

Without opening his eyes: "What?"

"You might want to try going to charm school."

"That so?"

"You don't, someday somebody's likely to rearrange your face so bad you'll drown when it rains."

"Have a nice day, Mr. Callahan."

I got into the Ford, feeling completely defeated both professionally and personally. I drove away.

Eleven

Sunday Morning, 10:45 a.m.

Thirty minutes later: FOR SALE.

I was not prepared for my reaction. The sight of the weather-beaten black mailbox set into concrete and brick brought tears to my eyes. I pulled to the side of the road and sat quietly in the trailing cloud of dust. The long, unpaved driveway was now overgrown with cactus and dried weeds. A man could still walk it, if he navigated carefully between the needled guardians. I had taken Hal's advice.

I had come home.

It only took me a moment to find the spot. A tiny stream still trickled through the low, gray boulders and fragile strands of water moss spider-webbed among small multi-colored rocks. I lingered there for a while, trying to sense her presence. All I could recall was the scent of her perfume, the way she brushed her long, dark hair, and then scattering her gray ashes over a row of blooming red roses while Daddy Danny sobbed helplessly. I could not remember my mother's face.

Rest easy, Katherine, I thought. *I wish I had known you.* I got to my feet and kept walking.

My chest tightened as the old, boarded-up buildings came into view, then the corral, the long metal watering trough, the barn. Old wagon wheels and rusted fragments of farm appliances littered the yard. The house was ruined now; the white had faded to something beyond color. The boards had splintered at all edges, and even the nails had begun to crumble. The well was bone dry, the bucket just a few slats bonded by bits of orange metal.

I paused on the porch, heart hammering in my chest. I could hear Danny Bell's voice as if echoing down a tunnel: *Goddamn it, boy, what are you, stupid or something? I told you not to touch that. Shut up or I'll really give you something to cry about . . .*

The door was nailed into place. I raised my left leg and kicked, then kicked again. After three tries, the wood gave way and I stepped into the house. I was astonished at how small the living room was, now that I was fully-grown. I sneezed in the dust and the gloom.

When I was in school I studied a variety of different therapeutic techniques, some more effective than others. Gestalt therapy works wonders. It allows clients to project their unresolved feelings for someone onto an empty chair. I decided to use the house itself.

"Hello, Danny," I said, feeling foolish. "How's it going?"

I leaned against the wall and closed my eyes. I reached for painful memories, activated them: Saw a scared, scrawny kid in a torn, striped T-shirt and jeans circling me in the dirt. His name was Willie Chambers, and his small hands were balled into fists, knuckles bruised and bloodied. Willie's eye was swollen shut and he was crying. Snot was running from his flattened nose. Daddy Danny and some friends were cheering and laughing, enjoying the contest. Danny seemed pleased and proud. *Put him down, boy. He's a goner now, sure enough.* I closed the gap and landed a right cross. Willie fell and curled up, trying to protect himself. *Pay up, pay up,* Danny called. *I told you he could do it.*

I felt sick to my stomach. I opened my eyes, looked at the house, and tried to believe it was a living thing. "Why,

Danny? Why did you make me fight those kids for money?"

The answer came. *To teach you.*

"Teach me what, for Christ's sake?"

We were seventeen, maybe eighteen years old and they sent us out into the bush, right into the tall green grass, all by our lonesome . . . What I "heard" was a pastiche of a dozen drunken, paranoid speeches I had endured over the years; it rambled like Danny had rambled . . . *I killed other boys, in close with a knife. I broke their necks with my bare hands. It screwed me up, kid. And what did I do it for?*

"I don't know, Danny. I went into the service to find out, but didn't learn anything I didn't already know."

My uncle fought the Krauts in a war that people said was a GOOD war. He got to stand up for something he believed in. They called him a hero for what he did, and they called me a baby killer.

"That wasn't fair," I said, so softly I almost didn't hear myself speaking. My chest ached.

I thought I was shaping you, boy, making you tough enough to be a man in this world. I wanted you to be able to fight the demons when they come.

"I'm fighting demons now, Danny. You got that right."

So what, boy? I fought 'em in the fucking mud and then in my nightmares. They followed me all the way to Nevada. You think I meant to lose my goddamned ranch to Lowell Palmer? I fought him, too.

"I know."

I did the best I could.

"I know that too."

Yeah, but you never looked up to me. You always had a mouth on you, Mick. I got no respect. I tried to help you grow some balls, that's all. Maybe keep you from being afraid of a little hard work.

105

"I never ran from the work."

There's evil out there, boy. It was for your own good . . .

"Yeah, you poor bastard," I whispered, "I'll bet you really believed that. You thought it was for my own good." A full catharsis followed. I tasted tears. "Did you ever manage to love me, Danny, even just a little?"

Silence, except for a slight breeze that whimpered at the broken windowpanes. I wiped my eyes, looked around. Nothing moved, no one spoke. It was over. I couldn't say whether or not it had done me any good. I waved at the house and left again. For some reason, I had to turn and say goodbye.

"So long, Danny. I'll see you around."

One lone cow was moaning again and a swarm of flies had found a pile of horse droppings near the steps. It was perhaps an hour later, but Will Palmer was still snoozing on his porch. He opened one eye as if he'd half expected me to return.

"Back so soon, Callahan? I thought you'd had enough of my persona."

I stepped onto the porch, my anger tightly controlled. "Persona. That was the Greek word for 'mask.' Did you know that?"

"Yes. Now tell me, how did that make you *feel?*"

"Oh, knock it off, asshole," I said. "Now you're starting to bore *me.*"

Will Palmer stiffened. "You're on my property, mister."

"Go ahead, be a fool. I've got all day." I dragged a chair across the wooden porch, allowed the legs to scrape in an irritating way. I flipped it around backwards, straddled it with my legs. *You want to see evil, Danny? Check this kid out.*

"What do you want, asshole?"

106

"Well, let's start with how grief-stricken and upset you are about the death of your beloved sister Sandy."

"Am I not performing to your satisfaction?"

"Let's just say getting stoned doesn't strike me as very . . . respectful."

"Well, that struck me as a crude attempt at psychological intimidation. Frankly, I think you can do better."

"You're right, I probably can. We got off to a bad start." I relaxed my face and body. "Can you tell me why you're being so defensive? I'd really like to know."

Palmer took the bait. "Perhaps you'll relate to this. I am the only young man around these parts to have gone to a prestigious college, Mr. Callahan. Have you read Camus? I am disreputable simply because I do not behave the way others *think* I should. I guard my emotional responses and disdain relationships. I comport myself differently than my fellows, and this has not made me popular."

"The ego defends itself."

"What?"

I stayed light. "I'm a therapist, remember?"

"Oh, that's right. Or you were before you reinvented yourself as an obnoxious lackey of the media."

"Touché." After a time, I pretended to remember something: "By the way, I know you saw your sister talking to me at the park."

"Half-sister. And your point is . . . ?"

I shrugged. *He's relaxed. Hit him.* I dropped my voice to a whisper. "I'll be straight with you. The point is that your soul is ugly as a bag of assholes. I think you and Bobby Sewell are two of a kind. Beyond that, I don't rightly know, but rest assured I'll be working on it."

Palmer grew flustered. "Fuck you."

"Tart retort, quite pithy."

His face reddened. "Callahan, I damn well don't like you. So remind me why I should be talking to you in the first place."

"You saw me talking with Sandy in the park."

"So?"

"So you want to know what she said to me. That's why you were smoking weed. You had to get a little faded first. Not because you're curious, but because you're scared."

He hid his reaction pretty well, but the mask slipped a bit. "Afraid of what?"

"Of me, because you know I haven't made my mind up yet. Because I might decide to talk to the authorities about what Sandy told me."

And then, having played my hand for the moment, I sat back. Waited. Silence can be a therapist's best friend, when it is properly employed. A flat, even countenance, devoid of emotion; no sound present but the rushing of blood and the beating of the heart. Such an experience allows intense emotions to surface, some of which can surprise.

Palmer sagged in his chair, seemed to weaken. "It wasn't my fault."

What wasn't your fault? I continued to bluff, defying a counter-transference that gave me a sudden and nearly overpowering urge to yawn. Depression oozed from this handsome man/child, making the atmosphere bleak and cloying.

"You know what?" he said defiantly. "It's none of your fucking business."

"Look, Will, Sandy made it my business." *What the hell are we talking about?*

Will got up, paced the porch. "You can't know what it's like living with my esteemed father. He who knows every-thing, who is always right, a man who wants to wring every

108

goddamned thing he can out of life every single day he lives it. We couldn't defecate without his permission."

I didn't want him to wind down, needled again. "You mean pity the poor little rich kid?"

"Fuck you," Palmer spat. "I knew you wouldn't understand."

"Try me. Maybe I'll surprise you."

"No camera, no recording device?"

"Nothing."

"I don't believe you."

"You'll have to," I said, and winked lewdly. "Unlike a lot of other folks around here, I'm not taking my clothes off for you."

Will Palmer snorted. "You know what? If you're going to do something, go ahead and do it. My father is God in this county, and you can't prove a thing."

"Not yet."

"Callahan, why do you even give a shit?"

I was honest. "I keep wondering about that myself. The only thing I can come up with is that she asked for my help." *He doesn't get it. In fact, he seems amused.* "I wasn't there for her, and I can't let that happen again."

"Give me a break, Callahan."

He's fighting down some intense emotion, has a facial tic. Why? "Maybe it doesn't make sense, but I prefer it to the alternative. Feeling like you feel."

"Huh?"

Will Palmer was depressed, narcissistic, and possibly a sociopath. That meant there was nothing inside of him but fear and driving need. *Oh, I think I understand you now, little boy.*

I bored in, speaking loudly at first, taunting him: "You couldn't sleep last night, could you Will? You know something is really wrong with you, but you don't know what. You tried smoking some dope, drank some booze, took some pills. You tossed around, sweating and thinking and worrying about getting caught. If you're lucky, you finally passed out somewhere during the night."

"Go away." *His hands twitched, his teeth clenched. I'm getting to him.*

I raised the intensity but lowered the volume. "Now you're sick to your stomach, you're shaking like a leaf, and your eyes burn. What was it Sartre said? That hell is other people? Well, you hate us, you hate yourself, and you hate your so-called life . . . you just don't have the guts to end it."

"Go away, Callahan." His voice was thick with emotion.

"You know that I can see right through you, see every disgusting little thought and habit you have. And you think I'm judging you for them, so you want me dead. You hate me because you can't stand it when somebody sees through you."

"Fuck you, man." *He's going to break. Keep pushing and he'll break.*

"Will, fuck your father. I already tried using everybody and not giving a shit. I tried being like you. It damned near killed me."

"Let me tell you something, Callahan . . ."

"WILSON!"

An old man's voice, coming from somewhere up on the second story. *Damn it, damn it.* The spell was shattered. Will Palmer flinched. "Yes, Father?"

"Who the hell are you talking to, you idiot?"

My stomach curdled at the tone of the old man's snarl, but Will gathered strength from it. He stood up. "It's some hick from town, Father. He wanted to offer his condolences."

110

"Well get rid of him, boy," Lowell Palmer spat. "I'm trying to rest."

The slender young man grinned at me. His arrogance once again as firm as a second skin. "Hey, you heard him."

I got to my feet. "Funny, it's hard not to figure Sewell and his bunch for this, but I think you know something, too. I haven't decided what I'm going to do, but I'm going to do *something*. Sandy asked me for help, and the fact that she's dead doesn't change anything."

"Get lost," Will Palmer said. He hawked phlegm, spat at my feet. "Don't let the gate hit you in the ass on the way out."

"Right."

I started the car, allowed Will Palmer a few seconds of satisfaction. Then I rolled the window down. "One last thing," I said, pleasantly. "Of course you knew Sandy was pregnant, right?"

Palmer went ashen. His hands fell to his sides. He sat down heavily.

"Of course they'll do an autopsy down in Elko. I just wonder what they'll find when they check for the DNA of the father. You got any idea, Will?"

"Get the fuck off our property," Will Palmer said.

"Relax, cowboy. I'm gone."

I drove away slowly, got some air into my lungs, and swallowed.

Man, what a sick puppy.

I started out the back way, towards the rear gate and the exit onto 93. The dirt road went past the grain silo and the three empty mobile homes. Between two of them were some large metal containers, as well as several bales of hay in random formations. Some of the bales had archery targets stapled to one side.

111

Twelve

Sunday Morning, 11:39 a.m.

"Check this out," Jerry said. We were in the motel office. He had multi-colored wires trailing everywhere and an old printer was grinding out pages.

I closed the door and dropped onto the well-worn couch. "What?"

"That dude Mex is an ex-felon named Jose Rodriguez, originally from the El Paso area. He did three years for burglary. He's auditioned for a couple more stretches, but nothing stuck. I've printed out his rap sheet and some background."

"The other one?"

"Donald Ray Wilson, a/k/a Wild Man, a/k/a Donnie Wilson, a/k/a Donny Boy. Born and raised in Nevada. He's got a substantial juvenile record, which the state has sealed, but I got into it anyway."

"You're a genius."

"Donald Ray was raised by an alcoholic mother who was a prostitute, mean as a snake. She ran some funky whorehouse down Jackpot way. The state records I hacked say she beat the shit out of the kid, claimed he fell down all the time. Donald probably would have been a dick anyway. He had a couple of busts for drug possession, but walked by milking that troubled childhood. Judge let him off with a promise to sober up and rehabilitate himself."

"I do believe the boy has a ways to go."

"No shit. He never showed up for rehab. He had an assault beef in Colorado, then skipped bail. The Colorado cops don't seem all that sorry he's down here in Nevada."

I heard a beeping sound. The largest television monitor lit up. "Don't tell me you . . . ?"

Jerry grinned. "Sure did." He pointed a small camera in my direction. His fingers flew over buttons on the console. An image coalesced from colored blobs, an older male with silver hair and a thin smile. Technology amazes me. Only a few hours had passed, and Jerry already had Hal videoconferencing into the motel office via a 21-inch monitor.

"Hello, Hal. Nice to see you."

"It's good to see you too, Mick." His lips moved, yet the top half of his head remained frozen. The effect was disconcerting, like a bad CNN report from Afghanistan. "I have something for you."

Jerry grew excited. "Stuff about Palmer already?"

"I knew that name sounded familiar," Hal said. His distinguished features rippled slightly as the image changed again. His resonant baritone sounded a bit tinny and muffled. "Lowell Palmer is a real *schmuck*. He was an investment banker, too. Out of Chicago, I believe, maybe originally over at the Board of Trade. Then briefly in New York City at around the time I made my residence there."

"And?"

"The point is, I seem to remember Mr. Palmer running afoul of the authorities, much as I did myself eons ago. Of course, yours truly could at least blame the dreaded disease of alcoholism for said inappropriate and maladaptive behavior. In Wilson Palmer's case, I believe he was merely your garden-variety thief."

"Oh, this is so *cool*," Jerry said. He bounced up and down in his chair. His voice broke on the last syllable. Hal peered into the European monitor and squinted.

"I beg your pardon?"

"That wasn't me, Hal. That was our hacker buddy."

"Oh. Callahan, for a moment I thought your voice was revisiting puberty."

"So this is where you learned to be a dick," Jerry said. Hal laughed out loud. The sound reached us two seconds before his face changed. Jerry shrugged and mumbled something about having strained his pixels.

"Hal, go on about Palmer," I said.

"He used to pull the pump-and-dump," Hal said. "This was perhaps forty years ago, long before the high-speed Internet version. One had to have a certain gift back then. You had to build a little penny stock very slowly and carefully and lure only the very best people. You used one person's capital to pump up the stock, hyped it as it rose higher, and then offered it to yet another and another as a so-called hot tip. Every *putz* involved thought he was in on a sweet little slice of insider trading. Spread a bit of carefully placed gossip, add some good old-fashioned bullshit, and *presto*. Your stock, which was of course entirely worthless to begin with, has now been successfully pumped."

"And the dump part is self-evident."

"Sure. You take the money and run," Hal said. "You see that was the portion of the scam that required such exquisite timing in those days. As soon as you had reached a truly insupportable level of face value, you would suddenly, and without warning to the others, dump all of *your* shares in a matter of hours. The stock would crash without explanation, and you would be gone with a profit."

Jerry laughed. "That must have pissed off a lot of people."

"Oh, most certainly," Hal Solomon said. "But, you see,

no one could come after him, at least not legally, because it was all insider trading to begin with. They could have gone to the authorities, but they would have been confessing to a felony. It was such a lovely scam." He sounded wistful.

"Hal, my friend, you still have a larcenous heart." I got up and stretched. "I doubt it was much fun on the other end."

"At the time, the pump-and-dump was almost an art form."

"And Palmer was a gifted practitioner."

"He was indeed."

I rubbed my eyes and thought for a moment. "What puzzles me is that the operative word would appear to be *was*. Because . . ."

"Because, as you indicated in our previous discussion, he still lives in a somewhat luxurious manner, even now."

"It's a decent-sized spread," I said, warming to the thought. "He's keeping it up and he's driving a brand new foreign car. He's not making money from my stepfather's old ranch or any of his other properties around Dry Wells. They've all been standing empty for years."

"So perhaps Palmer has moved out into cyberspace with his stock scamming?"

"I'm on it," Jerry said. "If he has anything wired, I'll run it down."

"Good." Hal's forehead moved; the mouth remained frozen for a millisecond. "I heard through the grapevine about numerous reversals of fortune. I know his reputation eventually preceded him into every undertaking. He might also merely have stashed quite a bit away. They say living well is the best revenge. Or perhaps the son is gainfully employed?"

I was pacing, lost in thought, so Hal started shuffling

115

through some papers on his desk. He drank from a bottle of mineral water that had a German label.

After a time: "Hal?"

"Sir?"

"The answer is no. I don't think Will Palmer has a job. I'd be surprised if he's ever been employed. Maybe that's relevant. Maybe this mysterious source of funds has something to do with the death of our girl."

"Let's hear from you, Jerry," Hal said. "What have you learned about the other gentlemen in question?"

Jerry scooted forward in his seat. He held a long, lined yellow notepad covered with scribbles. "I went asking around after Bobby Sewell first. He was a high school star, made all-state. I hacked the newspaper and college computers and even got this footage from the television station down in Elko. Check it out."

Jerry moved his hands. Streaming video replaced Hal on the monitor: Bobby Sewell, holding up a high school conference trophy. Young Bobby playing football, slamming his opponents to the turf. Bobby suited up and facing a quaking opponent, screaming: "I'll hit you so hard your houseplants will die."

"The various files say he got recruited by a bunch of colleges, including UNLV," Jerry said. "He wanted a good football program, though, so he ended up at Arizona State. Bobby got Cs in any class that wasn't basket weaving or finger painting. He played himself some damned good football, though. The Arizona Cardinals drafted him in the ninth round, but he got hurt in training camp, before he officially made the squad. He blew out his right knee. That left him with some minimal insurance coverage, but no serious bucks. I've heard he's still pissed as all hell about that."

"Life is a bitch," I said. The screen flickered to black and then Hal reappeared.

Jerry continued reading from his notes. "So our Bobby Sewell moves back to Dry Wells maybe six years ago, parties, and works a little on local spreads, tossing bales around. Couple of years ago he takes up with Sandy Palmer. He seems pretty tight with her family. That's about it."

I perched on the edge of the desk. Jerry cracked his knuckles. I jumped at the sound and shot him an annoyed glance. Hal, oblivious, yawned.

"Okay, Sandy claimed she dumped Bobby," I said. "And she wanted to talk to me about her boyfriend. So I don't know if she meant Sewell or someone who might have just entered the picture. If it was Sewell, maybe he couldn't handle losing her. He seemed pretty unstable."

"Possibly," Hal said. "What about our local representative of law and order, Mr. Bass?"

Jerry thumbed his notes, spoke again: "Glen Bass was born in Ely, and grew up around Elko. He never went to college. He served in Vietnam in 1970, this according to the newspaper story about his becoming sheriff. I knew he was with the 101st Airborne, so I found their website and started digging. Hal got me the rest of this from television archives, Mick."

The kid worked magic again. Old combat footage from Vietnam appeared on the monitor. Then some interviews with young boys at war; one of them was an incredibly young-looking Glen Bass. "He won a Bronze Star for valor on August 13th, 1970," Jerry continued, "when his unit assaulted a place called Hill 848 somewhere near Khe Ta Lao in South Vietnam. I guess half the North Vietnamese Army was parked there. Lieutenant Bass single-handedly killed five enemy soldiers while protecting two of his own wounded."

"Impressive," Hal said. We could now see his face again. "Bass was a brave young man."

"That's not all, though," Jerry said. "What got left out of the newspaper story was that he left the service in 1978 under suspicious circumstances. I e-mailed a couple of people, made a call or two, but all I could find out is that his ex-wife accused him of battery. He was arrested by the MPs, but the domestic violence charges were dropped when he resigned his commission and left the service."

"Something he might understandably neglect to add to his biography when applying for work as a law enforcement officer."

"Exactly, Hal."

"So we also consider Sheriff Bass. Perhaps we can endeavor to establish with certainty whether or not he and Ms. Palmer were an item at some point?"

"Whatever," Jerry sighed. "But this is getting to be one hell of a long list."

I shrugged. "It is what it is. Like I said before, this happened in broad daylight with most of the town nearby. Forget alibis, Jerry, we need to find motives and work from there."

"Okay, then," Jerry said. "Mick, you may be especially surprised to hear this. Your good buddy Loner McDowell might not exist."

My stomach lurched. "Come again?"

"I mean that Lawrence P. McDowell may not be your friend's real name. He claims to have been born in Boulder forty-two years ago, but turns out his biography on the website is pretty much bogus. If he has a driver's license or a Social Security number I couldn't find them, and I'm good. Ditto a credit card history. The news footage was all carefully controlled shit about his radio show. How well do you really know him?"

"Not as well as I thought. You're throwing me a curve ball with this one." I shook away a dark feeling. "Okay. Hal, one last report. Did you two geniuses find anything on Doc Langdon?"

"The good doctor is a licensed veterinarian," Hal said. "His record as a physician to stricken farm animals is pristine."

Jerry continued: "He always pays his bills on time, has one VISA and an American Express card. He owns his home. Doc spends most of his discretionary income on trips to Reno or Las Vegas. He stays in the best places and eats only the best food. I found several charges on credit cards that have 900 prefixes, so he digs phone sex."

"That's it?"

"Almost. He was also arrested for practicing medicine without a license, but eventually the charges were dropped."

Another bad feeling. "Explain, Jerry."

"I hacked the court computers and the cop files too. It seems Doc Langdon was making money on the side patching up mob soldiers when they got injured or shot. See, no pesky police reports."

Mob soldiers. I thought of the body in the alley, and wondered why Bass had wanted me to keep my mouth shut. He and Doc were good friends. "That's a little disturbing. It makes me less inclined to trust him."

"You think this ties in to Sandy?"

"Maybe, maybe not." It sure seemed to. A queasy feeling told me I didn't know people half as well as I thought. "Man, this damned town has secrets to spare."

Jerry dropped his notes. I sat on the edge of the desk and crossed my arms. "That's it, then. At least those are our only live ones for the moment."

"Yes," Hal said. His face was flickering again. "Young Callahan, I must say it does my old bones good to be focused and busy again. How did it go at the Palmer ranch?"

I filled them in on my strange confrontation with Will Palmer. When I explained how I had tried to provoke him, Hal seemed worried.

"Mick, you have indicated to townsfolk that you are in possession of potentially inflammatory information. The word will spread. Considering the other murder, there may be more here than just one angry lover. If so, someone already guilty of murder could assume two wrongs would make a right."

Jerry was picking at his teeth. He missed the reference to the second body so I let it pass. "Killing is kind of like eating peanuts? It's hard to stop once you start? Come on, lighten up, Hal. Something bad happened, but it was probably a crime of passion."

"I'm serious," Hal said. "You may as well have painted a target on your forehead, should Miss Palmer's demise prove to involve more than a simple case of jealous rage."

"He's got a point," Jerry said. "You carry a gun?"

"Guys, lighten up for Christ's sake," I protested. "I'm not planning on playing the hero here. If we find out anything of substance, we turn it over to the authorities. Providing our suspect is not the authority in question."

"Let us hope it isn't Bass," Hal said. "By the way, did you ever reach our obnoxious producer, Mr. Young?"

"I did indeed. He was not pleased."

"Did he allow you an extra day or two to reach the City of Angels?"

120

"He did not. He made noises about inquiring, but I think we're screwed."

"What are you going to do, then?"

"It's Sunday afternoon. I'm staying through tomorrow night, and then I'm going to Los Angeles. Listen, Hal, thanks for lending your ear and expertise."

"Think nothing of it. I am enjoying myself a bit. In fact, this investigation is as close as I dare come to pulling another sting without violating my fragile spiritual principles. It is bedtime here, good sirs. Good night to you."

The monitor clicked off. Jerry shook his head, rubbed his burn scar. "Jeez, does he always talk like that? How the hell can you understand him?"

I grinned. "Jerry," I said. "You are amazing. Give you a few hours and you give me the world."

"Sorry about the pixel glitches," Jerry said. "If something isn't moving, it tries not to refresh it, so the signals get thrown a bit out of synch. Also, the larger the surface, the more the pixels have to stretch to cut it. I used a pretty big screen, so I probably overloaded the video card."

"I'm impressed," I said. "You did a great job."

We grinned like possums, the way redneck men will do when they feel affectionate but homophobia gets the best of them. "Well," Jerry said, "what do we do now?"

"We go to lunch," I said. "We continue to spread the rumor that I know a lot about what is going on around here. We see what happens."

"And what if nothing happens?"

I didn't answer for a moment. "I'll tell you something, Jerry. I want to be on a plane for Los Angeles. I want to float around a pool with a beautiful woman and an unlimited supply of iced tea. And I mean *real* iced tea, not that pansy persimmon-flower stuff from West Hollywood. I want to make boodles of greenbacks talking to a camera. What I *don't* want to do is hang around here any longer than I have to." I stood up and cast a very long shadow. It was almost noon. "So if nothing of importance turns up by tomorrow evening, then by the end of this Memorial Day weekend, I intend to be out of here."

Jerry looked baffled. "Okay."

"I am in this for the *short* haul, and you can take that to the bank."

Thirteen

Sunday, High Noon

The little diner was nearly empty. Two aging migrant workers shared a beer and a bowl of chili in the far corner. Madge waited on us, collected their money, then returned to the kitchen. Annie was nowhere to be seen. I was staring down at my can of soda like it was the winning lotto ticket when I surprised myself by talking. "She was only twenty-three years old," I said. "I think I had something to do with her getting killed."

"What?" Jerry tugged his baseball cap down over the scar.

"I'm okay for long stretches," I said, absently, "but then suddenly I start to dream about her and I can't get her out of my mind."

"Who?"

"Bonnie."

"I don't know what you're talking about, Mick. Some client you used to see?"

"She was a blonde, like Sandy Palmer." It all came out in a rush. "I was doing this violence group with a colleague of mine, Angela Dorio. Sometimes I'd catch her client calls when she was on vacation."

"Oh. And this shrink lady was gone?"

"Yes. Bonnie paged me instead. Her boyfriend had threatened to kill her. She came in for an emergency appointment, really scared. Turns out she'd seen me on television. She'd recognized my name and my voice the minute I called her back."

This was not something I was used to talking about, and Jerry knew it. He didn't move, not even to take a sip of his coffee. I continued, now focused on another time and place.

"Bonnie was a beautiful girl. She was the kind who lit up a room. She looked a lot like Sandy, with blonde hair, blue eyes, a big smile. She could make a man eat his heart out." The migrant workers left through the back door, chatting in Spanish. "The boyfriend was older, thirties I think. He had been in jail a couple of times for assault and another time for beating her. The neighbors called the cops, and in California the law says if anybody has a mark on them, somebody has to go to jail. I guess Bonnie looked pretty bad that night, so they took him away. He never forgave her."

I sipped my drink. I resumed talking, almost in a whisper. "I hadn't had a lot of booze, maybe a couple of drinks, I don't remember. But I know it was enough that my judgment was impaired. I gave her the number of a shelter, told her to go there. I gave her my private number. I promised I would call her right back if she needed help. Then I let her walk out, and do you know why? I had to start taping a show in a couple of hours."

Jerry swallowed. "That doesn't sound too bad."

I ignored him. "Walt must have come along right about when my program aired. It's a safe bet he was calling her a slut and a whore, things like that. They usually do. When they found her, she had a split lip. She also suffered a concussion, a broken cheekbone, missing teeth, some kidney damage, broken fingers, and her ribs were in pretty bad shape. One of them had punctured a lung. So she was lying there drowning in her own blood; dying in her own kitchen, that Saturday night, while I was high on coke and booze and making fun of somebody on the air." I turned towards Jerry. "But you know what really fucks with me?"

"What?" Jerry's voice cracked.

"The cops found her cell phone a few feet away. Her broken fingers were reaching for it, and my number was already dialed in. She wanted to tell me all about her terrible evening."

"Mick, that's horrible. But how is it your fault?"

I grimaced. "Jerry, I didn't call her back. I got drunk and I forgot."

"Ouch. But look, you couldn't have known he would kill her."

"I knew it was possible. I started eating my shadow a long time ago."

"I don't understand," Jerry said. He obviously wanted to. But Jungian theory is dense and complex.

I thought for a moment. "Okay." I leaned forward. "We all have a shadow, consisting of all the elements of the psyche we don't understand. Carl Jung thought we had to examine and devour that part of us in order to be whole. If we do not accept and eat the shadow, it will eventually dominate."

"So therapy puts it in a burrito for you, or something?"

I laughed. "You might say that. We need light and dark to function. Evil is just the shadow without balance. But look, a man with no shadow also wouldn't have any courage. He wouldn't be able to fight for what he believes in. What's that old quote? Evil is just the absence of good?" I suddenly realized I'd left Jerry behind. "Sorry. I've lost you."

"That's okay," Jerry said. "But look, so you're an alcoholic. Why is that so unforgivable?"

There was one last bit of pus in the wound. I stared

down at the scarred plastic that covered the laminated table, studied the way it distorted my reflection. It made my features appear hideous. I felt my cheeks turn red. I eyed my dark twin without looking away.

"There was a groupie who used to hang out at the studio every night, kind of an airhead. While Bonnie was trying to call me, I was screwing her in a broom closet. I had turned my cell phone off so we wouldn't be disturbed. Get it now?"

"Jesus," Jerry said. "Yeah, I get it now. And that's why . . . ?"

"Sandy Palmer reminded me of Bonnie. I knew there was something oddly familiar about her, but I actually felt it in my bones over at Doc's place, while I was standing by her body. I was looking at Bonnie, too, and it made me feel sick."

"I get it, now."

"Hal knows me better than I know myself. He wants me to lose the guilt and start tilting at windmills again. He also wants to be a part of it because he's bored. So from now on, you and me, partner, are Don Quixote and Sancho Panza."

"Say what?" Jerry grinned.

"A knight in rusty armor. The trusty sidekick who helped him bought into his delusions of grandeur."

"Delusions of grander what?"

"Bad. Okay, I've got to see a man about a horse." I got to my feet, rocking the old wooden table. "Back in a few."

Annie Wynn was mopping the floor of the single rest room. She wore tight blue jeans and a white Dallas Cowboy tee. She looked edible. I stopped in the doorway, watched her for a while. Annie smiled with honest pleasure.

"Howdy. You need to get in here for some reason?"

"It can wait a minute. How are you? Was Loner annoying you last night?"

126

"Some," Annie said. She finished wringing out the mop, stood to face me. "He's a caution, that one. He's like Will Palmer, thinks he's God's gift to the ladies. I used to have a weakness for that kind of fool. These days, I don't even get accused of being a lady."

"I doubt that," I said.

Annie closed the distance. She looked up at me, bright brown eyes steady and focused. "I still make you nervous, don't I, Callahan?"

"Yes, ma'am," I said. "You surely do."

"You ever think how it was between us? How we were together?"

"Sometimes," I said, and winked, "especially lately."

"I never forgot," Annie said. "Not even with two loser husbands. You were always on my mind."

I backed up a step. "I don't know what to say to that."

"You don't have to say anything," Annie murmured. "Just take the compliment. Hell, Mick, you were smart, tough, pretty, and out of your damned mind. You were a genuine bad boy. There isn't a young girl in the world that can resist a combination like that."

We both laughed. "You were pretty wild yourself," I said.

Annie looked glum. "Yeah," she whispered, "a little too wild for my own good." She looked up, smiled sadly. "Could be I still am."

"I'd bet we're both older and wiser, now."

Annie's eyes sparkled. She cocked her head. "Wiser?" She moved closer and brushed her fingers up the crotch of my jeans. My body noticed. "Then just say yes."

I swallowed. "Slow down. A lot has happened in twenty years, Annie."

"Don't I know it?"

"Maybe a bit too much."

Her expression changed. She stepped away from me abruptly, as if another woman had entered her mind. "I'm sure we've both got our share of war stories."

"Mine are a matter of public record," I said. "It's going to be hard to live them down."

She gathered her thoughts. "You want to hear one of mine?"

"You want to tell me, I do."

I already knew the early stuff. Annie had grown up in a trailer park outside town. It was a broken home, and her redneck mother drank too much and found something wrong with nearly everything she did. So Annie had the kind of personality that both craves and mistrusts intimacy. She fucked and then fought, broke up and made up. Her heart was forever saying both "come here" and "go away" at the same time. She gathered herself, clearly uncomfortable with what she was about to say.

"I told you I lost a baby, right?" She cleared her throat. "It was an abortion."

"I see."

"You remember I used to talk about what I'd do, how I'd feel about having an abortion, if it happened maybe I got pregnant?"

I touched her face. "I remember."

"We were just kids then," she said. Her eyes went moist. "Then I didn't know if it was right that people were killing babies just for birth control. You recall that conversation?"

"I do."

"Well, the time came when I had to do that very thing myself." She sniffed and wiped her nose. "I was all alone, Mick. I didn't figure there was any way I could care for a baby. I was so young and stupid. But you see, you never know what's going to happen. It turns out the abortion messed me up. I can't have children. That was it, just that one time."

I stroked her hair. "Annie, I'm sorry."

"Me too, now," she said. "Sorry as hell." All the heat was gone. I gently put my arms around her. We rocked slightly to the left and right. After a moment we let go, and she looked up and chuckled. "Just when I start to think you're a prick, you do something like that."

"Huh?"

"You're a strange guy, always were." She moved closer. My pulse started to tap dance, my knees shook. Annie surely did have my number. "I never knew which Mick Callahan I was going to get. You went from cool and calm to hellfire and brimstone in a heartbeat."

"That's probably a bad thing."

Her breath was warm against my face and it smelled of fresh strawberries. "No, I like it," Annie said. "It makes you even more interesting." She quickly kissed me. And then, before I could respond, stepped around and behind. She slapped the seat of my jeans with an open palm. "You go on now," she said. "Do your business."

"Oh. Right."

In the restroom, I studied my face in the chipped mirror. I looked as confused as I felt. I splashed my face with water from the sink. I peeked back through the door for one last look. Annie went out onto the back porch. I followed the swing of her hips as she began to wring out the mop. Her clothes were soaking wet.

I flushed the urinal and washed my hands. The pipes were old and rickety and they banged and hissed, so I didn't hear anything. I walked back into the little diner and stopped dead in my tracks.

There were two of them, the Hispanic and the big one with the fuzz on his chin, the kid called Donny Boy. He and Mex had made short work of Jerry. My friend was on his hands and knees, trying to use his baseball cap to dab the blood from his lower lip. I felt oddly peaceful and enraged at the same time.

"Good afternoon, gentlemen," I said, smoothly. "Nice to see you again."

Panting. Jerry's low and muffled moan: "Damn. What the hell did *I* do?"

"For starters," Mex said, looking down, "you messed around with somebody else's pussy. Not a cool move."

"Yeah," Donny Boy said. "Say you're sorry, pizza face."

"Thorry," Jerry said. He lisped because of the swelling and the blood.

"And then," Mex said, "you started hanging around with Mr. Showbiz here."

"I guess that's my cue," I said pleasantly. "It seems like I'm the one you ought to be talking to."

"Not us," Mex said. "Bobby wants to see you. He's waiting outside."

"Okay. I'll be along shortly, as soon as I tend to my friend here."

My attitude confused Donny Boy. "The fuck?"

"He thinks he's really hot shit, because he was like a Green Beret or something," Mex said.

"Navy Theal," Jerry lisped.

They left. Annie came back in from the alley, where she had just finished dumping trash. She looked at Jerry with concern.

"What the hell is going on?"

"My friend could use a mother's love," I said. "Me, I've got some business outside."

I looked out the window. All the townspeople had vanished. People in Dry Wells sure knew when to disappear. I was completely on my own. Annie knelt by Jerry and handed him a paper napkin. "Oh, damn that's ugly. Hold your lip between two fingers," she said. "Let me get some ice on there."

"You think Sheriff Bass is in his office?" I asked.

"I doubt it, not this time of day."

"Then Jerry, soon as you feel up to moving around, it might be a good thing if you went looking for him."

"Hokay," Jerry said, into the napkin. He sounded like he had a mouth full of marbles. "Sure you don't need some help?"

"Help with what?" Annie asked. "Will somebody explain?"

"Thanks anyway, Jerry," I said, ignoring her. "I can handle this by myself. Maybe I've even got it coming."

"Got *what* coming?" Annie said. "I don't understand."

"That makes two of us," Jerry said. "Let's go find Bass." He struggled to his feet and stumbled to the door. Annie noticed blood on her fingers. She wiped them on her jeans, nodded quickly, and left.

I stepped out onto the porch, facing Main, where the three boys waited. Their harem wasn't far away: the hippie girl and the skinny brunette wearing beads were up on the sidewalk by Doc Langdon's clinic. The thin one, Jerry's sometime girlfriend, seemed upset.

Bobby Sewell was the theatrical sort. He had taken his shirt off to parade his six-pack and was strutting like a peacock. I looked around. Still not a sign of the citizenry of Dry Wells, as if this had all been neatly arranged. I shaded my eyes and looked south. A large, blue Mercedes was parked at the end of the block with the engine running. A young man with dark hair was inside, enjoying the air conditioning. He sat watching the street through a dust-streaked windshield that barely reflected the noonday sun. The man moved suddenly, and I saw the flash of clean, white teeth and a small puff of smoke.

Will Palmer.

I inclined my head in tacit acknowledgment. *Not a bad play*, I thought. *Let someone else do your dirty work.* I turned towards Sewell. Out of the corner of my eye, I saw a woman's face suddenly appear next to Palmer's. Her head had been buried in his lap. Palmer pushed it back down again.

I approached Bobby Sewell, my face pleasant. "Good afternoon," I said. "I hear you've got a problem."

"Don't go around asking questions about me and my friends. You got something to say, you say it straight to my face."

"Okay, Bobby," I said. "That's reasonable enough. Here goes. I think you're an asshole and you had something to do with Sandy Palmer's death."

The football players always charge at you, going for the tackle. Sewell screamed out a curse and rushed straight at my waist. I used my quickness, stepped to one side. Sewell was good; he caught himself and spun just in time, deflecting the fist headed for his jaw with an upraised elbow. We both backed away to take measure. I saw Donny Boy edging around behind me. "You plan on fighting me fair, Bobby, or you so scared you need to stack the deck?"

"Donny? Back the fuck off."

"Sure?"

"Yeah, I'm sure. Back off."

Donny Boy shrugged. I dodged a right cross, heard a man say: "Sounds like a good idea, Donny." It was Sheriff

Bass, walking slowly across the street. Had Will Palmer summoned him? Bobby Sewell seemed confused for a moment, but then Bass said, "This looks to me to be a fair fight. Let's just let them work this out alone."

"You got it, Sheriff," the one called Mex shouted. "Whatever you say."

Annie's voice: "Why, Sheriff! Aren't you going to stop this?"

"Naw, I don't think so, Annie," Bass drawled. "Thing is, I don't care too much for neither one of these boys. Wouldn't break my heart to see it go either way."

Bobby charged again, and a half-second faster. He slammed me into the wall by Annie's front window and started trying to batter my rib cage with his big, work-hewn fists. I tightened my belly and tried not to breathe. I grabbed Bobby Sewell by the hair and yanked, then brought one fist down sharply on the side of his nose. Blood spurted. Sewell shook his head and tried to bore in again, but I was down in the street, looking for room to maneuver.

"How about it, Bobby?" I taunted, although shouting made my ribs hurt. "Did you beat Sandy Palmer because she dumped you? Did you kill her?"

"Fuck you!"

Bobby charged. At the last possible moment, he realized his mistake and pulled back, narrowly avoiding a kick to the face. He circled more warily, panting. He hadn't expected this much of a fight. Frankly, neither had I.

A growling sound: At the end of the block, Will Palmer gunned the engine of the big Mercedes. He was obviously growing impatient. The girl reappeared. She edged closer, sliding her bottom across the leather front seat, but Palmer shoved her away. I saw her head bounce against the door and then the dash. She turned her face, as if crying. Palmer blew another plume of smoke.

Bobby and I danced around in the dirt as Donny Boy cried: "*Oh boy, oh boy*, come *on!* Somebody *do* something!"

What finally nailed me was an educated combination. Sewell bore in, jabs and crosses in a tight pattern, and the sudden shift to formal boxing threw me. One right struck home, and I found myself on one knee, rubbing my aching jaw. Frankly, I half expected Sewell to attack when I was down, but the boy held back.

"That all you got, man?" Sewell screamed. His nose was running bloody gruel. "You ain't nothing!"

I got up slowly and moved my chin around. "You hit like a mule."

I charged and knocked Sewell backwards. The sidewalk caught the boy by the heel, and I used my 220 pounds to crunch down hard, slamming Sewell against the concrete. I twisted my torso and brought a forearm down into his vulnerable neck, stunning the windpipe. Bobby thrashed like a fish out of water, nose bubbling with pink foam, unable to catch his breath. I remembered when Danny Bell had laid me out in exactly that way and how frightened I'd been. I softened, leaned in and whispered, almost kindly: "You can get some air, kid. It just *feels* like you can't. You won't die."

I let him go and got up, knowing I would be sore as hell in a couple of days. I turned away. In my mind it was over. Then Annie called out something unintelligible. Jerry hollered: "Look out, Mick."

Bobby smashed my skull from behind. For some reason, I thought of the dead man in the alley and his head wound. Time crawled, the way it does when you take one to the head. I heard my breathing grow absurdly loud and oddly slow. The entire world seemed to whistle and moan. My stomach rolled over, and lunch started to come back up. I was staggering, trying to stay on my feet. I looked down the street, towards the blue Mercedes. I managed to focus. Will Palmer was now laughing and pointing. The girl was still crying.

Bobby Sewell hit me from behind, this time in the kidney. The hovering sky went bright white for a moment. Now, I felt sleepy and warm and peaceful. I just wanted to give up and take a nap. Another blow whistled by the back of my head, this one missing by inches, but I didn't care.

Fight him you little bastard, Danny Bell cried from the depths of my mind. *This isn't a goddamned dress rehearsal. Don't you fucking quit on me, not now, not ever! You fight!*

I gathered myself; dropped low and spun around. I grabbed the crotch of Sewell's jeans with both hands and twisted. Bobby Sewell started making little yelping noises and bent over double. I freed one fist, yanked on his right ear. I tightened both grips and used them to run Bobby's blonde head into the outside wall of the diner, then dropped him on the sidewalk. Instinctively, I drew back my right boot to kick.

"Let's get him!"

Mex tackled me on the left side, Donny Boy from the right. They slammed into me at roughly the same time. A rib slid, and I felt a sharp pain in my chest. I slid to my knees, weary arms at my sides. Donny clubbed my jaw, Mex kicked at my chest. The world began to slip away. I dropped and curled up to protect my face and groin.

"Whoops," Bass called. "You'd best back off, boys."

Mex kicked again anyway. Donny drew back his fist, debating where to pop me. I opened my eyes, tracked the concrete. I saw a long trail of dust and sand and followed it to the rear wheels of Palmer's Mercedes. The car was leaving town, turning back out towards the lonely highway. I guess Will was satisfied.

"I said break it up!" Bass shouted. Donny Boy stopped the blow just in time. The sheriff walked over with one hand on his weapon. "We can't have fighting right out here on the city streets, can we?"

"No, sir," Donny Boy snickered.

"Mr. Callahan?"

"Why, of course not, Sheriff," I panted. I got to my feet and stood, swaying and shaking my sore hand. "We're all law abiding citizens here."

"Truly glad to hear that," Bass said. "Mr. Callahan, I do believe you said you'd be out of Dry Wells shortly. Can I assume that to be no later than the end of this holiday weekend?"

"You can."

He looked at Sewell with contempt. "Can you get up?" Bobby just grunted. Bass eyed me with what might have been a grudging respect. "You going to be okay?"

"Oh, sure," I lied. "They didn't lay a finger on me."

"Once you catch your breath, you come on over to my office. Maybe you can sign those two statements."

"Okay."

Jerry's lower lip had stopped bleeding. It looked like a flattened grape, slightly swollen and bruised. He kept trying to wave to the skinny girl, but she ignored him. I limped towards Annie, bone tired and feeling a bit immature. The ribs and knuckles hurt and my elbows and knees were all scraped and dirty.

Annie was standing near Jerry, wringing her hands. She was trembling. "I thought those bastards were going to kill you."

"They damn near did."

"Jesus, Mick. Did they hurt you bad?"

"I'm okay, Annie. Really. You go on back to work. Maybe I'll stop by and see you later on tonight."

"I'll hold you to that." She gave Bass a wicked look and walked to the diner. In the doorway, she glared at him again. "Sheriff, my ass," Annie said scornfully. She went inside.

Donny Boy, Mex, and the girls were now attending to Bobby Sewell. He was sitting up and croaking like a bullfrog about his broken nose and the pain in his balls. Donny Boy kept muttering, *oh boy, oh boy;* the one called Mex was calling me names in Spanish.

"You work pretty hard for five bucks," Jerry said.

I needed some rest. I smiled broadly at the Sewell gang and waved as we limped away. "Well, that ought to stir things up."

Fourteen

Sunday Afternoon, 2:35 p.m.

"Sorry I woke you up," Doc Langdon said. "But you probably shouldn't have gone to sleep anyway after a hit upside the head, just in case of a concussion."

"I know."

"Listen, you in some kind of contest to piss people off?"

I groaned as my bruised knuckles entered the bucket filled with ice cubes. The plastic container said *Dry Wells Nevada, UFO Country* on the side. It featured some garish slot machines and a little green man wearing a cowboy hat. The alien was strumming an electric guitar.

"Nothing got broke," Doc said. "I'd be careful of those ribs, and there might be some swelling in your hand, but this ought to help. Glad you got a little sleep right away, your body will need it."

"Who sent you over?"

"Why, Glen Bass," Doc said cheerfully. "Told me to fix up Bobby's nose and then get my sagging country butt over here. He thought you might go take *too* long a nap or something, or maybe just plumb forget to drop by his office. You got some statements to sign, and he wants to have a little talk with you."

I moved my throbbing fingers around in the ice. "God, I love this town. I can't get over how friendly you all are."

"It's your warm personality," Doc said. "We're usually not all that impressed with television stars, but we sure do like a boy who can mix it up a little."

"Have the state police called about picking up the bodies for autopsy?"

Doc shrugged. "There's some hard-core biker gang convention going on out to Ely, and it just may blow up on them, so they can't spare anybody until after Memorial Day. ME said to keep them both on ice. He'll be over early Tuesday morning to pick them up, maybe poke around the park and the alley a bit."

I leaned back with the bucket. "Doc, do you think somebody killed Sandy on purpose, yes or no?"

Doc looked amused. "Hell, who knows? I only work the livestock around here. I'm just your lovable old country vet."

"Yeah, but you're also quite a lot smarter than most of the people who live around here. What is your considered opinion?"

"Confidential like?"

"Off the record."

Doc stood up. "Can't say for sure, but I reckon during or maybe after somebody slapped her around, she slipped and fell. She was already barefoot on the rocks there, had abrasions on her heel. Anyway, she hit her head and passed out. But then I kind of lean towards the idea that the killer held her head under the water to make sure she was gone."

"Because?"

"What, the fall? Because of the way her skull got smashed, and because the wound looked very deep. The rest? Because like I said yesterday, I think the actual cause of death was drowning."

"Can you prove that?"

Doc shrugged. "Not without a forensic specialist right there at the site, and then only if nobody touched anything.

Forensics, now that's a strange kind of science. Those guys are real picky people, got to have everything exactly right, all down to the last detail. You can't touch a thing."

I opened and closed my fingers again. The bucket made a rattling sound. I winced at both the cold and the topic. "Then why *did* you move her so fast, Doc? You sound like you know better than to do that."

Doc gave me a look. "We all do what we're told in the end, don't we?"

"I guess so. Can we continue to keep this drowning thing just between you, me, and Bass? Might be I can use it somewhere along the way."

Doc studied me, thinking on it. Finally, he said, "Don't see why not. Now, come on. The sheriff is a'waitin'."

As I was locking the motel room door: "Incidentally, how well did you know Sandy Palmer?"

Doc Langdon was down in the dirt and two steps ahead. He laughed out loud. "That ain't very subtle, coming right out with it like that."

I followed him out into the sunshine. "I wasn't trying to be subtle. And I'm tired of the country bumpkin act, Doc. It was charming at first, but now it's starting to wear thin."

"Guess I'll have to work on my Elvis impression," Doc said, as he waited for me to catch up. "That's the only other good one I have."

I shifted attitudes. "Sorry, Doc, but I can't seem to stay out of this. It feels like something I have to do."

"Be better off you did stay out, boy."

"Maybe."

We walked for a while. I touched a rib and winced. After a moment of dead air, as we turned onto the street, Doc said, "Okay, then. Sandy Palmer. Truth is, I didn't know her very well, Callahan. I'll be straight with you though, it

140

was not for lack of trying. The girl got around, if you know what I mean."

Another tumbler clicked into place. I stopped in the dusty street. "No, I don't know what you mean."

"Come on, Callahan," Doc said. He seemed both amazed and amused. "Do you mean to tell me you didn't know Sandy Palmer was the town tramp?"

"No," I said, truthfully, "I didn't." That explained the mixed signals I had received from Sandy the day before, in the park. The intense counter-transference of childishness mixed with sexual heat. I felt a bit stupid for not having interpreted it correctly. "Sandy upset a lot of people, then, men and women both."

"Damn straight. Bass has got one long list of suspects to ponder. Look, that girl screwed every horny husband, son, and daddy in the county."

"I see."

Doc grew impatient and started walking again. He got a few steps ahead before I managed to react and follow. Meanwhile, Doc spoke over his shoulder. "I wanted her," he said. "Tell you the truth, I was pretty jealous of anybody got their chance with her."

"Jealousy can make a man do unusual things."

Doc snorted. "Oh, so now I'm O.J.?" His shoulders tightened but he kept on walking. "I said I never got in with the girl, Callahan."

I lengthened my stride and paced him. Then I stepped closer, crowding him a little. "I want to believe you, Doc," I said. "In fact, I almost do."

Doc laughed, edged away. He picked up the tempo. I realized he was in far better shape than he looked. He was old, but still strong and vital. "You're a rough bastard, aren't you?" he said. "You ought to ask Glen to deputize your ass."

We were approaching the sheriff's office at a brisk clip. "There's no easy way to say this, Doc. I've had a look at your police record. I know about the work you did for the wise guys, patching up soldiers."

Doc tensed, spun around, turned pale. There was a little wad of spit at one corner of his mouth. "Mind your own business, Callahan. I'm starting to comprehend why everyone around here dislikes you. You don't want me to join them, watch your mouth. You're running way low on friends."

"I've got enough friends," I said, lamely. I was trying to sound tough and indifferent.

That dog wouldn't hunt. Doc Langdon saw right through me. He stopped at the foot of the steps. "Is that so?"

I sighed. "No. Doc, I'm not sure I have *any* friends at the moment. But somehow I got myself into this situation, and now I have to ask some tough questions to get out again. I need to know what happened to Sandy."

Doc squinted and spat. He looked up and away, over my shoulder and into the pastel mountains. "You want it straight up, Callahan?"

"Sure do."

"Okay," he said. "Here it is, short and sweet. It would not surprise me a bit if somebody got upset at that girl and her round heels and decided to put her to sleep. Hell, son. Somebody took some video of her naked little butt a while ago and half a dozen copies were floating around town. So there you are. Okay?"

I was silent, perhaps for a bit too long. His words made me feel empty and sad. I studied the dirt. Doc was being honest, and in order to do that he had to avoid looking in my eyes.

"And why do you figure all this happened to her, Doc?"

"You're the shrink," Doc said. "You know as well as I do." His voice trembled a bit. "Somebody screwed that girl up, Callahan, probably years and years ago. She was a hot little twist, and she got around too much. That's all there is. You hear me?"

"I hear you," I said.

"Now, if you plan on raising more hell around here, you leave me out of it. I'm just a fat old man with a couple of black marks on his record. It's not much of a life to begin with, so don't you go and fuck with it."

Doc stalked off. I turned and went up the steps.

Fifteen

Glen Bass kept his office cool and dark, with virtually no dust. I saw some wanted posters, and lots of oak furniture, including a long wooden bench. The barred two-man cell seemed like something out of a western film. There were some awards for marksmanship on the wall above the large wooden desk. They were yellowed and seemed decades old.

There were a few photographs, the largest one of Bass with a unit of cheerful grunts in Vietnam. It was the kind of photo all handsome young boys took at the beginning of a war. I instantly sensed that only a few had returned alive. Another faded photograph showed a somewhat younger Bass crouched over the carcass of a dead buck with huge antlers. He was holding a long hunting bow.

I flashed on the dead man in the alley, his hands behind his back and fingertips sliced off; Doc had said he was killed with some kind of sharp object, perhaps a pick. What about a hunting arrow?

"A bow is an ugly way to kill something," Bass said.

I jumped involuntarily. "I've always thought so."

"Gets the job done, but it's cruel."

The sheriff was leaning against the wall behind the door, taking down a shotgun from the gun rack. He carried the weapon back to his desk. He sat down, spread some newspaper, and began to clean it. He did not look up.

"You prefer a shotgun?" I felt weak and sweaty and

144

wanted to sit down. But there was nowhere to rest, except for the bench, and I did not want to feel like his prisoner.

"I prefer a rifle," Bass grunted. "But I'm good with a bow, too. Thing is, the arrow hurts like hell, just slows the animal down so that he dies badly. That's not a clean way to kill."

"Why did you hunt that way, then?"

Bass looked up. I could not read his eyes. "That time? Somebody asked me to."

I decided on the lesser of two evils. Went to the bench, sat, and then leaned forward, hands on knees. "Who asked you to hunt with a bow?"

Bass finished scrubbing the barrel of the shotgun. He looked through, blew it out, put down the brush, and met my gaze. His tone was flinty. "Not sure that's any of your business."

"Just making conversation. Never much cared for hunting, myself. Especially bow hunting. My stepfather liked it."

"Killing is an acquired taste."

"Listen," I said, "since you and I are suddenly making nice again and all, can I go ahead and speak my mind?"

Bass put down the weapon. "Shoot."

"Unfortunate choice of words."

Bass did not smile. "Don't push me. I already asked you nicely to just shut up and leave town."

"In due time."

He bristled. "What the hell do you think you're playing at, kid? You're about to step in some deep shit here, and for what?"

"Beats me," I said, weakly. "Lately, I have this thing about playing hero. I suspect you'd know about that."

"The heroes I knew are all dead."

I wiped my brow. "That an observation, or are you threatening me?"

Bass leaned back in his chair. It complained and a hinge popped. He looked me over carefully. "Callahan, you and me, we've got some things in common. We both got hell whacked out of us growing up, both have world-class tempers. We both mean to do the right thing, but sometimes we screw up mightily. You recall that night?"

I shrugged. "Sure. Why the hell do you think I agreed to keep a dead man secret for a few days?"

Bass nodded. "Makes us even, I reckon. How old were you when I busted you, maybe seventeen?"

"Sixteen, probably," I said. "I was big for my age. I'd whipped Mayor Pepper's kid Greg in a money fight. His Daddy beat his ass again for losing, so Greg came after me with a box cutter and sliced my forearms up a little. I got it and threw it out into the fields." I paused, remembering, my face hot with shame. "Greg's head got bounced off that brick wall over by the old casino. He went down pretty hard."

Bass grunted. "I heard all the fussing, came around the corner while you were bent over the boy. I always meant to ask you, were you trying to help him or were you going to club him again?"

I thought for a moment. My throat closed. "I don't rightly know."

"Don't matter," Bass said. "That boy was bad, and you were just a kid. I didn't figure you deserved to go upstate for defending yourself."

"So you let me go."

"Jake Pepper was the mayor, Callahan. His brother-in-law was a senator. You and Danny Bell were white trash, at least to these morons around here. I made a judgment call, let you go. I'll stand by that."

"Maybe you're right," I said. "But I sometimes wonder. At least the kid lived. Whatever happened to him?"

"Greg drooled like a baby for a few months, then woke up and didn't remember shit. Last I heard he was living in Salt Lake and singing in some church choir. His asshole daddy died in '97. You were long gone."

"After Danny dropped dead and the ranch got repossessed, I hauled ass out of Dry Wells."

"As I recall, you enlisted in the Navy Seals. Made me proud."

"I never wore the trident. I got tossed out right after training." Bass raised his eyebrows. I sighed. "They got me for fooling around with the wife of an officer and fighting. It's a long story."

Bass nodded with something that passed for respect. "Okay. I don't talk about my days in the service very often, but it's Memorial Day tomorrow, so I'm going to make an exception. Listen up. This would have been late '68, maybe early 1969. They were inserting us into some fucking collection of huts and rice paddies."

Bass got a far-away look. After a moment, he continued. "There is a sound the chopper blades make, a kind of *'thock 'n thock 'n thock.'* It echoes through the metal, your butt kind of vibrates. Some boys would sit on their helmets, because they didn't want to get their balls blown off.

"This new guy called Cherry was maybe nineteen, like the rest of us, but he carried himself older. He was from California, had an education. We all figured he was fucking dinky dao for signing up. Anyway, so we are all in the chopper and you can't hear anything and your mouth tastes like dog shit and suddenly you're there. The doorway is open and we're spilling out into the razor grass wearing all

147

that gear. Some of us are falling flat, some running forward. The chopper doesn't stay down for thirty seconds because the LZ is hot. It's a trap, and they start cutting us all to pieces. Guys are screaming at each other and bellowing things into handsets and trying to get control, but this is so bad your asshole puckers until you could carve a washer off it.

"Near as I can tell, there is a machine gun nest right in front of the LZ, and since we got rice paddy and water all around us, that nest is blocking the only exit. Go out into the water, like some guys do, and you're lumbering along, all loaded down, and an even easier target. You can't go back, because that chopper pilot is out of there like a stripe-assed ape.

"And then the small mortar shells start falling all around us; guys blowing up and flying to pieces. I'm so scared I'm trying to sink into the mud so nobody can see my ass to shoot it. I wanted to see what I was made of. Hell, you can see what we're *all* made of in combat, and it's just red meat and gristle."

Bass stopped for a long moment. His eyes were dark, haunted slits. I had an urge to say something, but my mouth was too dry. I couldn't bring myself to speak. I was seeing through a window into my stepfather's past. I felt both fascinated and horrified. I tried to breathe quietly, through my mouth. Finally Bass continued.

"Cherry, his eyes are wide. You can't hear a fucking thing, but he's trying to tell me that he'll go up the fucking middle and I should cover him. Cover him! This kid watches too many movies. He gets up, he's a dead man.

"He gets up. And it happens to be right when Gunny and some boys start to run a shoot and scoot on the right flank, so the machine gunner turns to try to pick them off, and so does every guy Charlie's got. We have this lane we can see through, all of a sudden. Way down at the end of a dark tunnel there's a couple of dinks in black pajamas, and I am aiming and I fire and one of them goes down and then the other one does too.

"Cherry is broken-field running like a big fullback with the ball on fourth and seven when he has just *got to score* or the championship game is lost, you know? And he's firing from the hip as some little dink starts to replace the two I wasted, yanks on the gun and brings it around, but Cherry is there in the VC's face and puts him down. Then Cherry flips a grenade into the nest, where the gun and all the ammo and half the mortar guys are gathered, and starts running back towards me. And everything behind him just goes up, into fucking orbit, all red and yellow and black smoke. All the way back, Cherry is bobbing and weaving and dodging bullets and coming within millimeters of dying. Me, I'm frozen like a Popsicle right there in the mud. I'm blown away. I've never seen anybody do anything like that, before or since."

I wanted to stop him, for some reason. I cleared my throat. "Pretty amazing kid," I said. My own voice startled me. My mouth tasted terrible.

"Shut up," Bass snarled. "I ain't done yet."

I put my hands up, palms forward. "Sorry."

"The thing about Cherry," Bass continued, "is that he took a lot of crap from the guys. Calling him John Wayne, shit like that. He had an okay sense of humor, but I think it got to him. Not like it ticked him off, but that he *enjoyed* it a little too much.

"Couple months later, we get ambushed up around Hue. Two gunners this time, perfect fields of fire, got us in a crossing pattern. Cherry, he waits until one gunner is changing magazines, and he stands up and starts running again. The other gun swings around, though, and . . . Cherry just sort of flew into pieces. I don't know how to say it, except one arm went north and one went south and then the legs vanished too. His guts fell out. What was left of him dropped right there."

Bass seemed to return to the room. He smiled thinly. "He was a good boy, Callahan. And now that you're all grown up, you seem like you'd be an okay sort to have a beer with, too."

"Why did you tell me that story?"

"Because Cherry started believing he was some kind of a hero, instead of just plain lucky. Do you get my drift?"

I met his eyes and nodded. "I think so. You don't want me to go charging off foolishly, thinking nothing bad can happen to me. Something like that?"

"Exactly."

I shifted on the long, wooden bench. I had been stiff and motionless for a long time. The adrenaline from the fight had dissipated, so my muscles were starting to cramp up. "How many tours did you do, Sheriff?"

"One. That was enough for me."

"And you what, came back and got married?"

"Most of us did, back then."

"What happened with her?" I asked. "Just curious."

Bass stared at me. He moved in his chair and the wood cracked and moaned like a campfire. I saw his gears working. He decided to level with me. After a moment, he whispered: "I was crazy as a man can be outside a padded cell."

"Post-Traumatic Stress Disorder," I said.

"Whatever," Bass said. "I'd wake up screaming in the middle of the night. I drank too much, and sometimes I

150

went crazy for no reason at all."

I understood better than I wanted to admit. "Sounds familiar."

Bass eyed me. He shrugged. "I hauled off and hit my wife a couple of times, got busted down and out. They discharged me. That's it, beginning and end of story."

"Still have a temper?"

"Hell, it's been a long time since I teed off. I like it that way. Let me ask you a rhetorical question. Do you think a man needs to be ready to do violence in this world?"

"Yes."

Bass leaned forward, elbows on the desk. "Damn straight. The world hasn't changed all that much in a thousand years."

I choked out the question I'd been sitting on the whole time. "Sir, how well did you know Sandy Palmer?"

Bass moved the shotgun around so it was pointing at me. He resumed cleaning it; no sounds but the nylon brush against metal and my thumping heartbeat. Bass took his time, looked up. "You're a lot like Cherry," he said. "Born to be a chalk outline."

"I'm waiting."

"I knew her, Callahan. We talked. In fact, she was starting to open up to me when . . . but I wasn't sleeping with her, okay? Loner McDowell did, and Jesus, damn near everybody else did, but I didn't."

"I had to ask." *Loner, too?*

"Look here," Bass sighed, "when I asked you to keep your mouth shut about that body, I had my reasons. They just may have something to do with what happened to Sandy."

"What are you holding back, Bass?"

He glared at me. "You know something, smart ass? It

151

has crossed my mind that if the coroner's report does indicate foul play, it very well might have been you that done
it. You were the last one to talk to Sandy."

"Why don't you pin the other one on me while you're at
it?"

"Maybe I can, Callahan. Let's think about this for a
minute. Who's to say you *didn't* pop that man? Maybe I got
there before you could finish bashing his teeth in, so you
ran off and came back to act all innocent."

I nodded. "Or who's to say you didn't shoot him yourself, before I ran up? Then you considered killing me to
cover your tracks, but decided to trust me, call in an old
debt of honor instead."

"Listen to me," Bass said urgently. "I didn't hurt Sandy
Palmer."

"You didn't seem all that upset when she died."

Bass started putting the shotgun back together. "That's
probably because I wasn't too surprised."

"Excuse me?"

"Look, Sandy slept around, and some of the people she
got around with were pretty powerful. She was asking for
trouble. I kind of had an idea what might happen sooner or
later."

As Bass sighted down the clean barrels, right towards my
face, I said: "Just out of curiosity, Sheriff, you do plan on
telling the state police you knew her when they get here on
Tuesday, right?"

"You mean do I plan on withholding potentially vital information in what might turn out to be a murder investigation?" Bass pulled the triggers. SNICK. SNICK. I flinched.
Bass said, "Leave this to me, Callahan. I'm on top of it.
Quit poking around things you don't understand. Your
mouth is starting to write checks your body can't cash."

"Maybe so," I said, truthfully, as I got to my feet. Bass rose too. Suddenly the room seemed a whole lot smaller. "But I'm sticking around anyway."

"You know what? You look a lot like another stubborn Irish kid I served with. He died too. I am going to say this one last time, in as friendly a way as I can. Leave town. I will straighten this out."

"I'd have to believe you folks would do the right thing on your own," I said. I put out my hand to shake. "No offense, but I'm starting to have trouble trusting anybody." He ignored my hand. I lowered it again. "Besides, what's going to happen if I don't leave?"

"You will find out that you're no hero," Bass said. "Like Cherry, you've just been lucky so far."

I limped out into the afternoon sunshine. Annie was sweeping her front porch, half a block away, and she waved to me. Small puffs of dust spun around her ankles. Bass slammed the door shut behind me.

Sixteen

Sunday Afternoon, 4:20 p.m.

I limped on back to the motel room, turned on the noisy air conditioner, and stripped. I examined my body for bumps and bruises. My chest ached. Bobby Sewell and his boys had put a hell of a lot more miles on my odometer. Finally, I took a long shower and let the hot water massage my sore muscles. I toweled dry and sat down to think things over.

I had stirred up a lot of trouble, taken a pounding, and collected a lot of biographical information, but in the end all I had learned was that Sandy was promiscuous. The answer, if there was one, was hiding in the psychological profile of someone who was secretly a murderer. But who?

To a therapist, the *Diagnostic and Statistical Manual of Mental Disorders* is the Bible. I had a battered, dog-eared, soft-cover copy of DSM IV in my luggage. I sat in my underwear, thought about various people in and around the Dry Wells area, and drank a cold can of soda. Then I reviewed some sections in the book. I thought some more, then slipped into a fresh pair of jeans and a clean shirt and opened my copy of *Paradoxical Interventions in Existential Psychology* by E. M. Markoff.

> *It may be said that death anxiety, ergo the attempt to avoid confronting the impossibility of further possibility, is the underlying cause of all character disorder. The three other difficult existential givens of (a) assuming responsi-*

*bility for the self, (b) constructing meaning from meaning-
lessness, and (c) coping with the isolation of the human
experience, all arise from the fourth; the reluctance of the
ego to face its own fragility and impermanence. Also, as
all addictive behaviors are clearly avoidant in nature,
they are ultimately traceable back to this one root cause.*

I closed my eyes for a moment, pondering the concept of
unconscious death anxiety. Something Loner McDowell
had said kept nagging at me. I read for a bit to refresh my
memory, and then meditated. Finally, I replaced the book
in my suitcase and went back out into the sunshine.

The radio station's front door was unlocked, so I let myself in. The red "ON AIR" light was lit, but that probably
meant that Loner was taping an interview. There was a
small monitor box above the head of the stairs. I heard
Loner say, "I'm glad you could take the time to be with us
today. I know you have a busy schedule."

A female-sounding voice, very low and husky, replied,
"I'm delighted to be here Mr. McDowell, and it is exciting
to meet you in person."

"Before the commercial break, Loretta, you were telling
me about the first time you had the . . . experience."

I stopped by the huge fish tank at the foot of the stairs.
The tropical fish looked hungry, so I fed them and listened
to the interview. It was vintage Loner. "Now, I believe you
said you had been reading in bed? A romance novel?"

"Yes," the guest gushed. "I was still just the teeniest bit
awake and suddenly the lights in my bedroom began to
flicker on and off, on and off. The television had a picture
but there was no sound at all, just this strange moaning."

"Moaning."

"Yes, and I couldn't imagine where it was coming from.

155

And then the closet opened and out came a creature tall as an average-sized man, but smooth and hairless. It had a round head on it, with one big eye. I don't mind telling you I was scared to death."

"I'm getting scared just listening."

I grinned and began to poke around the office. The interview droned on. The small desk in the cubbyhole behind the fish tank held nothing but a fountain pen and some notepaper. The large front window had recently been cleaned. The wooden arms of both the couch and stuffed chair placed strategically in the waiting room smelled of polish. There were several storage cabinets downstairs, and a random assortment of metal and wood structures and bookcases. I searched them.

The woman said, "It was terrible. I'm almost too embarrassed to go on. He . . . it . . . forced me to have sex."

"My stars."

I opened a storage cabinet, went through some papers. The woman with the low voice continued, "When he had had his way with me, he went back into the closet. The lights came back on as if nothing had happened."

"So you never actually saw a spacecraft?"

I looked carefully at some of the titles on the tape boxes in one cabinet. The shows contained titles too absurd for the National Enquirer. MY SON HAD AN ALIEN BABY, THE ALIENS BUGGED FIDEL'S UNDERWEAR, MONICA LEWINSKY WAS NOT OF THIS EARTH, and more. I put one pile to the side and picked up another.

"Oh, yes! I looked out the window into the night and saw it floating straight up towards a large mother ship. It was quite beautiful, all big and round and milky to look at, almost transparent, and it had a long tail that wiggled."

"Sort of like a sperm."

A chilly silence followed. Then, "I suppose you could say that."

"I think I just did say that. Now, was that the only time you were visited by a lover from outer space, or did he come back for seconds?"

"I did not come here to be disrespected," she said.

A fat manila envelope spilled open. It was stuffed with hotel brochures targeting Vegas "high rollers," and also held several signed markers, or gambling notes. One, from a Reno casino called the Wagon Wheel, was for over forty thousand dollars. Loner owed some serious people some very serious money. I put the envelope back where I found it, feeling guilty. Meanwhile, upstairs, the show was falling apart.

"You owe me an apology," said the guest.

"I'm sorry to have offended you," Loner protested, but his voice was trembling with mirth.

"You certainly should be."

I was running out of time. I briefly examined some videos. There was only one unmarked cassette. I slipped it into the small TV/VCR and used the remote to fast forward. Somehow I knew what I would find. A woman's face swam into view. It was Sandy Palmer and she was masturbating for the camera. I closed my eyes, rewound the tape, and put it away again.

I closed the video cabinet, started up the steps. The second stair made a loud squeaking noise, and I paused. I looked beneath it, saw that one side of the board was coming loose and a nail was bent. I left it alone. No sense in hammering something down during the taping.

Loner was wrapping up, so I went back to the couch and sat on one arm. After a few moments I heard Loner's big finish, the patented Halloween music and vocal button. A

157

tall, morbidly obese man with white hair pulled back into a ponytail came bumping and thumping down the stairs. He was dressed as a woman, in a garish and loose-fitting dress, but clearly had a five o'clock shadow. Now I understood why the second step had sprung loose and started squeaking so loudly.

"Well, I never!" the guest said. "You were mocking me!"

"No, Loretta," Loner chuckled. He was following him/her down the stairs. "I was only making some observations."

"Look, McDowell, I'm trying to make a buck here just like you," the guest shrieked. "You could have cut me some fucking slack." He spotted me on the couch and immediately went back into character. "And when the aliens finally come for us, *you* will be left behind, Loner McDowell. I can personally guarantee that!"

He glared at me. "Don't you go on this program! This man is a cynic and a fraud and I intend to expose him."

I somehow managed to keep a straight face, nodded in agreement. "He is kind of an asshole, ma'am."

The guest slammed the door hard enough to run a fingernail crack along the bottom edge of the front window. Undiscovered dust flew everywhere. After a few face-twitching moments Loner began to laugh, and then so did I. It was that good, gut-wrenching kind of laugh between friends that relieves tension and clears the air. When it was over, we were both close to tears. The two of us ended up sitting on the floor, panting.

"What a way to make a living," Loner wheezed.

"You're out of your mind."

"I have to be. Jesus, Mick, I'm glad you were here to see that. Not a soul on this earth would have believed I didn't fake it. I'll tell you something, I can't wait to figure my way out of this business."

"What do you have up your sleeve?"

"Me and my partner, we got some ideas, but I can't talk about them yet."

"Partner?"

"A 'beaner,' name of Manuel," Loner said. "I'll tell you about him sometime."

"I've always meant to ask you how you got into doing this. I've told you my story a couple of times over. What was *your* first job?"

Loner stretched out flat on the floor. "On the air? An FM station in Dallas, back in the early 1980s. I did that middle-of-the-night, Barry-freaking-White low voice thing. Most of the listeners were devastated to find out I was a white bread cowboy from right there in Texas."

"You're from Texas?" I asked. "I had it in my head you were from Arizona or someplace."

"That's from my bullshit web bio. I hail from Paris. Texas, not France. But I don't advertise the fact."

"You still have family there?"

"I doubt it. My folks are dead." Loner stood up and dusted the wide seat of his black jeans. "Maybe I still got some distant kin in the flats around there, who knows. Say, haven't we ever got around to talking about this before?"

"Don't think so."

"Then why ask now?"

I rose too. "I was thinking that in this business you can work around a man, get hired by him out of nowhere, and still not know his real first name or where he's from. Just struck me as odd."

"Based on the other night," Loner said, "I was figuring that there was more than curiosity behind those questions. Okay, here we go. My first name, and I will break your jaw if you ever repeat it, is Milton."

My jaw dropped. "What? Excuse me, I didn't catch that."

"Fuck you, Callahan."

"*Milton?*"

"Goddamn it, if you were named Milton McDowell and wanted to be an outlaw radio star, wouldn't you change *your* name to Loner?"

"I guess I would at that," I said. I sat on the couch, motioned for Loner to park in the stuffed chair. "So Milton McDowell from Paris, Texas is an FM jock somewhere, changes his name, and then what?"

"Some lady called in to tell me some ESP story instead of a request. I was bored, so I put her on the air with me. People called in to the station the next day and said that they dug it. The genius part is I realized most of them weren't calling to make fun of that lady. They liked listening to her and wanted to *believe* what she was saying. It hit me that there might be a market for oddball stories told straight. Then when I heard that there was this little radio station in Dry Wells that was for sale, I went for it. I knew I could pump doing this show from a place known for UFO sightings. With syndication, I could send it out *anywhere*. Plus, I like my hookers legal, and I flat *love* to gamble. Nevada made sense." Loner realized how much he'd revealed. He squinted at me and cocked his head. "Seems to me you gave me some crappy excuse for asking me so many questions a couple of minutes ago. What was it again?"

"Some kind of bullshit about wanting to know you better, I think."

"Oh, that's right. So what's the real reason?"

"Okay," I said, studying the big man's eyes. "I'm here to ask you what you know about how Sandy Palmer died."

Loner shook his head. "Well, I'll be damned."

"What?"

"The other night when you were asking questions I thought no, not Mick Callahan. The Mick I know is burned out. He's too busy trying to keep himself out of trouble to worry about somebody else's problems." McDowell motioned to the door. "You walked to talk? Okay, but let's go get us a beer."

We stepped outside and Loner locked the door. Out on the street, he seemed uncharacteristically subdued. "Mick, what do you know about the Palmer family?"

"I know that Lowell Palmer made a lot of money, most of it the wrong way. I know the rumors about Wilson not keeping his pants zipped. What else is there?"

"A lot," Loner said. "And you didn't hear it from me, okay?"

"Fair enough." Our boots drummed the dirt for a moment.

"You want to understand," Loner said, "you got to ask yourself something. How does a man who went belly-up three times, the big BK and everything, end up with a large ranch and nice cars anyway? How does an old dude in a wheelchair whose son don't do jack all day but knock up women, how does this old man pay the bills? You getting my drift?"

"That had occurred to me."

"Good," Loner said. "Because I can't go a lot further than what I just said. I'm too fond of breathing."

I stopped in the street. "Give me a break, man. Save the melodrama and just tell me what people around here are so wound up about."

Loner shook his head. "Can't do it, friend." He lowered his voice, but kept his facial expression pleasant. "Not right out here in the middle of the street, in front of God and everybody. Let's go inside."

Tap's plywood bar was deserted. Sunlight streamed in the window and danced a jig with motes of dust. Loner dropped a mangled bill on the counter. He reached into the refrigerator, popped open a beer, and offered one. I shook my head. Loner laughed. "Don't you get tempted?"

"Not today."

Loner took a long pull, belched, and leaned over the bar. "I don't understand you, man. I mean, you were more fun drunk than you are sober. How long has it been this time?" I didn't like the subtle emphasis placed on *this time*.

"A while."

"And what has it gotten you? You don't have any more good times. You make less money than you did when you were high. You probably ain't been laid since you got cleaned up. What does this sobriety shit do for you?"

"I enjoy remembering where I was yesterday. I don't have as many bad dreams. Let's just say it's for the best."

Loner downed the rest of the beer, left a second bill on the counter, and popped open another bottle. "This thing you started fooling around with here in Dry Wells, it probably ain't for the best you keep it up."

I waited, my expression blank.

After a moment, he continued, "Small towns are funny. Everybody knows everybody else's business. You take Sandy Palmer there, the little girl just loved to party, and she wasn't particular about who she partied with. But then, right after you got it on, she'd not talk to you for days. Act like she was pissed, or maybe nothing personal even happened. She was a strange girl."

I studied his face carefully, then broke eye contact and fiddled with a coaster. "It's clear she had problems," I said.

"That would be an understatement," Loner said. "She'd say things while you was necking and getting ready, like

'Can I call you my boyfriend?' And you'd always say, 'Sure thing,' even though you knew it was crap and that she was saying the same thing to everybody else. Hell, I probably would have felt sorry for the kid if I had stopped to think about it."

I looked up again, my gaze cool. "But then, you never were the stop and think about it kind, Loner."

Loner howled. "Ain't that the truth? I never was, not like you, Mick. So anyhow, the way I see it, Pop Palmer had to know exactly what was going on. Both of his brats were way out of control."

"He didn't interfere?"

"Not even before he had the stroke and got stuck in that chair, assuming he really is crippled. He's a piece of work, that one. But the kids just ran wild. Maybe Lowell didn't give a damn."

Someone walked by outside, big black boots thwacking the cracked pavement. Loner looked nervous, but no one entered the bar. He waited for the sound to fade away before resuming the conversation. "Way I figure things, Lowell screwed up so bad being gone and in trouble with the law; maybe he didn't have the heart to crack down on his youngsters. You got to believe a Pop loves his kids, right? Of course, I may be being a bit too charitable."

"Maybe."

"Why are you looking at me that way, Mick? I'm your friend, okay? Not some poor bastard you got trapped on camera."

I just stared.

Loner said, "*What,* damn it?"

The heat in my gut blossomed and rose to my cheeks. I thought of the porn video, gritted my teeth. "A young girl is dead, Loner," I said. "And to tell you the truth, it doesn't

163

sit well with me that nobody gives a damn."

Loner looked uncomfortable. "Hell, Mick, I've always been a pussy hound. You know that. Leopard don't change his spots."

I closed the distance, leaned over the table, my tone sarcastic. "You held her in your arms, Loner. You touched her skin and kissed her and ran your fingers through that long blonde hair. And then you told her lies."

"So did a lot of guys." Loner was squirming.

"And they can speak for themselves. What I'm seeing right here and now is a selfish, inconsiderate, narcissistic prick who can't even suck it up enough to take pity on a dead girl."

McDowell twitched in his chair. I kept my hands loose and in front of me, in plain sight on the table, and held my breath. Loner sat back again. After a long pause, he said, "Fuck you, Mick."

I breathed out again. "I'm sorry, Loner. I don't know what the hell has gotten into me lately."

"You didn't mean that?"

I wasn't calm enough to lie. I shrugged. "Let's just say I didn't have the right to say it."

"Christ. How about some sensitive therapist talk?"

"It's my day off."

McDowell sighed. He took a moment to peel part of the Coors label off the beer bottle. I waited him out. A fly buzzed by my ear. "Okay," Loner said. "I'm a dick. I know that. I did care about the girl, man. I'm not totally heartless."

"You could have fooled me."

"Maybe it *did* fool you. This is confidential, right?"

"Probably."

"Now there is a comforting answer. Look, she was beautiful. She was funny. She was full of energy, and she was a fucking great piece of ass. Of course I cared about her."

I rolled my eyes. "I'm listening."

"But it's pretty hard to let yourself have deep feelings for somebody who is screwing half the town at the same time, you know? It's hard on a man's ego."

"Especially if he didn't know."

"Huh?"

I leaned forward, elbows on the table. "Did you find out about the other guys before or after you started sleeping with her, Loner?"

"Jesus, you really are wondering about me too, aren't you? You think I would do something like that, hurt a girl?"

"Oh, I think you did plenty to hurt her."

Loner turned red. "Who the fuck are you to judge me? A man has got to live before he dies. Just because you can't rock and roll doesn't mean the rest of us need to be preachers."

"True enough." I broke eye contact to ease the tension. I had pushed all the right buttons.

Loner was frothing at the mouth. "I've had my own rough row to hoe, partner," he said. "I did a three-to-five stretch with hard cons, real white trash. I was living with weightlifting queers and sick tree-jumping child molesters twenty-four seven. Don't you go telling me I can't enjoy my freedom any damn way I choose."

"The truth is I don't generally much care about what you do," I said. "But you still didn't answer my question. Did you find out about the others before you slept with her, or after?"

"Oh, come on, Mick. This is a tiny little fucking town, where everybody knows everybody. That's why my partner Manuel and I are trying so hard to get the hell out. I've lived and worked around here for a few years now. I knew the Palmer family and that Sandy had a reputation." He finished his beer. "You want to talk to somebody who might have been surprised, try that Bobby Sewell, the kid you punched out this morning. That boy is dimmer than a hillbilly IQ, and he's got a nasty temper."

The most dangerous moment had passed. I felt the tension leaving my body. "What do you know about Bobby, Loner? I know he was set to play pro ball and got hurt, but that's about it."

"Hangs around with a bunch of whacked-out kids like Donny Boy, the one with eyes like a bull on loco weed."

"How does Sewell make a living?"

"Most of those boys can stay busy doing one thing or another on somebody's spread. Even in the dead of winter, cattle got to eat, so somebody has to take the bales up into the hills and feed them. A boy with a strong back can make three squares and a cot almost any time, if that's all he's looking for."

I started to get to my feet, but Loner dropped two more ones on the bar and waved me back to the stool. He popped a third beer for himself and a can of Diet Pepsi. "Got to have some kind of a drink with me," Loner said. "Leaving so soon ain't neighborly. Now what are you up to, here?"

"Poking around," I said, and sipped the soft drink. "I'm just talking to people, trying to put all the pieces together. I feel like I'm interviewing a dysfunctional family, and nobody is being straight with me."

"It's one non-functional town, all right. Don't mind telling you I'm flat sick of it. Like I told you, I've been waiting on this hombre I do business with, a little guy I believe is going to help me get the fuck out of here for good."

"How?"

166

Loner tapped his skull. "Might sell the station. I got a brain for business, Callahan. That's all there is to it."

"You surely do."

"Gotta ask you something," Loner said. He wasn't angry any longer, but I had come pretty close to getting punched in the nose.

"Shoot." The soft drink was ice cold, and tasted pleasant. I took another sip and waited.

"Did you insult me a minute ago on purpose, thought about it carefully before you did it and all?"

"Sure did."

"You were trying to shock me into saying something I didn't mean to say, weren't you?"

"Yeah," I said. I took a long gulp of the drink and finished it. Loner looked at me differently, seemed vaguely impressed.

"You play some dangerous games."

I crushed the Pepsi can in my fist and examined it for a time. There was nothing else to say. I yawned and got to my feet. McDowell looked up, bleary-eyed. He was becoming maudlin, now. He'd be hugging me soon, telling me he loved me.

"I'll tell you something, Loner," I said. I started for the door. "You end up in a bigger place someday, one that has shrinks; you might want to go."

Loner guffawed. "Oh, come on."

"You're a fun guy to hang around and a lot of laughs, but I think there's a little piece of you missing."

Loner seemed amused. He leaned his bulky body back in the wooden chair and smugly finished the bottle of beer. "And what piece is that?"

"The one that would let you love."

Seventeen

Sunday Afternoon, 5:45 p.m.

In the high country, there is a space in the late afternoon where the air hangs heavy and the minutes slow to a crawl. Evening shadows color the ridgeline, as if gathering strength in the mountains before moving down to darken the desert floor. Nothing seems important. Whatever is about to take place has already taken place countless times. The earth is vast, it is implacable, and not in a mood to change.

Hal smiled on the video monitor, and his image was crisp and clean. Jerry seemed proud. "It is nearly one here in England, and I may leave for Zurich tomorrow, but I have some more information on the Palmer brood." Hal paused and squinted. "But first, I can't see you very well. Jerry, how is your lower lip?"

"Fine, if I ever want to work as a circus clown. I hit the computer right after Mick called me. I have some stuff to tell you guys about McDowell."

"Then by all means, go first."

I popped a Diet Coke, pushed back the chair, and swung my legs up onto Jerry's metal desk. "I'm all ears."

"I hacked my way into the central files of the great state of Texas." Jerry said. "I got the name of a legitimate Texas Ranger and his ID, and then used his identity to poke around. There *was* a Milton McDowell born and raised in Paris. I conned a deputy name of Brewster who didn't have much going on this afternoon. He told me McDowell was born on one of those places where they barely raise enough."

"Explains his love of money," I said.

"There were three brothers in that family, two a lot older than Milton," Jerry continued. "Both brothers did time; one is doing life for a double murder during a robbery, the other got executed six years ago. Deputy Brewster says Milton was kind of a mommy's boy, since his daddy ran off when he was six. He got into trouble all the time, like the other brothers, just not as serious. Milton was always able to snake his way out of it."

"Smart kid?"

"Way smart, the deputy says. To quote him exactly, 'That boy is master of the grip and grin and likeable as hell, but he'll pick your pocket.' Says Loner had a knack for charming cops, judges, and other men's wives."

"Sounds like our boy," I said. "Did he have a rap sheet there?"

"The last screw-up was so bad he couldn't bribe his way out of it. Seems he went to work for some old dude owned a body shop and started doing some radio spots, really funny ones. Only problem is, he was also doing the old man's pretty young wife."

"How colorful," Hal said. His face stretched on the monitor, making him look briefly like a Halloween pumpkin. The screen rolled and settled again.

I raised my eyebrows and Jerry sighed. "That's because I have thousands of dollars of gear plugged into a cheap strip from the hardware store. Give me a break."

"Go on, kid."

"Somebody who didn't like the old man told him all the gory details and sent a couple of photos taken through a motel window, the kind that showed McDowell's butt cheeks and her high heels. The old man goes bonkers. He hires a couple of goons to rip the kid apart like greasy fried chicken. The two big guys corner him at the body shop, but Loner puts both of them away. He finishes up by whacking their hands with a ball peen hammer for messing up his new clothes."

"Ouch."

"I guess he goes back for the young wife, or maybe just for one last piece of ass," Jerry said. "The old man tries to pull a gun on McDowell, and McDowell slaps the crap out of him. And then in front of the wife, who is all screaming and bawling and threatening to call the cops, he spills all the gruesome details of how and when he did the girl so the old man won't ever be able to forget. He steals the old man's new Caddy, beats feet out of town."

I had always known Loner had a shadow. I hadn't realized it was long enough to cover the tri-state area. "They ever catch him?"

"Outstanding warrants for grand theft auto, assault, and if you can believe it, something called alienation of affection. Seems they got a statute of limitations on a lot of stuff down there, though, and the deputy thinks it ran out years ago."

Hal asked, "I wonder why it stays so fresh in his mind, then?"

"Everyone in Paris hated that old man," Jerry said. "His bitchy little wife wasn't popular, either. So the locals still tell that story and laugh about how they both got theirs because of the McDowell boy. In fact, the local law isn't all that inclined to arrest him."

"So the deputy has no legal interest in finding McDowell, assuming our Loner is indeed the same man?" Hal asked. On the monitor, he was rubbing his temples and looking down. I had given up trying to make sense of those images.

"Probably couldn't charge him with anything if he could."

"That would motivate a young kid to hit the road," I said, "and it's just tawdry enough he'd be reluctant to disclose the details. It looks like he was honest when I asked him directly."

"It would appear that way," Hal said.

"What else do we have to go over?" I asked.

"I have some things," Hal said. "Shall I continue?"

"Please do."

"As for Palmer, court records show that there have been seven attempts to prosecute him for fraud but he fought them all off successfully. He also settled three different cases of sexual harassment out of court in the 1990s. Also, both Palmers have settled paternity suits out of court. A number of lawyers adore them."

"A lot of expenses for a man who has twice declared bankruptcy."

"Yes," Hal said. "So I began to wonder where in the world these sizable sums could be coming from."

Where in the world? He had gotten my attention. I swung my legs around and sat up straight. "Go on."

"It was Jerry who found the original accounts and traced them," Hal said. "With the numbers, and by virtue of my connections, I was able to ascertain that Mr. Palmer has a number of offshore accounts in the Netherlands Antilles and the Bahamas. Most of the money came from these foreign accounts, all of which, I might add, appear to be formidable in size."

"Were you able to find out if he has paid taxes on any of that money?"

"Not according to the IRS files," Jerry said. His eyes were red from staring at the screen. He started shuffling papers. "I stole them a few minutes ago. I've got the last ten years printed out in case you want to see them."

I frowned. "Isn't that a felony?"

"Only if I get caught."

"Lastly," Hal said, "if one were to believe the tax forms submitted by his accountant, who appears to have an impressive imagination by the way, old Lowell is poorer than a church mouse. He is practically destitute, except for his land, which is now virtually worthless. The ranch is, of course, locked up in a living trust and thus fully protected."

"I'm with you," I said.

Jerry was lost. He started looking back and forth between the color monitor and me, much like a drunk watching a tennis match.

"So you had better move quickly," Hal said.

Jerry sighed. "What the hell are you guys talking about?"

The room turned red, then blue, and then red again. A horn honked twice in the motel driveway; a siren howled and then went silent. Jerry jumped to his feet and yanked on the blinds. "It's Sheriff Bass!" He started shoving papers into cardboard boxes and shutting down the equipment. I felt an overwhelming sense of dread.

"Hal?"

"Yes, Mick?"

"We have to run. Go to sleep, and I'll e-mail you or get back to you in the morning."

"All right. *Shalom.*"

I turned off the monitor. Jerry closed up the computer gear and we went back into the front office. I took a deep breath and motioned for Jerry to open the front door. I walked out onto the porch, hands in the side pockets of my jeans.

"Afternoon, Sheriff."

Bass stepped out of his patrol car and leaned on the open door. "Callahan," he said, "I need your professional opinion about something, and I'm going to be too damn busy to drive you back here. I want you to follow me."

I grabbed my jean jacket and motioned Jerry into the shotgun seat of the old green Mustang hatchback. Bass sped out of the driveway and I followed. As we pulled out onto the highway, Bass fired up the siren.

"What the fuck is this?"

"Beats me, Jerry. Fasten your seatbelt."

Something was chewing at the back of my mind and a cold chill came over me. We had found some important information, but just a little too late.

Jerry was totally confused. "What's going on?"

"Let me think." I clicked on the radio and let the plaintive wail of Emmylou Harris fill the car. She was singing "Too Far Gone." Jerry made a face, but I ignored him. We drove towards the gathering darkness; it would be sunset soon. As Linda Ronstadt began an old Roy Orbison tune, we hit the turnoff onto Highway 93. After a moment, I recognized "Blue Bayou." I ran the facts through my mind again, backwards and forwards. I went over that initial encounter with Will Palmer. I didn't like what I was thinking.

"Jerry, there appears to be an awful lot of Palmer money offshore. Many zeroes worth of money, hidden God knows where."

"So?"

"The old man may be dying. If the ranch is in a living trust, and that money is outside of the United States in fraudulent accounts, then one person in particular stood to gain a great deal from the death of Sandy Palmer."

Eighteen

Sunday Evening, 6:44 p.m.

We left the cars by the two-story house. I heard the obnoxious buzzing of flies as soon as we neared the grain silo. Bass walked briskly ahead through the lengthening shadows past the old barn, then entered the tack room. There were well-worn saddles along one wall and bridles on another. Dust motes, hay, and the odor of horse manure. Leather creaked in the evening breeze. Time stood still.

He swung from the rope like some grotesque piñata, blackened tongue protruding from the right side of his mouth. His eyes were bulging bullfrog-wide, and his nostrils dripped mucous. This had been a bad death, with much struggling and kicking, as if there had been second thoughts. The scuffed wooden footstool lay on its side perhaps one yard away, and his bare toes still seemed to stretch desperately in that direction.

Doc was already on the scene. "I already took a mess of pictures," he drawled, "and measured pretty much everything out. I do believe I'm starting to get good at this."

Jerry said, "Oh, Jesus."

"That ain't Jesus," Doc said, "that there is Will Palmer. You recognize old Will, don't you Callahan?"

I swallowed. "He's looked better."

Sheriff Bass and I stared at one another. Was he thinking about the street fight that Will Palmer had orchestrated, and whether or not I seemed surprised enough at finding

174

the body? Me, I was starting to wonder if I'd trusted the wrong man . . . and how much longer I'd be willing to keep his secret.

Doc spat in the dirt. "Sheriff, has everybody gone plumb crazy?"

Bass seemed weary. "It's beginning to look that way. Has the old man come down out of the big house?"

"Told me he don't want to see it."

"You let me know when you got all your notes, Doc," Bass said.

"Nearly done now. Those facial vessels seem pretty occluded, but that's likely because he fought it so hard after he'd dropped. See there? His face and neck are a pretty red."

"So?"

"So the coroner will want to check for a strangulation bruise on the base of his neck, just to be sold this was really a suicide. Seems pretty damned obvious, though, and the pictures ought to show it."

"Why did you bring me here, Bass?" I couldn't bring myself to look Will Palmer in the face. I kept wondering if badgering him might have contributed to what appeared to be a suicide.

Bass pointed towards a pile of hay a few feet away. A large sheet of plain typing paper lay upon the straw, weighted down by the handle of a pitchfork. "Mr. Callahan, tell me what you think of that, but don't touch it."

I crossed the floor, barely breathing. The hand-printed letters were large and written with a felt-tipped pen. I knelt in the dirt; examined the note and everything concerning its placement.

PLEASE FORGIVE ME POP. I FEEL TERRIBLE ABOUT WHAT HAPPENED TO SANDY.

175

Harry Shannon

In 1957, two researchers named Shneidman and Farberow analyzed the handwriting and content of sixty-six suicide notes. What emerged is that suicide notes have "positive," "negative," or "mixed" emotional content. Genuine suicide notes had a great preponderance of so-called "neutral" thoughts. The author is already dead inside.

I heard a dry, retching sound. Jerry was outside, vomiting into the dirt. I tried to ignore the foul odor of excrement. The note seemed casually placed, which seemed odd. I read the words over and over: *Please forgive me Pop. I feel terrible about what happened to Sandy.*

"What do you think?"

"I don't know," I said. "This boy didn't strike me as having much capacity for remorse. Could you get a sample of his handwriting?"

"Already on it."

"Don't bother," Doc said. "The boy had terrible handwriting. He printed everything, so that somebody else could make sense of it."

I nodded, casually. "And you know that because . . . ?"

"He left me notes on livestock. One about a castration, for example. Hell, if I'd have done what I thought it said, I'd have cut the nuts off *him* and sent the bill to his prize bull."

I stood up and dusted the knees of my jeans. "I want to talk to the father. I'd like to do that as soon as possible."

Bass shook his head. "Maybe you haven't been paying attention, but Lowell Palmer owns this town. If he doesn't want to see anybody, I'm not going to try and make him."

"You're the law, Bass."

Bass gave a shark grin. "He's the *law*, Callahan. I'm just the sheriff."

"I'll be back in a little while," I said. "I'd be obliged if you'd wait for me."

176

"We'll be here," Doc said dryly. "We still got to cut this boy down. Hurry on back, you don't want to miss out."

Jerry, still kneeling in the dirt, watched me walk by. His cap had fallen off and the burn scar was dark with blood. He didn't say a word. Hungry hens scattered out of my way as I approached the two-story building. The interior lights were already on. I knocked once on the front door and waited for the devil to answer.

"Who is it, damn it?"

With courtesy: "My name is Mick Callahan, Mr. Palmer. I was here earlier today, talking to Wilson about Sandy. I need to talk to you, now."

"Go away."

The lie: "Mr. Palmer, Sheriff Bass and the state police have both asked me to speak with you."

"No."

Respectful pleading: "Mr. Palmer, I'm sorry for your losses. I truly am. But this can't wait."

"I said no."

Authoritative: "Mr. Palmer, you want me on your side, not against you. Trust me, it is in your best interest that we speak."

A silence, then, "You can open the goddamned door for yourself, can't you?"

I entered a humid darkness, caught the faint scent of lemon wood polish. As my eyes adjusted to the lighting, I saw expensive antique furniture, a few oil paintings, and Oriental rugs. The décor put the room in a kind of time warp, back to the early 1900s. Then I heard an odd whirring sound, oddly mechanical for the setting. I looked up and to my right.

Lowell Palmer was in the wheelchair, descending the side of the staircase via a special elevator platform. His long white hair was unkempt, and the hands working the controls were contorted by age and arthritis. He had a checkered blanket in his lap. He was scowling. His presence seemed to chill the room by several degrees.

"You have five minutes," Palmer said. His tone was brittle. "What the hell is it that could not wait?"

I decided to ease in. "Five minutes, then. As I said, I am sorry for your losses. I can't imagine what it must be like to lose a son and a daughter on the same weekend."

Lowell Palmer grunted.

"You know how they found Wilson?"

"I do."

"Do you think he was upset enough over Sandy to have committed suicide?"

"Who knows? My pathetic son is dead. My worthless daughter is dead. I am now all alone in the world. Ask me later what I think."

I felt like I'd been kicked in the gut. The clock seemed to tick more loudly. "I have my own reasons for being here, sir. They are important. I apologize for this intrusion, but I need to know the answer to that question and a couple of others."

Lowell Palmer slid off the platform and on to the garish Oriental rug, rubber wheels hissing, electric motor humming. He rolled over to face me. His large eyes were steady and devoid of emotion. I felt the short hairs at the base of my neck flutter and come to attention, stroked by an atavistic dread. I felt somehow small, defenseless, and out of place on this turf, but I kept my face a blank screen.

"Were your children close, sir?"

Palmer sneered. "My children were *very* close, as if that is any of your business."

I wanted to lower myself to Palmer's level. I located a

footstool. I sat down, consciously relaxed the upper body, softened my voice, and leaned forward a bit. I did not like being near him. His breath was sour and his skin had a strange odor.

"Poor Will must have been in shock," I said, softly. "But then I suppose you both were."

Palmer reacted instantly. "Will was merely upset. I was *suffering.*"

"I believe you," I said, following his lead. "Really suffering."

"This is a terrible thing," Palmer said. "You don't know."

"You're right, I can't know." I forced myself to reach out and take one of Palmer's liver-spotted hands. I patted it gently. I had the sudden fantasy I was stroking a rabid dog.

"What are you doing?"

"I am so sorry for your suffering. It must be enormous."

"That's true. I am in such pain," Palmer said. He pulled his hand away with suspicion, but found it difficult to resist having a rapt audience.

"How can you be expected to deal with this?" I carefully left a space and waited. For a time it did not seem as if Palmer would rise to the bait again. Suddenly, he did.

"I am an old man," Palmer whined. "Who will look after me now?" One solitary tear rolled down a wizened cheek. "They left me all by myself."

"It must be a frightening thing," I said gently, "to be old and suddenly alone like this."

"It is," Palmer cried. "You have no idea."

"No," I said. "I'm sure I don't. But I would like to know. That is, if you are willing to tell me."

"You are that therapist person, aren't you?" Lowell Palmer eyed me suspiciously. Then, just as abruptly, he relented. "I suppose I should talk to someone. Why not?"

I nodded. "Good," I said. "That's good."

Palmer laced his crooked fingers. "What did you want to discuss?"

"I just need to have a sense of you, and of your family and its history," I said. "It's a long shot, but perhaps I can contribute to an understanding of this tragedy."

"My whole life is a tragedy," Palmer sobbed. "Look at me. I sit in this chair, helpless, unable to enjoy my wealth and true standing. And I have always been surrounded by such weak, ineffective people. Now my worthless children are dead and gone, both on the same weekend. These should be my golden years!"

I decided to bore in on the obvious narcissism. He had the whole package—arrogance, the callous exploitation of others, a distinct lack of empathy, the glaring sense of entitlement. This was a textbook case. Palmer cocked his head, disturbed that I was ruminating rather than listening. I leaned in even closer to display my enthusiasm and thought, *keep him talking.*

"Can you explain what you mean by worthless?" I asked. "It sounds like your children have been a terrible disappointment to you."

"They have," Palmer sighed dramatically. "And I gave them my love, I assure you. I gave them all the love in the world."

The sentence hung in the air like static electricity. I stopped myself from speaking; forced a thin smile and an expectant expression. "Go on."

"I know what love is," Palmer said finally. "It is freedom. Did you know that, mister . . . young man?"

He didn't remember my name. I was not a person to him. "Callahan. I think I'm following you. Please, do continue."

Palmer struck a pose, cupping his chin in one hand as if trying to project wisdom. "True love is the freedom to love in any way one chooses, without restraint and without limitation."

"I see."

"Do you? I taught my children that kind of love."

"Without limitations."

"Yes. And now look how they have chosen to repay me!"

"By abandoning you." Palmer nodded and manufactured tears. I forced myself to pat the old man's hand again. "I'm enjoying this discussion, Mr. Palmer," I said. "And I promise you, I'm listening very carefully."

Nineteen

Sunday Night, 8:02 p.m.

The ride back: tires moaning on blistered asphalt. The high beams sliced ahead into the night, occasionally catching the wide, mysterious eyes of a nocturnal hunter at the roadside. Jerry played with his sore lip, wriggled his brows, and sat there brooding. Perhaps he was embarrassed that he'd been of little use during the afternoon. Finally, he couldn't take the silence any longer.

As we passed the weathered radio station and entered Dry Wells, Jerry spoke. "You're not really buying this, are you, Mick? Don't you think this is all a little too convenient?"

"You saw the note," I said.

"So Wilson Palmer killed Sandy, and then decided to hang himself the very next day because he felt so bad? And that's it?"

"That is entirely plausible, given the facts. Jerry, I know you want to believe otherwise and why you want Sewell to go down for this, but we have no proof."

"Look, I don't buy fucking a word of it," Jerry sputtered. "And I can't believe you do, either."

"You saw the note. Bass will get the state police to hire a graphologist, but let's assume the handwriting matches Will Palmer's. If nothing else turns up as evidence, it may be that simple."

Jerry sulked. "And old Bobby Sewell is a choir boy, or

just kind of misunderstood? Come on, Mick."

"I can dislike somebody without having to think he committed a couple of murders. Besides, what would Bobby Sewell have against Will Palmer?" But then a few more tumblers clicked in my head.

Jerry felt a change in the environment, and suddenly turned towards me. "What? What were you just thinking?"

"Nothing," I said. "Let's drop it. Look, we tried. We came up empty. Tomorrow, I'm out of here."

I pulled into the motel lot, parked in front of my room. I shut off the engine and searched for something else to say. Jerry hopped out of the car. He stopped a few feet away, fists clenched, visibly upset.

"I'm not leaving," Jerry said. "I still think Sewell killed Sandy."

"Maybe you're wrong."

"He's a fucking bully, and she dumped him. Man, she said on the air that *she was afraid of her boyfriend.* I don't know about Will Palmer. Maybe he just did himself out of grief. But I feel damn sure that Sandy was murdered and that it was Bobby Sewell who killed her. I'm going to find a way to prove it."

A lone coyote wailed a blues riff, perhaps a mile or two south. "What if you do and Bass doesn't care to listen?"

"Then I'm going to call the state cops. Mick, I have to get Skanky away from them before something bad happens to her, too."

"You do what you have to do," I said. "Me, I'm leaving tomorrow. You may not believe this, but I don't really have a choice."

"Fine," Jerry said. "I never thought I'd see this."

"See what?"

He started pacing, rubbing the scar on his forehead,

working himself up. "The hot-shot crusader I used to look up to is bullshitting himself. You know something stinks to high heaven, but you *want* to believe it's over. Man, your old self would have been all over this town with a television crew a couple of years ago. Now you're fucking off, even if you've got to close your eyes to the truth."

"Jerry, listen to me . . ."

"You really let me down, man."

Jerry slammed the car door and vanished into the gloom. I don't know how long I sat there in the dark car, listening to that one miserable coyote wail his guts out, but it was long enough to know that Jerry had a point.

Twenty

Sunday Night, 8:30 p.m.

"I'm sorry I woke you."

"I don't mind," Hal said. "Tell me the rest." There was a slight echo on the line. All I could hear for a moment was *rest, rest, rest* tapering off into transatlantic static.

My eyes traced a crack in the ceiling. It had the odd look of a phallus, pencil-sketched on the wall of a toilet stall. "I've read about this," I said. "First time I've ever seen it. I asked this old man about his two dead children and I got virtually no affective response, no emotions of sadness or grief. So I probed him a little about the tragedy of his *own* circumstances, and he broke down and cried."

"What do you make of that?"

"Total self-absorption. At first I thought he was lost in some kind of denial. I asked him to tell me about Sandy's mother and he described her as a harridan who tormented him with her neediness. I asked him about his first wife, Will's mother, and he described her as demanding and annoying. Oh, he would add the occasional requisite disclaimer like, 'I hate to speak ill of the dead, but . . .' or 'I know she did her best, but . . .' Hal, his meaning was clear. He was too good for everyone." I reached across the end table, checked the time, and wondered if I would sleep tonight.

"I was listening intently to the meta-message. I'm telling you he didn't mean a single kind word he said, only the disparaging ones. Underneath it all was such emptiness. I've never seen such a mentality of victimhood and self-righteousness."

"Unpleasant."

"Analyst Otto Kernberg's definition of evil was 'malignant narcissism.' "

"Let me play devil's advocate," Hal said. "Perhaps you were somewhat predisposed to hate him because he helped to destroy your stepfather all those years ago?"

I considered. "Perhaps I was, yes."

"We already knew he was a sociopath. Could his advanced age have anything to do with the rest of it?"

"No. This was more than just a character disorder. Let me finish, and you'll see what I mean. You'll see why I feel disgusted."

"Go on, then."

"I kept on sympathizing with him. Sometimes he would look at me suspiciously, but I made it safe for him to complain. Hal, he even started trashing his children. Will was a dilettante and a womanizer who'd never been any good. He called Sandy a slut and a disappointment. In other words, he had a nifty list of everyone else's shortcomings but absolutely no sense of his own culpability. No grief, no sorrow for anyone but himself. The old bastard was as close to pure evil as anyone I have ever encountered."

I stretched out flat on the motel bed and turned out the light. It felt safer in the darkness, with warm starlight streaming in the open window. "I never wanted to believe in evil, but after a few years of this work, you see things. Hear things. It slowly comes to you that there probably is something that has nothing to do with abusive or neglectful parenting. A genetic freak that comes along, once in a while."

Hal said, "I suspect there is more to this story."

"Bass, Doc Langdon, and Jerry were waiting, so I took some chances. I asked him if he thought he had been strict enough with his kids. Hal, *he thought about it*. He allowed as to how he had probably been too loving and lenient with them. He took that question and turned it into a statement about his superiority as a parent."

"How does it all add up now, son? Do you think that Will beat Sandy and then went over the edge? What happened?"

I lay there wishing I hadn't quit smoking. Or drinking, for that matter. "We'll probably never know. I think it's likely that she was arguing with, or perhaps about, her brother. If it was Will who beat her, then that's what he felt guilty about. But he had a lot of other things on his mind."

"Such as?"

I gathered my thoughts. "Here it is. I have an evil old bastard who is apparently terminally ill. Both of his adult children are dead. I did not see him under professional circumstances, but I have no witness to what he said. So why bother?"

"Bother with what? You've lost me."

I squirmed. The springs squeaked, and my mind gave me some more unpleasant sexual images. "Incest. Palmer wants to believe he's progressive in some way, but he's just a damned pedophile. He said kids should be encouraged to play with one another, and that adults should be allowed to 'pleasure their own kin.' His words."

Hal sighed. "That's foul."

"Let's just say I'm satisfied that there was enough mental illness in this family to account for a mysterious and devastating pregnancy, a homicide, and the subsequent suicide of the victim's brother by hanging. And ironically, none of that has to tie in to that first body to make sense."

"What a weekend."

"Tell me about it. And if there is any more psychopathology in this stinking town I don't want to know about it."

"I don't blame you," Hal said. "But the important thing here is that you have tried to do the right thing. Have you given this enterprise your best effort?"

"Yes, but it all seems to have come to a dead end. I can't tell you how much I want to leave this place. I am half-tempted to pack up tonight."

"Perhaps you should."

"It's late. I think I'll go for a run, get some sleep, and drive to the airport early in the morning. I can still make my meeting on time."

"Darin Young? That's still on?"

"He wouldn't let me reschedule."

"He is a penis."

"He is indeed. How is the weather in Zurich?"

"The sun will be shining on the Banhofstrasse shortly, and I intend to take a stroll. I will indulge in a dab of fresh yogurt, a hot buttered croissant, and *eine milch café* to start my day. You have a pleasant jog and a decent sleep, young man. I believe you have done an important thing here."

I snorted. "What the hell have I done?"

"You have allowed yourself to truly care about someone, to grapple with the circumstances of her suffering. That is an important step. Responsibility may be the bane of a boy's existence, but it is the true content of a man's. And you know I am fond of saying all that is necessary for evil to triumph is for a good man to do nothing."

"Is it that simple? I can say I tried?"

"Perhaps."

"We'll see. Have a good morning, Hal. I will call you again from L.A."

"Do that, please. Now repeat after me. I never had it so good."

"I never had it so good."

"*Shalom.*"

I changed, went outside. The evening air was surprisingly brisk. I tried to hold myself back and jog lightly, but the emotional pain was too great. I felt angry, weak, and ineffectual. My shame drove me into a full run perhaps a mile too early. I burst around the corner, jumped across the railroad tracks, and raced through the park, panting, under an impassive night sky. The skyline was black velvet, rimmed with dark blue and speckled with silver stars.

My breathing grew ragged. I rounded a tree and loped along beside the creek where Sandy had drowned.

I could not bring myself to stop there.

I increased my pace yet again, right side stabbing with pain, stride becoming a stagger. When I could no longer bear the hurt, I slowed to a jog and then, panting, walked down Main Street. I heard someone coming. I froze, sweat dripping from my face, and once again flashed on the dead man in the alley. Instinctively, I stepped back into the shadow of the storage bin behind Doc Langdon's office.

Doc Langdon and Bass were strolling up Main from Caldwell, moving towards the sheriff's office. The sheriff was smoking a cigar. They were arguing. When they were on the opposite side of the street, across from Annie's closed diner, I heard what they were saying.

"I don't like it, Glen."

"You don't have to like it. Just do what you're told."

"And then?"

"And then this little problem we got will work itself out."

"You think this is a *little* problem?"

"Of course I don't," Bass snarled. He bit down on his cigar and the orange tip sprayed miniature fireworks. "But I don't have any good choices here, Doc. Neither do you."

Doc stopped, almost directly across from where I was hiding. Bass took a few steps and then turned. Doc raised his arms up in frustration; lowered them slowly as if surrendering. "How you feeling, Glen? You sleeping okay these days?"

"Fuck you."

"No," Doc said, "fuck the both of us."

Bass resumed walking, and eventually Doc followed. When they resumed their conversation, they were out of earshot. I turned back towards the bar. Tap's place seemed warm and inviting, and the addict voice in my mind whispered: *What's the difference, man? You can't change the world. It has always sucked and it always will suck. May as well party, right?* I looked down and found my hand on the ancient, dented brass doorknob. I had no idea how long I had been standing there, or how I had gotten so close to a relapse.

I yanked myself away, moving almost comically, and began to jog again. I deliberately added another mile to punish myself, and then finally limped back into the motel parking lot. The office was closed. Jerry's red scooter was missing. I felt exhausted, emotionally and physically; it was a welcome release. I stopped at the bottom of the steps, searched for the room key.

Someone was crouched above me in the darkness.

I jumped back, my hands balled into fists. The figure stood, stepped forward out of the shadows. The old gray cat hissed, meowed, ran a few steps, and crouched down again.

"I knew you were scared," Annie Wynn said. "But this is ridiculous."

I sagged. "You really spooked me. I didn't stop by. Sorry."

"Why didn't you?"

"I'm not having a great night."

"Maybe I can improve it some," she said. "I came by to officially invite you to be my escort to the fireworks in Starr Valley tomorrow."

"Unfortunately, doesn't look like I'll be in town," I said. "I'm flattered, though. Maybe you'll give me a rain check?"

"You're leaving?"

"For California. It's business."

"Shit."

She sat down on the porch and lit a cigarette, offered me a drag. I shook my head. "One of the many things I've given up." I sat next to her on the top step, still slowing my breathing. I was enjoying her presence.

"You smell like a horse," she said.

"Sorry."

"No," she said, edging closer. "That's okay. I like horses." And then she kissed me. Her lips were full and soft, and the first I had tasted in more than a year. I felt myself hardening. It took all of my willpower to not take her right there, on the porch, under the stars. Finally it stopped. She blew her breath out and giggled.

"What's so funny?"

"Chemistry," she said. "No way to explain it, but it's there or it isn't. You and me, we always had bushels. I've missed you, Mick. I don't want you to go."

"I have to," I said. "And the truth is I don't know as I belong here any more."

"Truth is, I didn't want to come back to Dry Wells either," Annie said. "Mom needed me, though. Getting old alone is a sad thing." The cat strolled by her feet, on the way to somewhere mysterious. She scratched his tattered ears. "He's your cat, Callahan," Annie said. It wasn't a question.

"What makes you say that?"

"He's all beat up but still a stud and he doesn't have a regular place to live. Seems like a fit."

"I guess you're right," I said. We held hands and looked up at the night sky. The blues singer howled again, and a second coyote joined in. A few wordless moments slipped away.

Annie grew pensive. "You ever think about lost chances?"

"Sure. An analyst friend of mine calls it 'the road not taken.' We ponder that old sweetheart, the career mistake, the big investment opportunity we missed. Everybody does that."

Annie lowered her head. She smiled a wry smile and said, "Mine was you."

"I'm honored."

I hugged her. Stark images of her trailer-park childhood, alcoholic mother, and abandoning father flooded my mind. I remembered how we had been as troubled teens; how we'd counted on and idealized one another. The sexual magnetism had been, and still was, intense. But I wasn't a kid any more, and neither was Annie. And I couldn't un-learn what I knew, not even for a second chance.

"Callahan, can I ask you something?"

"Sure."

"What was that fight with Bobby Sewell all about?"

"Boys will be boys," I said, dismissing her concern. "It was one of those size-of-the-dick kind of things."

"Come on, I'm serious," she said. "Just what are you up to, and why are you pissing everybody off?"

I searched for safe words. "I wanted to try to put things right."

"Past tense?"

"Most likely."

"You said you were sticking around because you knew something about Sandy's death. And then I heard you say those nasty things to Bobby Sewell. Tell me the truth, do you think somebody drowned Sandy Palmer?"

I sat for a long moment before I answered her. "We may never know for sure, one way or the other."

"What happened yesterday? I wasn't there."

I shrugged. "Sandy talked to me, I walked away. She died a few minutes later."

Annie shook her head in the darkness. "How'd you ever get tangled up in a mess like that?"

"That's a long story."

She snuggled in close and stroked my arm. "I've got nothing but time," she said. Her body fit mine so comfortably I trembled. She knew. "Tell me all about it," she said. "Don't bullshit me. I mean, if something bad *did* happen to Sandy, why would anybody be all that surprised?"

"A few townspeople have told me they saw trouble coming."

Annie chuckled dryly. "The world has changed a lot since the pill, but not that much. There's still a huge double standard. Women can't get away with things that a man does every day."

"Yeah."

"And those Palmer kids? They always were trouble. Look, I even made the mistake of dating poor Will a while back."

I straightened. "You're kidding."

Annie nodded ruefully. "Unfortunately I'm not. I knew

193

his reputation, but I thought . . . I really liked him. And then I got my ass kicked. Sometimes you got to learn things the hard way, right?"

I thought about my own history. "Right again."

"Sandy never learned, though. Look here, Mick, a girl who chases down every man a little town has to offer is just asking for a world of hurt. One of them is bound to go loco on her, sooner or later. And that's probably what happened."

"She made me feel sad," I said, abruptly. "I remembered her as a child. I felt sorry for her."

"I can understand that," Annie said. "But a slut took my last husband. Callahan, think about it. She was little Miss White Sunflower Dress, twitching her cute little butt all over the park, making men fight over her day in and day out."

"What are you driving at, Annie?"

"You shrinks are supposed to be big on taking responsibility, Mick. Isn't she to blame too, in a way? What did she expect?"

"Yeah," I said. I felt intensely uncomfortable, all of a sudden. "You're probably right."

"Damn straight," Annie said. "Sandy wrote her own story."

"What about you?" I asked.

"What about me?"

I slowly inched away. I was still trying, but failing, to keep sex out of this conversation. "Are you back in Dry Wells for a reason this time, or did you just have no place else to go?"

"No place else to go," she said, honestly. "My first husband was a deadbeat, so I dumped him. Like I said, the second one, he was a dumb-ass rodeo cowboy, kept fucking around on me. He made me crazy denying it, but I knew. So I followed him around one night. I caught them together."

"Ouch."

"No shit."

"He's still breathing?"

"Actually, yes. But she was bleeding when I left." Annie laughed. "Anyway, I found myself suddenly single. I waited tables in a casino for a while, but you got a brain, you get sick of it pretty quick. There's good money in those tips, but you have to get used to strange men groping your ass."

" 'Strange' being the operative word."

"Maybe 'ass' being the word," Annie said. "Now, 'strange' you get to take for granted, after a while, when it comes to men."

"Present company included?"

She didn't answer. I could smell her perfume and something else. It was the musk scent of the two of us together. I swallowed and edged further away. Annie noticed. "What's wrong," she said. "I got fleas or something?"

"No," I said. "It's not you."

"Didn't think so, not the way you kissed me a minute ago. Can I get me another one of those, cowboy?"

I ran my fingers through her hair. She reached for me, but I turned my head and kissed the tip of her nose. "I just can't. Not right now."

Annie looked baffled. "Let me get this straight. You're a man. You're sweaty and half-undressed. You're out on the empty porch with a beautiful woman you used to get it on with, and it's all on a hot spring evening, and you say sorry but not *now?* Mick Callahan, what the fuck is your problem?"

"It's really complicated," I said miserably. "I'm sorry."

Annie got to her knees and dusted the seat of her jeans. "I meant it when I said I never forgot you."

"I know."

"Mick?"

I couldn't see her, but her voice trembled. "The baby I lost, that abortion that screwed up my insides? It was *your* baby, Mick."

Against my will, my mind pictured a little child with my dark hair and black-Irish features. I felt stunned, slapped in the face. "My God, Annie. Jesus."

"I thought you should know."

"I don't know what to say."

She sighed and her breath teased my neck. "There's nothing needs saying."

"I am *so* sorry."

She sensed my resolve and pulled away. "But the answer is still no?"

I did not reply. She got to her feet and stretched. Her breasts were outlined by the cool, yellow moonlight. I looked away and down at the ground. Annie bent over and pinched my face. "I think I get it, now. This is about some other woman, right?"

After a long moment, I said, "Maybe it is. Something like that."

"Okay," she said. "I've been waiting a long time. I can wait a little longer. You'll be back."

"Could be," I said.

"Oh, I'll have you all right." Annie walked away smiling, with an exaggerated swing of the hips. She called out over her shoulder, "It's your loss, cowboy."

I moaned. "Don't I know it."

Annie flipped me the finger. She vanished into the gloom. I sat still for a while, waiting for the rush of sexual

196

heat to die down. I couldn't explain it to her because I didn't fully understand it myself. My mind was in a kind of spasm. Something was going on in the unconscious. I needed time alone to think, which was difficult when I felt like a horny teenager. I took a long, cool shower. I hummed an Irish ballad Danny Bell taught me, "Believe Me If All Those Endearing Young Charms." I wondered, not for the first time, if my mother had known it. The thought of another woman dying young depressed me even further.

I toweled off and then lay naked on the bedspread in the darkness, willing my mind to slow. I meditated for a while, thought things over.

From my readings about Taoism and Buddhism, I knew that a wise teacher would discourage "dualism" and the illusion that distinctions such as good and evil are meaningful. In the East there is only the one universe, which is a cohesive whole. It is said that polar opposites have no place in an enlightened mind. But such abstractions were of little comfort now, because although I told myself that evil did *not* exist, I could not stop seeing Lowell Palmer's obsidian eyes, so bottomless and dispassionate. They had seemed entirely devoid of empathy, curiosity, or virtue. The man had a presence that was truly chilling, and very hard to define.

Please forgive me, Pop. I feel terrible about what happened to Sandy.

I pictured the dead man in the alley, hands tied behind his back and fingertips sliced away. Saw that ugly wound at the back of his neck, made by a pick or perhaps a hunting arrow. And I wondered how the hell he factored into this chaos.

I opened my copy of *Synopsis of Psychiatry* and read about Borderline Personality Disorder. BPD sufferers are intense, self-involved people who are impulsive, lacking in

197

boundaries, out of control in areas like spending and sex. They can be prone to melodramatic outbursts and angry, tempestuous relationships. I refreshed my memory, then rubbed my eyes and put the book away. My eyes wandered back to the clock.

I swore and looked at the time again. I debated, then grabbed my cell phone, opened and dialed it. The phone rang and rang. I rubbed my face. Finally a woman picked up. I made myself sound happy. "I'm calling for Darin, please. This is Mick Callahan speaking."

"Just a second," she said, curtly. She was clearly un-impressed. I heard rock music and laughter. Several moments passed. I forced a wide, toothy smile and whispered a variety of obsequious opening sentences. I felt like a prostitute and loathed myself for doing this.

"He said to tell you he's busy," the woman said.

"Excuse me?"

"He's out in the pool playing volleyball. I'm supposed to tell you to call back and leave a message on the machine."

"But . . ."

"Bye, now."

I closed the cell phone and massaged my temples. After a moment I opened the telephone again and hit the redial button. I waited through the voice mail message. "Hey, Darin old buddy, it's Mick. You wanted me to call you back regarding our meeting Tuesday afternoon at five at Warner Brothers. It looks like it's going to be fine, okay? And I'm *really* up for it. See you then."

I slowly closed the phone, dropped my head into cupped palms, and shuddered. I wondered if I had set a high enough price for my very soul. I sat for a long moment, then jumped to my feet, went to the refrigerator, and poured some milk into a saucer. I opened the door and clicked my tongue. A few seconds later, the old gray cat strolled over and wound itself around my ankles.

"How's it going, Murphy?"

The cat purred.

"That's your name, you know. Murphy, for Murphy's Law."

More purring.

I put the saucer down and listened to the animal drink. I stroked his scarred ears and matted fur, savored the ragged, affectionate sounds he made. When Murphy was finished, he farted and strolled away.

"You're welcome."

I went back inside and tried to sleep.

Twenty-One

Monday Morning, 8:45 a.m. . . . Memorial Day

Sandy Palmer's blue eyes looked up at me through inches of clear, cold water. Her mouth spewed bubbles as she begged for her life . . .

I struggled; thrashed around and coughed; fell out of the bed and onto the area rug. The crash woke me. I stayed on all fours, panting, and watched several sweat drops splash down onto the heavily varnished floorboards. The clock ticked. I looked up and saw that it was nearly nine.

"Goddamn it!"

I got up on toes and fingertips and did push-ups until my muscles started shrieking; then rolled over and did stomach crunch movements until my abs were on fire. I considered going for another run, but decided to hustle. I took a long, cold shower and scrubbed myself, desperate to rub away the dream. And then I thought of Annie Wynn and the touch of her fingers.

No doubt about it, I thought. *It is most definitely time to get the hell out of Dodge.* I grabbed the telephone.

"I am sorry sir," the Swiss clerk said with precision. "It seems that Mr. Solomon has left the hotel. He mentioned that he might take a train down to Ticino. That is very near Italy, by the lake of Lugano. There are many fine restaurants there."

"Thanks." I set the phone down. It was all up to me now. I considered my choices. I was a blur of motion the

200

millisecond the decision was made. I closed up the computer and packed it away in its black padded case. I circled the room, tossing clothes and books and yellow note pads into the worn, plaid suitcase.

Outside, I tossed my baggage into the hatchback and slammed it shut. I walked briskly over to the motel office and knocked, without really expecting an answer. I knocked again. Jerry's red scooter was still missing. A cold feeling swam into the pit of my stomach. *Maybe it's already too late.*

"Glad I caught you," someone said. I whirled, my hands coming up.

"Whoa, bubba!" Loner cried. "Easy there."

"Christ, you scared me."

"Sorry about that."

"What are you up to, Loner?"

"Gonna be quite a fireworks show tonight. I'll be watching from the station because we're on the air live. But hey, you look like you're already on your way out of town."

"You're right."

"Then I better do it," McDowell mumbled.

"Do what?"

Loner seemed pale and tired. His eyes were red. His hands were trembling. He cracked his knuckles, scooted his left boot through the dirt awkwardly, and cleared his throat. He looked twelve years old. "I don't know how to say this."

"Just say it."

"I'm an asshole, Mick. I've been thinking about what you said about me not caring about anyone. First it pissed me off but then it really started to bother me."

I just wanted to get this over with. I shrugged, smiled gently. "If it bothered you, maybe that proves me wrong."

"Hear me out," Loner said. "This isn't easy. I've done a lot of stupid and selfish things. Never gave them much thought. To me, that's the way the world is. You take what you can get. But somebody is dead, and here I am acting like nothing happened. I don't like seeing that in myself."

"Two somebodies are dead. Will appears to have hung himself yesterday."

"Oh, shit. Damn." Loner sagged as if he were about to lose his balance. "What the hell is going on?"

"Lots of people seem to be wondering that very thing."

Loner sighed. "That does it."

"What?"

"I'm gonna finish up tonight with the Memorial Day program, and the live broadcast of those fireworks out to Starr Valley, and then I'm outa here."

"You? But you own the radio station."

"Got an offer last week. I just decided right here and now that I'm taking it."

"What about your friend Manuel?"

"Fuck him. I've waited long enough."

"I'm surprised," I said. "You seem to like it here."

"I have a serious need to raise some cash, Mick. It seems my partner ain't coming, so I'm on my own, and I've got some king-sized gambling debts to settle. There are other jobs and other places. I always did like Tahoe too, you know." Loner couldn't look me in the eye. "I'm actually glad you're going, old buddy. There are a lot of weird things going down around here. I don't want you to get mixed up in them."

"What things?" I asked, not really expecting an answer.

"Better you don't know," McDowell said. "Let's just say there's a lot of money involved. Sorry I dragged you up here and got you mixed up in all this."

I shook my head, ruefully. "Not half as sorry as I am."

McDowell grinned. "I believe you."

"I'm tempted to ask you to explain what you just dangled out there. But the truth is I got it in my head to get the hell out of here. And I'm gonna stick to the plan."

"Believe me, I understand."

I looked around, hands on hips, and tried my best to seem annoyed rather than worried. "Loner, you got any idea what happened to little Jerry? Have you seen him this morning?"

McDowell shook his head. "I'm looking for him, too. I just dropped by to say goodbye to you and pay your room charges. Seems like the least I can do."

We shook hands. McDowell punched me on the shoulder. It hurt. "Good luck over to L.A. I like you, even if you did make me admit I'm an asshole." We smiled, nodded at one another. Finally we hugged.

"Thanks for the job, Loner. Stay out of trouble."

Loner nodded. "That's what I'm going to do," he said, turning away. "And it's smart of you to do the same." He threw back over one shoulder: "Gotta go, the show will be starting early today. Don't you worry about Jerry or the motel bill. I'll handle all that."

"Thanks."

"*De nada.*" Loner stopped. He looked at me for a long moment, seemed about to say something. Finally he shrugged. "*Adios, amigo,*" he said. He walked away.

I stood there until the big man was gone. I contemplated my situation one last time, went over what I knew and what I now suspected. Several moments passed. I became aware of a distant, scratchy voice blaring from a loudspeaker and brass band music coming from the park. The Memorial Day show had begun. It was time to leave.

I willed myself to move, but my body remained still. I re-membered the dream I'd had about Sandy Palmer and shivered, although the day was turning hot. I pondered everything and went over my options.

I didn't really have any.

Once the decision reaffirmed itself, I turned and got into that old green hatchback Mustang. I started the engine and drove rapidly away from Dry Wells.

Twenty-Two

Monday Morning, 10:15 a.m. . . . Memorial Day

I took the 93, cut south and drove on past the Palmer ranch, looping off towards the west without a sideways glance. I almost missed the back entrance because a thicket of tumbleweeds and a pile of old cement blocks obscured the start of the dirt road. I grabbed my cell phone and clipped it to my belt. I parked the hatchback on the far side of the dead brush. I swallowed deeply, opened the trunk, lifted the spare, and removed the body of the jack; hefted it, testing its weight as a weapon. It would have to do. I stayed low to the ground, hunched over, and moved as quickly and quietly as possible onto Lowell Palmer's property.

I could smell the sage and my own dank fear. Blistering sunshine pounded my shoulder blades. Horse flies buzzed and a horde of grasshoppers began to click and rattle. A solitary cow mooed from low and to the left; she was probably grazing down in the gully. I stopped from time to time, just to avoid being a constantly moving image on the barren desert floor. I scanned the horizon, then the windows of the houses to see if I'd been discovered. Saw nothing; caught my breath and moved on.

I came upon the three empty mobile homes near the back of the property. I would have to cross a long open stretch to reach them. Between the dented fenders of two of the old vehicles, I spotted three very large, chest-high steel containers. I braced myself.

I raced brokenly across the empty, dusty driveway and into the space between two of the mobile homes. The tall steel cylinders were marked TOXIC GAS and labeled as Hydrogen Chloride. With those contents, a simple valve failure or breakage could suddenly create an unguided missile. I set the jack down in the dirt, knelt by one of the containers, and put my shoulder to it. It rolled easily; it had already been emptied. I eased up the metal wall and tried to peer in one of the windows. It was closed, shuttered, and locked. I tried another, then one a bit more weather-beaten, and peeked through a tiny crack. I saw containers of red phosphorous and others marked as holding iodine.

I sniffed the air, caught the faint whiff of heated chemical agents and knew this was a very dangerous place to be. I concentrated on what I had come here to do. I knelt and picked up the jack. I found its heft comforting.

When it felt safe, I sprinted across the second open space, slid under a broken wooden fence rail and into the back yard of the big house. I stayed in the shadows behind the vegetable garden, my nose burning with the odor of concentrated fertilizer. The two-story house seemed quiet. I slipped over to the far end of the garden and around behind the bunkhouse. I heard some chickens clucking. A nearby horse whinnied.

Jerry's red scooter lay half-hidden in the brush by the watering trough, only a few feet away from a tall haystack.

Four large bales were covered with several paper targets, all of them well punctured. An old white Ford Fairlane was parked on the property, as was the battered red pickup truck I had seen the day before. I stayed in the gloom for a few moments, quieting my breathing, and then sprinted for the back porch of the two-story house. I vaulted the railing, the jack held aloft in my right hand, then rolled and came to a stop by some patio furniture. I was surprised by how little noise I had made. Waited, listened.

I heard nothing but my own hoarse breathing and a sprinkler hissing repeatedly from somewhere nearby, probably watering the parched lawn at the side of the building. I crawled across the splintered porch on my hands and knees, got to the back screen door and slipped it open. I winced at the whine of the creaking hinges.

I opted to enter the house standing up. I eased the door open, stepped in, and gently closed it behind me. I slid down the wallpapered porch wall and stopped by a large laundry basin to get my bearings. Through a hall door I could see the living room, where I had first confronted Lowell Palmer. To the right, I saw the stairway with its elevator platform. I heard the ticking of the antique grandfather clock.

"Wait up a second," a female called, from perhaps thirty feet away. Another voice, male: "Hey fuck you. You just hustle your ass up."

"Go to hell, then. We'll wait here." The sound of male laughter, some hooting and hollering.

I heard a vehicle, its tires spinning for traction in the dusty road. When the sound of the engine had faded away, I let out the air in my lungs. For a brief moment, I considered running away. *Goddamn it, you stand and fight them, boy,* Danny Bell said. Stomach-curdling shame followed and when that feeling passed, the white heat of anger took its place. *Let's do this.* I stepped into the living room, the hair on the back of my neck standing rigid.

The area was still polished, immaculate. I turned and checked out the doorways. I opted to slide low below the long glass picture window, then clutched the jack to my chest and rolled lightly to the foot of the stairs. I wiped my

face. It suddenly hit me that somewhere along the way—
possibly out in the garden—I'd lost the damned cell phone.

I had intended to corner Lowell Palmer and somehow
negotiate a solution. Because of what I'd seen in the abandoned mobile homes, I now knew that the situation was
more dangerous than I'd realized. I needed a new plan.

"Well hell, that isn't *my* fault," someone said. She
sounded close, perhaps only a few feet away. Within seconds
she would be passing the porch. "Why are you guys always
blaming *me?*"

"Shut the fuck up," a male voice said. Maybe the one
called Mex? "You're always whining."

My heart leapt into my throat. The screen door was
opening. I looked around for somewhere to hide, decided to
sneak to the second story. Moving on my toes, angry with
myself for wearing boots, I stepped on the corners of the
stairs and jogged rapidly upward.

The screen door slammed, and someone moved through
the room below and out into the kitchen area. I heard rum-
maging. The male voice again: "Don't he keep any goddamned beer?"

Something dropped to the kitchen floor and splattered.

"Shit. Oh, here we go."

Clanking of glass, a twist top. "*Ahh.* That's better. It's
hotter than a bitch out there, man. You want one?"

"No," the girl said. "We better get back to work. The
Boss will be way pissed off if he catches you."

"He ain't gonna catch me," Mex said. "And I ain't afraid
of him."

"Maybe you should be. I'm going back to work."

"Pussy," Mex said. But he followed her out the door.
The screen banged closed again. I blew air like a horse
ridden too hard. My palms were drenched with sweat, and I

had to shift the jack to both hands in order to hold it. I moved to the top of the staircase and stood by the elevator seat, my eyes darting about. I went looking for Palmer.

The first room was a guest bedroom of some kind; it was furnished in a somewhat nondescript, Western way. It was dusty and hadn't been used in a very long time. I closed it up and slipped into the next room.

The hinges squeaked, and I jumped a bit. My flesh writhed as I sensed something bleak and soulless lay within. I turned sideways and pushed the door the rest of the way open.

It was Will Palmer's bedroom; there were photographs of him with several smiling young women. Will in high school, Will at college dances. In every photograph his cruel eyes seemed flat and empty. Some of his dark clothing was now scattered about, and there were pornographic magazines and videos by the bed. I saw stubbed-out marijuana cigarettes in an overflowing ashtray. An oddly eclectic collection of posters dotted the walls, a mixture of rock-and-roll and modern art. Several classic books lined a ceiling-high wooden shelf, and sloppily framed a multi-disc CD player littered with plastic cases. The room smelled musty and foul, as if somehow infected by the manner of his death.

I leaned the jack against the wall for a moment and wiped my palms on the legs of my jeans. As I passed by the window I peeked down into the driveway below. The red pickup truck was gone. The old white Ford was still parked in the shade of a weathered oak tree near the bunkhouse. Mex and the girl had returned to work, probably somewhere in the mobile home area. I was thirsty, so I stole a few sips of water from the tap in the dead boy's bathroom. I splashed some on my face and examined my sweat-matted black hair and slightly crooked nose in the mirror. I had never looked so boyish in my life. *Hail the conquering hero.*

I stepped back into the hallway. The ticking of the grandfather clock seemed louder than before. Something small, with tiny claws, scampered through the attic. I moved on.

The next room was Sandy Palmer's; I knew because of the gentle fragrance and the pastel colors. Infused with melancholy, her room seemed to belong to another dimension. I saw one photograph of her, laughing with her brother. In another Sandy, perhaps eleven years old, was riding bareback on a handsome Palomino.

I eased back out into the hallway, stole a quick glance backward, and then stepped briskly to the threshold of the master bedroom. I shifted the jack to my left hand, tried the brass knob, and got a small static shock. The door was unlocked. I slipped inside and looked around. The room was spotless, with little warmth or charm, and cold as frozen bones. The very air felt wicked.

The bathroom door was open, and I could see handicap bars by the toilet and the tub. Lowell Palmer lived here. There was an inner door, solid oak, and it too was closed. I kept my boots on the thick, ornate area rugs to muffle my steps and tiptoed over. The blood sang in my ears. *Toughen me up, Danny. Here there be monsters.* I opened the door and stepped inside.

The closed-up room was like a furnace. There was a massive four-poster oak bed with a canopy, pale yellow in color. The bedspread was pulled up high, despite the heat, and molded in the shape of a human body. I could see an old man's wizened arm and hand above the covers. A flesh-colored Ace bandage had come undone and trailed away towards the foot of the bed.

Lowell Palmer's wrinkled face was frozen in a silent

scream; his eyes were wide and spider-webbed with blood. The large, clear plastic bag had been tied over his head, probably while he was still sleeping. He had awakened to find himself unable to breathe. His wrists had been tied to the bedposts by the bandages; his right arm was still bound there. He'd untied his left, but had apparently been too weak to free himself completely. The old man had died slowly, in agony, gasping for air.

He's all yours now, Danny. Make him pay what he owes. I set the jack down on the carpet and turned away from the body. I was swallowing air, trying not to vomit, when I heard a sound like distant thunder.

Someone large was coming up the stairs, moving rapidly, two steps at a time. I looked around desperately, darted into the closet; sliding mirrored door, blackness, and the scent of mothballs. I stood frozen, face and palms soaking wet, and then realized with horror that I'd left the car jack lying near the head of the dead man's canopied bed. Before I could correct that mistake, someone else was in the hallway. I groped around in the darkness, but found nothing I could use for a weapon.

Someone entered the bedroom. Silence. An explosion of air, followed by a male voice saying: *"Oh boy, oh boy!"* The one called Donny Boy. He called out at the top of his lungs: "Hey, this old motherfucker is dead, dude. He's stone cold dead."

Muffled response from downstairs. "I shit you not. Old man Palmer is way dead up here."

Donny Boy trotted out of the room and back down the stairs. I slipped out of the closet as soundlessly as possible, grabbed the jack, and froze when I heard footsteps running across the floor and coming back up the staircase. I got back into the closet in time, jack in hand, and held my position in the darkness.

"Well, I'll be damned," said the one called Mex. "He looks awful, don't he?"

"We better tell Bobby," Donny Boy said. "He's not going to like this."

Mex laughed. "Hell, he probably *did* it!"

Whispering? Maybe, I couldn't be sure. After a long and uncomfortable silence, I heard the footsteps walking away. I waited as long as I could, slid the mirrored door open, and stepped back into the room. Lowell Palmer lay as before, his bulging eyes staring up through the plastic. I slipped over to the window and looked out. No one was in the yard. I thought about slithering down the latticework on the side of the house, rather than risk the stairs again. But I'd be hanging out in the open for a long while.

I considered using Palmer's phone to make a quiet call, but who, if anyone, could I trust? I held the jack in my left hand and walked over to the door. The silence screamed obscenities. I listened to some wasps as they square danced through the attic. I peered into the hallway, and then moved out of the room.

"Oh boy, oh boy!"

The ragged breathing and the whisper tipped me, but too late to avoid the blow. Donny Boy brought a raised fist around hard and caught me right on the side of the jaw. My knees buckled and my torso went limp. The jack slipped from my fingers. I heard circus music. My skull bounced off the wooden door. Then I was kneeling on the rug, trying to shake the punch. Donny Boy was dancing around like a delirious prizefighter. I groggily tried to locate the jack. His boot caught me in the midsection and I crumbled.

"I told you so," Donny Boy shrieked. "I told you somebody was here. I saw the jack and then it was gone and I told you so."

Two powerful hands gripped my throat and squeezed. The world became a black screen with flickering white dots. I felt too weary and broken to care. *Don't you fucking quit on me, boy, fight back!* I grabbed the thick wrists and began to struggle. I broke the choke-hold, pushed up and away.

"Oh boy, oh boy," Donny said. He punched me in the jaw again. Meanwhile I gasped for air.

"Easy," Mex said. "Don't kill him yet. Leave him for Bobby."

"Donny, Mex, look," I croaked, thinking fast. "Listen to me. Let me try and explain something."

"Shut the fuck up!"

After the next blow to the head, I pretended to be unconscious. Donny Boy kept hitting me. Finally, I passed out for real.

Twenty-Three

Near Noon . . . Memorial Day

The world smelled terrible and it was very dark. I was staring at something ugly and wriggling, something that had a fat, waxy body and too many legs. I flinched and watched the insect scamper away onto a pile of potatoes near my head. I was sideways in the dirt, and my hands and feet were bound. There was something in my mouth; a rag that smelled faintly of oil and gasoline and tasted of rich soil. The insect vanished into the shadows.

It was a potato bug. I hate those filthy suckers. I was on the floor of the potato cellar I had seen towards the front of the Palmer property. It was half sunk in the earth and half above it, with a large wooden door. The only light emanated from a lantern several feet away. I tried to move my feet, and was able to loosen the bonds slightly, but my hands were well tied. My head throbbed with pain whenever I moved.

There was a sudden racket and sunlight filled the enclosure, blinding me. I closed my eyes again, but not before I saw that I was facing the wall, lying with my back to the doorway.

"Is he awake yet?"

A girl's voice answered, from nearby. "No. He hasn't moved." She sounded frightened. "Maybe he's a goner. I think we should just leave, Mex. This is turning bad fast."

"I ain't going anywhere without my money. You stay

214

here and make sure he stays down. You got to, you bop him on the head with that shovel."

"Okay, okay," she said.

"Bobby is righteously pissed. The little one showing up last night was bad enough, but now we got two of the assholes to worry about. You watch them good, bitch."

The big wooden doors closing. Cool darkness returned. I thought I recognized the girl's voice, but was unable to place it. Her tone seemed gentle. Had she seen me move and lied about it? One way to find out. I moved again, made a soft moaning sound. The girl came over and knelt in the dirt beside me. She stroked my head gently and her fingers came away bloody and dark in the gloom.

"I'm so sorry, mister," she whispered. "Really I am."

I shook my head and tried to indicate that she should loosen the gag.

"I can't. They'll kick my ass if I do."

I made a pleading sound. After a few seconds the girl got to her feet, moving away, and I thought I'd failed. But she returned with a canteen and loosened the gag to give me some water. I drank gratefully.

"Easy," she said. "You get sick, you could throw up in that rag and drown in your puke."

"Thank you," I said. "I was really thirsty."

"You're welcome," she said. She started to put the gag back in my mouth.

I blurted out: "Wait a second. Just let me breathe some air. I won't tell anybody or yell."

"Nobody to hear you if you did, except for Mex and Donny. And then we would *both* be in a world of hurt. I'm not safe here, either. These boys are crazy, mister."

"Tell me about it. Do you know what happened to my friend Jerry, the little guy with a red scooter?"

"They got him last night," she said. "He was poking around the mobile homes when Mex and Bobby caught him." Her voice tightened in the gloom. "They beat the shit out of him."

"He's alive?"

"He's right over there."

I tried to roll over but couldn't manage. "Help me, okay?"

She leaned down and turned me. I could see Jerry; crumpled in the corner, bound and gagged.

"Can you please check on him again?"

The girl had long black hair and was wearing blue jeans. I saw the row of beads around her neck and recognized her from Jerry's office and the park. The girl he loved, the one called Skanky.

"Did Jerry come here looking to see you?" I asked.

"He's sweet," she said. "Don't matter to me he's ugly, I like him. But coming here was stupid." She started to replace the gag. "Look, I'm not going to risk getting into trouble again."

"Don't I know you?"

"You don't know me," she said. She put the gag back in my mouth and moved away. I just looked at her evenly, letting her see the lack of anger or fear in my eyes. Eventually she went over to Jerry and felt his wrist and his neck. She leaned down to make sure he was breathing.

"I think he's okay," she said. "He ain't dead, anyway."

"Thmp hhmp."

"What? Oh." She undid the gag again.

I made a melodramatic show of gasping for air. "I said thank you."

"You're welcome."

"I do know you. I saw you leaving Jerry's office day before yesterday, in the morning. And I know your voice too, don't I? You called the show. I remember the way you say things that start with the letter H."

"Wow. Yeah. That was me."

Don't think about the bugs, Callahan. Keep talking. "You started to ask me for some advice. You were on a cell phone, where there was music playing. Sounded like a party or something. Somebody called you and you hung up without telling me what you wanted."

"You've got a good memory."

"We could start again," I said. "You could ask me what you wanted to."

"I was just worried about Jerry and what they'd do if they found out he was my friend," she said. "I wondered what I should do."

I tried not to sound as desperate as I was feeling. "So you care for him. I do too. Maybe I can still help you to sort things out."

"I don't think so, mister. I don't know if anybody can help any of us, now. Please don't get me in trouble. They hurt me real bad when I get into trouble."

"What are those big drums for, honey? They have enough chemicals in those mobile homes to blow up this part of the state."

"You're scaring me."

"They're making crystal meth here, aren't they?"

The girl was quiet. It probably occurred to her that her answer wasn't likely to make much of a difference. "If you mean speed, yeah. Crank."

"That's dangerous," I said. She fell silent. I heard some insects scrabbling around a sack and shivered.

The girl spoke again. "I didn't know anything about that when I started hanging out with Mex. Honest, I didn't."

"I believe you," I whispered. "But I hear that crystal can wholesale for around five thousand dollars a pound. Once they step on what's out there a couple of times, that one batch alone could be worth more than one million dollars on the street."

"Wow."

"That's one reason why they might be a little too willing to kill people."

"Look, I shouldn't have been with Jerry the other night," she said. "And Mex finds out I'm talking to you, he will kill me for sure."

"Maybe. I know he plans on killing Jerry and me before this is all over. You don't want to be a part of that, do you?"

"N-n-n-o," she whispered. "But I can't get in trouble. I'm scared."

"I'm not doing too well myself. I about wet my pants when he came in just now."

She managed to giggle, a good sign.

I said: "You think I'm kidding. I came pretty close. What's your real name?"

"Never mind."

Get the name. Connect with her. "I remember. You called yourself Mary when you phoned my radio show."

"Yeah. Nobody around here knows me by my real name."

"Mary," I said. "This is a bad situation. For all of us."

"You stop talking to me," she said abruptly. "You'll get me in trouble."

"I don't want to get you in trouble. I'd like to keep you *out* of trouble."

"It's too late for that. Leave me alone."

"Listen, Mary?"

"Huh?"

"Do you think you can loosen the rope on my wrists just a little? Then you can go back to guarding me."

She shook her head frantically and backed away from me, kicking up dust. Some of the fat little insects, startled by her movement, clicked and slid along behind the foul smelling stacks of potatoes.

"You called my show, Mary." I used her first name as often as possible, to stress intimacy. "People do that because they need some help. You wanted me to help you then, and maybe I still can."

"I don't think so."

"What do you think they'll do to my friend Jerry and me, Mary? Let us go?"

"I don't want to know."

"But you *will* know. You'll know for the rest of your life."

"Maybe we'll just leave and you can get yourself free later. I'll ask them if we can do it that way."

"I think you know better. There's a lot of money at stake. Worse yet, I saw the old man lying murdered in the big house up there. It's too late for that kind of wishful thinking."

"Palmer? God! I don't want to know anything about any of this."

"Mary, I don't want to die, not in this place. I don't want Jerry to die. If you give me just a little help, I can do the rest on my own."

She was crying now, and I saw her rub her eyes.

"Please, Mary."

"You can't tell, you promise?"

"I promise."

She reached behind me and dug at the thickly-knotted rope binding my wrists. She stopped twice, swearing under her breath, when nails broke or fingers were sprained. Finally one strand came loose; I could just catch it with my fingers. Mary backed away, edged around in front of me on her hands and knees. She put the gag back in my mouth, but gently this time. She did not tie it at the back.

"You hold this here," she said. "So they won't know. And don't you tell anybody I did anything."

I shook my head that I wouldn't tell. She rolled me over, facing the wall as before. I struggled to loosen the rest of the knots. Mary sat in the scary dark with me, beneath the yellowish glow of the lantern, and began to rock back and forth. She started humming something familiar. After a few bars I recognized it as "All the Pretty Little Horses," a child's lullaby. She seemed close to the edge of sanity.

Jerry stirred. Mary saw, and looked back and forth between the two of us, considering. She shook her head. "I done enough," she said. "I'm not doing any more."

I strained with my fingers, but the ropes wouldn't budge. I could feel the slick of blood on my hands, a nail starting to give. The pain was intense, the alternative worse. Absurdly, someone knocked on the large wooden doors, as if politeness were appropriate. Skanky got to her feet and yanked one side part of the way open. Another girl slid through. I caught a glimpse of her and thought I recognized her from the park; she wore torn jeans, a T-shirt, and had long reddish hair. She seemed drunk or stoned. She slid clumsily down a pile of potato sacks and giggled.

"I'm gone, girlfriend," she said. "I am *so* out of it."

"No, Frisco! You didn't get high on me, did you?"

"You got to take an hour or two more," Frisco giggled. She was already half asleep. "I got to nod off."

"But it's your turn to guard them."

"Just lemme sleep," Frisco mumbled. She began to

snore lightly. Skanky got up, furious, and kicked a sack of potatoes. "God *damn* it! I just can't catch a break."

"The fuck you hollering about?"

Male voice: Mex. He must have been standing outside, right above the wooden doors. Skanky backed away, scooting on her bottom. She started panting for air and whimpering. "It's cool."

The doors flew open behind me, and even though I was still facing the rear of the cellar I had to close my eyes at the sudden light. I kept my hands still.

Mex apparently saw Frisco passed out. "Stupid," he said. Then, referring to Jerry and me: "They still out?"

"Still out," Skanky said. "Nothing going on down here. How is everything at the shop?"

"Boring as a motherfucker," Mex said. "I been thinking about you. I just had to come visit again."

"I don't feel so good," she whined. I heard noises: rustlings, breathing, the sound of a zipper. "Don't," Mary said. "Not down here, okay?"

"Shut up."

I froze, felt terrible for the girl. Mex moaned and swore. Some fabric ripped. When the wet smacking sounds started, I began to work furiously at freeing my hands. Perspiration helped. When I pulled hard, one hand slipped free. The groaning was becoming more intense. Gambling, I slowly brought my legs up and began to work on the knots around my ankles. Suddenly Mex wailed and went silent. I could hear the girl, crying softly. I slowly returned my body to its original position.

"That was good," Mex grunted. The girl continued to sob quietly. "Oh, shut the hell up."

Skanky said, "What are we going to do about them?"

"Those two? What do you think, dipshit? Bobby says the

kid is more of a hassle because he's been living in town. The radio guy was due to leave today anyway, so nobody will give a damn when he disappears."

"Can't we just leave them to get loose on their own?"

Mex chuckled. "The big one here saw old man Palmer with a baggie on his head. That changes everything. It don't matter who killed the old fart. This could mean the needle. I heard back in the '90s, down there to Arkansas, it took one goddamned executioner more than forty minutes just to find a good vein. Fuck 'em both."

Mex began kicking at something. I heard mumbling and complaints in a female voice. "Get up, you cow!" Mex hollered.

"Leave me be," the one called Frisco whined.

"Get the hell out of here and get it together," Mex said. He forced her up the steps and out of the cellar. She went off, snarling in protest.

I heard boots scuffling in the dirt, coming my way. I kept my eyes closed. "I'm gonna do him right now," Mex said. I heard the long, cool snicker of a knife blade leaving a leather belt. Mary gasped in horror. Ice cubes formed in my gut. I wasn't sure if my limbs were completely free.

"You do it," Mex said suddenly. There was an odd lightness in his tone, a macabre touch of humor.

"Do what?" Mary asked, after a moment.

"*You* cut his throat."

"N-n-n-o."

The sound of a slap and the girl's choked sob of pain. I tested my legs, still wasn't sure if I could free myself. I could be caught helpless, on my back like a roped calf.

"Skanky, you do what you're told. You take the blade like *this,* and then you draw it across like *that.*"

"I can't do it," she whimpered.

Another slap and I was tempted to roll over and go for the boy; take my chances. Then Mex emitted a throaty, jeering laugh. "You're not good for nothing."

She just sobbed. I tensed my body and waited for Mex to return to my side, but he wasn't going to kill me.

"You can't even take a joke," Mex said.

"J-j-joke?" Mary said.

"Killing is a man's work, babe. You stay here. Don't worry, one of us will be back in a couple of minutes to take care of it." The doors opened, slammed shut. We were back in the foul darkness.

Twenty-Four

Monday Afternoon, 5:56 p.m. . . . Memorial Day

"The fuck?"

I was not where I was supposed to be. Donny Boy reacted at once. Quick as a snake, he jumped down into the cellar. I was expecting Mex, and aiming the shovel blow to the area of the shorter man's head, so I only caught Donny with a glancing blow to his shoulder. It hurt, but not enough. Down on the cellar floor, in the bright patch created by the open wooden doors, Donny lost his balance momentarily. He fell to his knees. Mary was crying, Jerry was awake and writhing.

I threw myself down from the second step and onto his muscular chest. It felt like a Coke machine with a head on top of it. I bounced off, smacked down into the filthy dirt, and rolled away into the darkness. Donny Boy's eyes were still used to the sunlight. I'd only have a few more seconds.

"Skanky, you bitch," Donny Boy hissed. "Bobby's gonna kill you for this." And he kicked at the shivering girl. As his leg went up I rolled again, out of the shadows, and kicked hard for the side of the locked right knee. I was a half a second late. Donny Boy slammed a huge fist down onto my left ear. It hurt like hell. I found myself right where I didn't need to be, on my hands and knees. Donny laughed and tried to kick at my testicles. I spun, grabbed his boot in mid-air, and savagely twisted the extended right leg. Donny cried out and fell. I jumped forward and brought my fist down hard on the kid's jaw. It connected. The shock ran up my arm to my shoulder.

I rolled away and got to my feet, waiting. Donny moved more slowly. He was rubbing his jaw and he now favored his right leg, only gingerly put his weight down on it.

I locked on the boy's eyes and closed the distance, hands rotating up in the dusty air, palms open and knuckles half closed. Donny still had some quick stuff left, and he landed a sharp right to my chin. The world went blurry and bright for a second.

"Stop it," the girl cried. "Just let them go."

Donny Boy was glaring at me. He wasn't used to getting hurt, and he felt humiliated and enraged. My lip seemed slightly swollen and tasted of copper. I wiped my mouth with the back of my hand and saw blood. I surprised myself by smiling.

"She's right," I said. "This could all stop right here. You let us go, and by the time we tell anybody, you're long gone."

Donny Boy didn't answer, just whispered, *oh boy, oh boy,* and then he lunged forward and grabbed the left sleeve of my shirt. He yanked the arm away and down and landed a strong shot to my exposed ribs. I cupped my palm and put my full force behind a slapping blow to the kid's right ear. I felt the contact and the sudden suction and registered the subsequent cry of pain. I snarled with satisfaction. I was in the rhythm of the fight now, not thinking about avoiding it or wondering how long it would last, just concentrating on inflicting as much damage as possible.

Donny Boy suddenly stood straight up tall, a soldier on parade. His expression was child-like: eyes wide and bewildered. Then he fell like a sack of cement. Mary had freed Jerry, grabbed the shovel, and slammed the back of it into Donny Boy's skull.

I held my ribs, leaned over, and checked for a pulse. The slender girl seemed horrified by what she had done. She was shaking her head back and forth in the shadows.

"He's alive," I said. "But he'll be out for a while. Thank you, Mary."

"They'll kill me for sure," she said.

"Now they will, yeah."

"Oh, my *God* . . ."

"You have to come with us, Mary. We have to get you the hell away from here."

Jerry was sitting up, shaking his head. "What's going on?"

"We're leaving," I said. "And I mean right now."

We stumbled up the steps, leaning on one another, and went out into the afternoon heat. Someone had lifted my watch, so I checked out the angle of the sun. "I make it to be maybe 4:45 or 5:00. We can try for the Memorial Day picnic on Starr ranch. Or maybe we go into Dry Wells and look for help."

Jerry stumbled and fell. His eyes were bloodshot and he had a shiner and some facial contusions. "Jesus fucking Christ, Mick. I can't believe I'm still alive. Why don't we just call the law?"

"I'm still not sure whose side the law is on, Jerry."

The girl was sobbing helplessly. I looked around, spotted Jerry's red scooter by the cars. Jerry followed my gaze. "Oh man," he sighed, but he seemed in agreement. We staggered towards the vehicles. He stopped at the scooter, spoke rapidly. "Skanky, you get on this thing and ride south. In about an hour's time there is a town with a bus station. Are you listening?"

She nodded, trying to pull herself together. They were both crying, holding on tight. "Shit," Mary sobbed, "I'm never gonna see you again, am I?"

"You got money?" Jerry gripped her hand.

"No," she answered. "Nothing."

"When you get there, you sell my scooter," Jerry said. "You get on a bus and get out of the state."

"But, Jerry . . ."

"Go," Jerry said. "You'll be safer this way." He looked down. "And then maybe someday . . ."

I interrupted him. "Mary, where are you from?"

"A little town in northern California," she said. "By Grass Valley."

"It's time you went home again."

Jerry started the scooter and she got on it. He kissed her and stepped away. "What if my folks won't have me back?" Mary asked.

"One step at a time," I said, and recited a simple 800 number. "If you ever need help, you call that number and ask for Hal. He'll know where I am, and then I can put you back in touch with Jerry."

"Mick," Jerry said nervously, "she'd better move it."

I nodded. "We'd better haul ass, too."

Mary repeated the 800 number. She leaned over and kissed Jerry. She smiled weakly, gunned the little engine, and then she was gone. Jerry touched his face where her lips had been. He looked terribly sad. I put a hand on his shoulder.

"You'll see her again."

"Maybe," Jerry said. "If we live. Let's boogie."

We moved through the settling dust. I pointed to the red pickup. "Hope you can still remember how to hot-wire that truck, because we need to get the hell out of here. And I mean yesterday."

"Sure I remember," Jerry said. He crawled into the

truck, fumbled around beneath the dash, and the engine fired. Country music blared from the tinny radio, somebody who sounded a little bit like Merle Haggard: *Oh I'm so sorry* . . .

Jerry got behind the wheel. I shrugged and rode shotgun. My raised eyebrow asked him if he was up to this. "I used to steal them, remember? I'm used to making getaways."

"If you say so," I said. "But you'd best prove it right now. We're running out of time."

So sorry . . .

"Come on, Jerry, let's move it."

And right then Donny Boy came lumbering up the cellar steps, screaming, *oh boy, oh boy, oh boy,* like a banshee. Jerry spun the wheel and started toward the front of the property. I peered into the dust and swore under my breath.

"Goddamn it."

I'm so sorry I hurt you baby . . .

"What?"

"The metal gate has a chain and padlock," I shouted. "Head out the back way. Go!"

Donny Boy threw something that smashed into a corner of the windshield, leaving a spider-web pattern and a sizeable dent in the safety glass. I had barely registered that it was a cement block before it bounced off the hood and into the dirt. I started coughing from the dust and tried to roll up the passenger window. There wasn't one.

The rear tires spun out as we drifted into a ditch in the yard. Jerry fought for traction. We could see Donny Boy approaching in the rearview mirror, dragging the shovel.

"Jerry?"

"What?"

"Get us out of here. I think that good old boy is seriously pissed off."

The tires caught some rocks, and Jerry thumped them up onto the lawn. He drove right through the vegetable garden; twine and sticks and fertilizer went flying. He aimed the old red truck at the back gate.

"Shit."

As we left the garden, Mex appeared from the right, sprinting like a wide receiver. He was carrying a pitchfork, and he aimed straight for the tires with the sharp prongs. Out of pure reflex, I elbowed open the passenger door and slammed Mex with it, sending him flying. But I lost my balance as well, fell out of the truck and flopped down onto my belly in the parched earth. Jerry sped away. I groaned and struggled to my feet.

Maybe this is how it ends. I felt a small, pinched sadness in my gut, and a stinging in my eyes. I hadn't lived the life I'd wanted. It seemed a shame to die this way. Mex grinned and closed in for the kill.

The training kicked in. Time slowed down and I felt loose, like this was just an exercise. Mex came at me with the pitchfork. I knew Donny Boy was closing the gap behind, shovel in hand. I needed a weapon, but decided I'd relieve one of the boys of theirs. I settled in and waited for Mex, hoping I'd judged the relative distances correctly. Mex came in low, stabbing for my groin. I jumped away. It was only a feint; Mex had seen Donny approaching and wanted to drive me backwards. Instinct made me duck just as the shovel whistled past my shoulder; I had missed being decapitated by a matter of seconds.

I charged Mex, feinted right, and lunged left. The prongs narrowly missed. I slammed into Mex with all of my strength. The boy flew backwards, dropping the pitchfork. I kicked at his balls, grabbed the weapon, rolled, and then rolled again in yet another direction, trying to keep Donny

229

Boy off my ass. I got to my feet, swinging the fork back and forth at chest level. Mex was up again, swearing.

Baby, I am so, so sorry . . .

Donny Boy didn't see the truck coming. It clipped the shovel right out of his hands and sent it spinning away. The force of the blow must have rocked his arms to the shoulder blades, for he dropped to his knees and looked stunned. Jerry drove right into the surprised Mex, the hood of the big red truck striking the kid about chest-high with a sickening thump. Mex disappeared under the front of the vehicle and there were some more thumping sounds. I didn't wait to see what came out of the other end.

"Get in!" Jerry shouted.

I jumped back into the passenger seat and Jerry gunned the engine and took off again, screaming towards the back gate.

"My car is in some brush by the highway," I said. "Maybe we should split up?"

"Bullshit," Jerry said. "There's strength in numbers, my man."

We passed the mobile homes. The girl called Frisco was seated on a bale of hay, smoking another joint. She looked stunned to see us roar by. The wooden gate was halfway open, but Jerry didn't even try to avoid it. The gate splintered and gave.

We bounced up and down through ditches and over clumps of sagebrush. A few seconds later, when we arrived at the old Ford hatchback, we saw that the tires had been slashed and the hood was open. Someone had already cannibalized it for parts.

Jerry paused at the highway. "It's your call, Mick," he said. "Down to Starr Valley or up to Dry Wells?"

"Safety in numbers, you said? You're probably right. Let's

head for the picnic in Starr Valley. Maybe we can slip away into the crowd and buy some time to think things over."

"Hey, Mick?"

"What?"

"You came after me. Thanks."

"You came back for me, too, so we're even."

"Can I change the radio to a rap station?"

"Just drive, kid."

Jerry turned the wheel, shifted, and headed south. As he hit the accelerator, someone returning from a hunt stepped out of the sage to the side of the road. He was big, well-muscled, and carried a wicked-looking black crossbow. He reacted instantly, bringing the crossbow up and firing. I pulled Jerry down onto the seat and the metal arrow screeched right through the left side of the windshield and buried half of its length in the front seat. I peeked up, saw the hunter's hands were busily re-loading.

"Like I said, let's head for Dry Wells."

Jerry slammed into reverse. The second arrow took the side mirror right off the body of the truck. We spun around and started south, towards town. Just then, the old white Ford Fairlane came roaring out of the front gate of the Palmer ranch. Donny Boy was hanging out the shotgun window, holding a long bow. He seemed intent on our tires.

"Side road," I shouted. "Down there, by the creek bed. How are we fixed for gas?"

"We ain't got dick," Jerry said.

We left the highway and then slid down a gravel rock face toward the flowing water. There was a small concrete retaining wall, but we sailed over it. Jerry seemed to anticipate every bump, but I slammed my head into the ceiling of the cab several times.

"Jesus, Jerry."

"Hey, you want to drive, we can pull over!"

We hit a small dirt road that went back into a grove of cherry trees, went through some tall pines and then up the side of the mountain. We passed a small building that might have been an old power station. Jerry turned to avoid a tree trunk, and scattered some deer. It was getting late and the sun was melting down into the western hills.

"Headlights don't work," Jerry said. "That could be a problem."

"Don't say that. We don't need any more problems." I looked over my shoulder. For the first time, there was no sign of pursuit. "How do we avoid leaving tracks in this thing?"

"We don't."

And then we pulled out into a clearing. I immediately saw that we were trapped. The rock face went straight up for perhaps thirty feet; it had a small waterfall flowing down the face and a clear fishing pool at the bottom. Some rusty old car bodies were stacked up to the west of the little cove, blocking any exit.

"Back up?"

"Can't. Better turn around."

Jerry gunned the engine, but now circumstances slowed us to a dangerous crawl. We had to go forward a few feet, back a few, painfully edging the truck around to go back the way it had come. It was noisy work. And then the truck stalled completely.

"Oh shit," Jerry said. "We might be out of gas."

Without a word, I jumped out of the passenger door and raced away. I moved up the side of the cliff and into the trees, crouching down to bury myself in the leaves, brush, and dirt.

Jerry, down below, had already lost sight of me. "Mick?

232

Where the hell did you go?"

"*Oh, boy*. You move, you die," Donny Boy said.

I was lying in a mound of brush and dirt, watching through some leaves. Jerry looked to his left and saw the drawn bow and the vicious tip of the arrow.

"Your friend turned rabbit," Donny said. "Easy, take your hands off the wheel. Do it now."

Jerry lifted his hands up. The girl called Frisco stumbled out of the trees, panting for breath. They must have left the Ford a bit further up the road and followed on foot. I held my position. My nostrils made the leaves tremble.

"Where's the other one?" Frisco asked.

"He ran," Donny said. "We'll catch him. *Oh boy, oh boy.*"

Jerry said, "Hey, listen . . ."

"Hey, I feel like a cop," Donny Boy said. "You, step out of the truck. Frisco, you get behind him."

"Why don't you shoot?" she asked. "What are you waiting for?"

"Shut up," Donny said. "I'll tell you in a minute."

They tied his hands. Jerry seemed more dazed than frightened. Donny Boy was picking his nails with a hunting knife, muttering. I started to move, but just then he looked up and scanned the tree line, so I waited.

"What are you going to do?" Jerry asked. I could barely hear him. Donny looked down again just as Frisco finished tying his legs. She shoved and Jerry fell to his knees and onto his left side. He was going to die. For a moment the only sounds were the water singing down the falls and the growl of a distant engine. I could smell the teeming life in the freshly turned earth and the faint stench of gasoline. The green of the trees was darkening to a dusty rose as the sunlight began to fade. The colors were vibrant, thick, and beautiful. Night was close, now, in more ways than one.

I slipped out of my position and edged down a few yards, wincing every time pebble rolled or a leaf crunched. It seemed to take me forever. I leaned against a tree and carefully stepped over some pine cones.

Jerry screamed. I looked down. Donny Boy had used the knife on him. That voice: *oh boy, oh boy.* Jerry began to mumble prayers.

"Now you cut him," Donny said. "Do his throat."

"I don't know how," Frisco said.

"I showed you on the deer," Donny snapped. "Just do him like that, across the neck."

"This like some fucking club we all gotta join? I mean, what *is* that?"

"I said cut him."

Jerry gurgled in terror. He began to sob in short, shallow gasps. The couple continued to bicker, now fully engaged in their macabre conversation. I made my move, came out into the open.

"Like this?" she said, drawing a crescent moon in the air with her tiny fingers. She seemed bleary-eyed and stoned.

Donny Boy smiled. "Not bad," he said. "But press down with your thumb as you go, like this." He made a sharper, cleaner move and gave the knife back to her with a flourish.

"I do this, you'll get off my ass?"

"It's rad," Donny said. "Just remember to jump back out of the way of the blood."

Frisco knelt by Jerry. She grabbed his hair with one hand and yanked his head back. His throat was exposed to the cool evening air. To me, the stars seemed huge and getting closer because I was too far away and still searching for a weapon.

"Don't!" Jerry screamed. "Don't fucking do it!"

"Oh, shut up," Donny laughed. "Don't be such a pussy. You won't hardly feel a thing."

The huge rock hit Frisco right in the center of the back. She dropped the knife, made an odd, kittenish sound, and then curled up into a tiny ball of agony. Donny Boy whirled and went for his bow, but now I was standing two yards behind him and already had it in my hands. I undid the taut bowstring and flung the bow out into the trees. Seeing my calm face and cold eyes, Donny Boy seemed frightened for the first time.

"You're going down, now," I said, evenly. "This can go easy, or it can go hard."

"Fuck off," Donny Boy said. He gathered himself to fight. I walked over to Jerry; knelt, grabbed the knife, and cut the rope around my friend's wrists. Donny Boy kept his eyes on the knife. I handed it to Jerry, who began to free his legs.

Donny sprang, going for the open field tackle, but I was faster. I spun and landed a hard left hook. It snapped his head back while he was falling forward. He rolled face down. I had a smaller rock in one fist. I stepped to one side and brought that fist down onto Donny Boy's kidney. Then I dropped the rock, held the boy by the hair, and slammed my knee up twice, catching him under the chin with the second strike. Something snapped and Donny Boy went down. I stepped back, breathing slowly, watching without emotion. *Good job, Mick,* Daddy Danny said. *But he's not done.*

Donny Boy was bleeding profusely from the mouth and nose. He got to his knees, swaying, and struggled to get up. While he was still on all fours, I stepped to the right and kicked the side of his head. Donny Boy cried out in pain and went down hard.

"Don't get up," I said. "I might kill you."

Donny boy wheezed and then struggled back to his feet. Before he could focus his eyes, Jerry stepped in front of me. He started to pound away with his fists, emitting little grunts and cries of rage.

I let it go on until Donny was unconscious, grabbed Jerry from behind. He fought me for a few seconds and then went limp. I felt warm wetness on my open palm. Jerry was bleeding on the left side. I checked him out. The knife had sliced deeply into fatty tissue, missing vital organs, but he was losing a great deal of blood.

"Can you walk a little ways?"

"I think so."

"Dry Wells is close. Doc has some medical supplies in his office. We'll take the Ford."

We hog-tied Frisco and Donny Boy together and left them to spend the night in the open. I wished them nightmares in the dark.

Twenty-Five

Monday Night, 8:36 p.m. . . . Memorial Day

Jerry and I got out of the car near Doc Langdon's office. Outside, we heard brass band music echoing through the foothills. We paused for a moment and watched as a spotlight began to slice through the black spring sky. The celebration in Starr Valley had begun. Jerry picked the lock and we went inside.

The telephone on the antique desk wasn't working. "The main line's probably been cut," Jerry said. "I'll bet it's down from somewhere out near Palmer Ranch."

"Lie still." I did not want to turn on the lights, so I worked near the desk, under the glare of the high intensity lamp. Jerry groaned and leaned back in Doc Langdon's swivel chair. The harsh light made his facial scar look scarlet.

"That hurts," he said.

"All I can do right now is disinfect the area and pack it with gauze."

"How bad does it look?"

"It's bad, but you'll live. You're going to need a ton of stitches, but I don't have the talent or the time."

"No shit," Jerry grunted. "Bobby Sewell is probably out there looking for us. At least we helped poor Mary get away. And admit it, Mick. It sure looks like I was right about that sonofabitch, doesn't it?"

"Not much doubt about it," I said. "The boy's been

237

dealing drugs with the Palmers, and he may be guilty of a murder or two. Now, you try and rest. Nobody knows you're hurt, so I don't think anyone will come looking for you here. I'll try to get us some outside help."

"Mick?"

I was moving fast, but stopped in the doorway. "Yeah?"

"Do you think I'll ever see her again?"

"Mary? I think so."

"Good," Jerry said. "You sure you don't want me to go with you? Maybe we can make it to where I have my gear stashed. I could get the word out over the Internet."

"By now they've either trashed all of your stuff, or they're waiting there for someone to try and use it."

"Mick?" Jerry said, theatrically. "This is where I'm supposed to tell you to be careful, right?"

"Yeah."

"Well, screw you. I'm thinking about me. Don't get killed, get back here with some dope."

I was outside again and slipping behind the wheel of the Fairlane. I drove it back towards the sheriff's office and parked it down the road from the Saddleback Motel, hoping to throw any pursuer off Jerry's trail. Now all I had to do was move through the virtually empty town without being spotted and find a way to get some help.

The first house was dark. The second had a radio playing in the kitchen, and the porch light was on. I could hear Loner McDowell's voice, describing the holiday fireworks. I knocked softly, but no one answered. I tried the knob, but the door was locked. There was no car in the small driveway.

"What a beautiful sight this is," Loner said over the radio. "Bright colors that just plain light up the night sky. All you folks should be here to see this for yourselves."

238

The radio station. *Of course* . . .

I was moving before my consciousness fully registered the sound, a millisecond before I actually heard the sudden, loud buzzing; like some angry hornet flying too close to my ear. The air contracted and then expanded again, as the metal hunting arrow split the wooden doorjamb with a dull *thwack*. I threw myself over the porch railing and down onto the lawn. I landed awkwardly, rolled away, and sprinted towards the next house. I feinted, as if going for the front door, then vaulted the waist-high chain link fence and ran in a jagged pattern through the back yard.

A man, whispering: "Callahan? Come out and play."

I stopped by an overflowing trashcan to catch my breath. I had to disguise each destination until the last possible moment. If I went in and out of the various yards there was always the slim chance someone might be home and in a position to offer assistance. I decided that I'd cut back and forth across First Street, and if I failed to lose the pursuer I would run down the alley behind the abandoned garage, up Caldwell Street and then over to the radio station. It had an emergency backup system. They could cut the central telephone lines, but they couldn't stop the broadcast without shutting down power to the entire area. Besides, I'd be leading the hunter blocks away from Jerry.

I heard footsteps cross the porch next door, grunting, and the sound of the metal arrow being retrieved from the doorjamb. I waited for the man to step down onto the grass on either end of the porch, so I could set the location in my mind. The hunter traced my steps, coming closer. When he stepped off the right side of the porch and began moving towards the back yard, I bolted again, heading across the street at an angle for the next well-lit home.

The man, the hoarse whisper still disguising his identity:

"Come out and play with me."

Boots make a racket in gravel. I slipped in the driveway and tore out the knee of my blue jeans. I swore softly and rolled behind an old Chevy that was up on blocks in the middle of a blotchy front lawn. I could see the man following me, but only from the waist down; camouflaged hunting pants on big, muscular legs. The man started to cross the street, the metal crossbow loaded and hanging low at his side. I looked around frantically. I grabbed a sizeable stone and threw it into the kitchen window of the home. Glass shattered. I waited for a voice, for an alarm, but nothing happened.

As I'd hoped, the man assumed that I was trying to enter the house, perhaps get to a telephone. His big legs turned towards the kitchen of the house and he broke into a trot. I inched around behind the Chevy, smelling the sweat and motor oil on the scattered rags. My fingers touched a screwdriver; large, flat-headed, handle wrapped in duct tape. I slipped it into my belt and duck-walked behind the car, wincing at the noise my boots made in the gravel.

This guy was formidable. He was wearing a sleeveless hunting shirt, camouflaged in brown and green, and in the shadowy light his arms seemed abnormally muscular. The wicked-looking black metal crossbow was up at his shoulder now, as he stalked the front of the house and closed in on the kitchen window. Discretion seemed the better part of valor. I planted the toes of my boots in the gravel for traction and shifted my weight up onto my fingertips, like a fullback. When the man arrived at the broken window, his back to the old car, I took off again.

The hunter tried to lead me as I ran broken-field across the road, back where I had started, but two houses closer to Caldwell Street. I came to a vacant lot surrounded by a tall, piecemeal wooden slat fence. I kicked in a board and pushed through to the other side, but trailed my left leg for a moment too long. An arrow caught the fabric of my jeans and tore some flesh from my calf. The pain was blinding, especially when I yanked the barbs free of my skin. I bellowed.

The man whooped with excitement and charged across the street, notching another arrow.

Leg throbbing, with sweat pouring down my face from the stress and the pain, I limped across the lot. I found an open spot on the other side of the fence and broke through it. I was vaguely aware that the pursuer had once again stopped to pick up the expended arrow. I had planned on making a foot race out of the last hundred yards, but with a wounded leg the odds were against me. I needed an advantage. I made another broken-field run towards the abandoned garage.

A missile raced past my ear and smacked into the lower end of the corrugated tin roof, missing my head by a few inches. It buried itself in a wooden beam. In the few seconds it would take to load another arrow I cut through the long-dead gas pumps, aiming for the empty, shuttered hotel next to Margie's Diner.

"Take your time," the hunter whispered hoarsely. He was right behind me. "As far as I'm concerned, you can drag this out all night."

I kicked at the boarded-up window of the old hotel. Nothing gave. I looked over my shoulder, peering back into the gloom, and in the faint glow of the stars and a porch light I saw the man coming. He was taking it easy, swinging the crossbow and whistling, as if he had all the time in the world. A huge ball of red, white, and blue soared up into the sky behind him and then blew apart into gigantic sparklers. A crowd cheered faintly, the sound carrying from far away in Starr Valley.

I planted the better leg, kicked, and felt the shock burn the wound in my calf. The boards gave way and I stumbled inside the old hotel. Inside, I sneezed. Dust flew everywhere. I had to feel my way across the darkened lobby. Some furniture had been covered with tarps and left behind, clumped like terminally wounded patients in a battle zone. I tripped over a cardboard box and heard glass shattering. I moaned, clutched the injured calf, and scrambled behind a sofa. I looked back, chest heaving and mind racing.

The large hole I'd left in the wooden barrier was now sprinkled with starlight and the rainbow traces of fireworks from the southern sky. I saw no sign of the man.

I weighed my chances. If he flanked me and moved further up towards Caldwell Street, I'd be pinned down, or turned back towards the center of town. I remembered the screwdriver and felt for it. It was still hanging from my belt. I was lucky it hadn't been driven into my own flesh.

My eyes began to adjust. A row of abandoned, long-empty slot machines saluted silently. I used them for cover and moved as quietly as possible; duck-walked back the way I had come, closer to the makeshift entryway. *Come on fella,* I thought, *be macho.* When I reached the end of the row of slots, I was only a couple of yards from where I'd broken in. I paused, awaiting his decision. I had to sneeze again and pinched the end of my nose. My fingers stank of fresh blood.

The hunter appeared in the open space, weaving like a black hole among the stars. More colors burst high in the desert sky behind him. The man was playing it safe, standing back a few feet with the crossbow raised to his shoulder. He held it pointed at the opening in the boards. He edged closer.

I slipped the screwdriver into my hand and held it low, point forward, to drive it up into the guts. I steeled myself.

The man was still. He took his time, gauging the distance and the risks involved. He came forward boldly, right into the opening, with the crossbow upright. He moved into the lobby, momentarily blocking out all light, and then stood still. He waited for what seemed like hours before sliding away to search for me.

I let him get several yards into the room, waited for the sounds of boots crunching through the broken glass I'd left behind. I waited until there was no way the man could spin around and aim the crossbow in time. I waited until I couldn't stand the waiting any longer, and then I launched myself at the patch of starlight as though I were trying to tackle the next burst of fireworks.

"Shit."

And I was through the opening and out into the night, slamming down onto the cement. I gathered myself and sprinted as best I could, racing down the sidewalk past the dead or dying businesses, and there it was at the end of the block and just a little beyond: the phallic tower of the dilapidated radio station. I heard the pursuer cursing and fumbling his way back through the boards behind me, and knew I had a lead of at least fifteen or twenty yards. My leg hurt.

I darted to the left and then the right. The radio station loomed closer. Suddenly another series of white bursts lit up the night sky behind us. I was exposed, like a soldier crossing no man's land under flares. I zigged again, and then zagged back the other way. The station was only yards away. I had a bad stitch in my side and my calf muscle was cramping; it had started to stiffen the whole leg.

An arrow thumped into the dirt perhaps two feet to one side of me, right where I'd been just a second before, and I reached deep inside for one last burst of power.

I slammed up onto the porch. The door was locked. I had given Loner back the keys. A huge rocket went off in the night sky a few miles off and the echo of the faraway crowd went *oohh* and *ahhh* behind us. I used the screwdriver to smash a small hole in the huge plate glass window, dropped it. I covered my face with crossed arms and slammed my shoulder into the window. I stepped away and flattened against the wall as the huge shards of glass crumbled and fell.

The hunter was standing tall in the middle of the street surrounded by red, white, and blue fire, calmly notching another arrow; drawing a bead on me. His face was still obscured. I started back towards the door, then spun and threw myself sideways through the window, hoping to clear the glass on the lower side. I took some of the sharp fragments with me and knew I'd cut up my lower back. I slammed into Loner's big office desk and heard the old rotary telephone go flying. I narrowly missed the large fish tank, crashed into the side of the staircase and slid to my knees. I'd made a huge amount of noise. Would McDowell hear?

I sat there in the darkness, thinking, looking up at the large and consummately ugly tropical fish in the lighted tank. I was hurt. I was tired. I was running out of time. Most of the pieces had finally come together, but I only had a few seconds to plan a way out. My mind went into overdrive. And then suddenly I knew what to do.

Footsteps crunching through the broken glass again.

I went charging up the stairs. I skipped the step that groaned, almost without realizing it, and just as I turned the corner I heard the hunter coming into the lobby behind me. The speaker above the door was playing some John Phillip Sousa. I opened the studio and stepped in.

There was no sign of McDowell.

"Loner? Loner, goddamn it, are you here?"

I sagged in total exhaustion. Had Loner taped all this in advance and left town? He wasn't on the air live at all. *But how could I be so wrong?* Just then a commercial kicked in. The final piece came to me.

I limped over to the console. I lowered myself behind it and down into the engineering chair with a loud groan. One way or another, it was nearly over. There was only one way in or out; I was right, or I wasn't, there was nothing else to be done. Someone large bounded confidently up the stairs. I ran my practiced hands along the console and then looked up.

Bobby Sewell stepped into the tiny booth. He was panting and shaking his head in grudging admiration. He wore a large white bandage over his flattened nose. "Christ, Callahan," he said. "You would have been one hell of a football player. You're not real fast, but you sure got some moves."

"Bobby Sewell, it is you," I said, as mildly as possible. "Well I'll be damned. I thought that was just too obvious."

"Too obvious? The fuck you talking about?"

"Jerry thought it was you from the start. I didn't think so."

"Callahan," Sewell said with a shake of his head, "you are too fucking weird."

"Most folks around here seem to agree with you."

Sewell raised the crossbow. "You fucked up my nose, man," he said. "You owe me."

"Maybe I do at that, Bobby Sewell." The room got

bright and clear. The hair on my arms and neck stood tall and my mouth went dry with fear. I swallowed. "What are you going to do?"

"I feel like being nice tonight," Sewell said. "Tell me where you want it. In the head or in the heart?"

Then Bobby stiffened. Loner McDowell stepped out of the closet behind the smaller fish tank. He held a large .357 Taurus revolver in his big paw. The gun was aimed right at Bobby Sewell's forehead.

"What the hell?"

"Easy, Bobby," Loner said. "Lower that bow and set it down there on the carpet. We wouldn't want it going off on us, now would we?"

"What are you doing, Loner? I thought you left town." Bobby did as he was told.

"I did," Loner said. "I got to thinking, and then I came back."

"Thinking about what?"

"About how my partner Manuel never showed up here in Dry Wells like we planned. See, Doc Langdon had a few beers tonight. He let slip how Bass found some stranger's body Friday night, all trussed up like a Thanksgiving turkey with the fingerprints sliced off."

Bobby flinched. "Loner, listen . . ."

"I figure you did Manuel to try and run me off, Bobby. You made him strip, tied him up, and then shot him in the back of the head with this here crossbow."

The guy in the alley had a name, now. Manuel. For some reason that felt satisfying. I leaned forward and put my head in my hands. My lips were almost touching the mike. "God, I'm wiped out," I said. "Loner McDowell, if you weren't so ugly I would kiss you."

There was a blur of motion from just out of the corner of

my eye. I flinched and ducked my head.

"Don't," Bobby cried.

The gunshot was deafening, and the room instantly reeked of cordite. I looked up as Bobby sank down the wall and disappeared from view. Sewell's bandaged face was now a blotchy red, white, and gray mess.

"Goddamn it," Loner growled. "Why did he go make me do that?"

I fingered my ears. They wouldn't stop ringing. McDowell moved slowly, the handgun loose in his fingers. He stepped around Bobby, his back to the doorway, and picked up the crossbow with his other hand. He looked down at Sewell's body, shaking his head.

"Dumb bastard," Loner said. "You okay, Mick?"

"I guess so," I said, stupidly. "You all right?"

McDowell looked back and forth between the weapons in his large hands, from the crossbow to the pistol. "What a mess. I don't know how the hell all this got so out of control," he said.

"It's like eating peanuts." Suddenly I felt lightheaded. I leaned back and almost giggled.

"What?"

"Once you get started, it's hard to stop."

"Mick, I'm worried about you," Loner said.

"You know, I think I've pretty much figured it out."

"Figured what out?"

I sighed. "Oh, come on. Don't play me for a fool any longer."

Loner nodded solemnly. "It was beautiful while it lasted," he said. "Poor Bobby here, he and I used to party together. He was the one that first hit on me about putting up some money. Palmer just gave us a safe place to work. Pretty soon we were all raking in the green, you know?

People just can't seem to get enough of drugs, Mick."

"So I've heard."

"But lately, me and Bobby been kind of at each other's throats. You know, like two big dogs in the same back yard. One of us had to go." I stared at him. "Don't look at me that way, man. I'm not proud of hustling drugs, but I owe people."

"Mob people, Loner? Like the ones who had Bobby Sewell hit your partner, Manuel, and leave him in the alley without any teeth?"

"Damn, boy," Loner said. He whistled. "You're pretty smart. Yeah, I have me some serious tabs in Vegas. I guess they wanted to send me a warning."

"That's why you're trying to run."

"I needed dough. So I put up some money to make the crystal, I set it up with Palmer, and I took a nice cut for myself. That's all there was to it, Mick."

I cleared my throat. "Don't."

"Don't what?" McDowell said, innocently. He turned his body slightly to the left without breaking eye contact.

"Listen to me, Loner. Don't do it. Kill me too. It won't save you."

"What are you talking about?" Loner said. He had a puzzled look on his face, but the crossbow was now up and pointed at my chest. "I don't mean to kill you, old buddy."

"You only made one mistake."

Loner grimaced. "And just what was that, Mick?"

"The suicide note for Will Palmer. He would never have said, 'Forgive me Pop.' He always called Lowell 'Father.' I'd have thought you would have noticed that, close as you were to the two of them."

Loner sighed. "He came at me about Sandy, Mick, and tried to give me a ration of shit about her dying. I didn't mean to strangle the prick. That crystal can make you crazy, once you've been up for a couple of days. Anyhow, then I had to improvise. The thing is, Will woke up just as I kicked that stool out from under him. He got to die twice, and I got to watch."

"I don't know if anybody deserves to die like that."

"Oh, he did," Loner said. "But like I said, somehow everything got a little out of control."

"Well, now with Bobby and all the Palmers dead, you'll walk away with at least two million in drug money, enough to settle your debts."

"And then some."

"Only one thing bothers me. What is it, now, Loner? Four dead people in three days? With me, it'll make five. That's quite a mess to explain. You're smarter than this, man. What the hell happened to you?"

Loner was wearing gloves. He'd thought it out pretty well. He shifted his weight so that he'd have perfect aim with the crossbow. I realized the story would be that Bobby and I had killed each other when Loner was already out of town. Why the radio station? Well, after all, I'd worked there. I had talked on the telephone with Sandy Palmer from there, only a couple of days before. It wasn't bad, actually.

"Damn it, Mick," Loner said. He looked genuinely sad. "I really don't want to hurt you. I wish you could have minded your own business. Why didn't you just leave town when I said?"

Talking fast, heart in my throat: "Because of Sandy Palmer, Loner. You know how it was. She was special."

"Oh Jesus," Loner howled. "You *too?* Goddamn it, boy. Not you too."

I lied desperately: "You got mad at her for being pregnant. You went way crazy. Sandy told me all about it."

"Huh?"

"You didn't want the baby, right?"

Loner laughed. "Nice try, Callahan. A little shrink stuff, even at the end. I didn't give a shit about her having a baby."

I believed him. *But then what the hell had set Loner off?* My mind whirled in circles, seeking an answer.

"She was about to tell you my secrets, friend. I was warning her to keep her mouth shut. I slapped her around a little bit and she fell backwards. She hit her head on a rock in the water, and I thought *shit,* well, that tears it. Figured I'd better make tracks, so I took off."

"Was she dead?"

"Then? She was still breathing. But I didn't want anybody to see me there."

I grunted. My chest filled with rage, but I kept my features empty. "Did you ever wonder whose baby it was, Loner? Yours, or maybe her brother's? Maybe that's what got you so angry at Will. That he was screwing his sister? No, I know. Maybe it was that the baby was really Lowell Palmer's? Could he still get it up?"

Loner was growing red-faced. "That baby-raping bastard?" he snarled. "He probably could. You know, Mick, the old tree-jumper really got scared. He thought that there would be cops crawling all over Dry Wells soon, because you were poking around wondering how Sandy died. He told me he wanted to shut things down. And he wouldn't pay me any of the money he owed me. I couldn't have that, man."

"I suppose not," I said. "Did you watch him die, too?"

"Oh, you know it. And I'll watch you right soon, now."

I was seconds away from death. I played my last card.

"Wait one second. I know something important, Loner. Something you don't know."

"Go to hell, Mick," McDowell said pleasantly. "I'll meet you there soon enough." And he started to pull the trigger on the crossbow.

"Wait," I said, my voice cracking. "We're on the air live."

Loner snorted. "Sure."

"Just so you understand what's up. All of this has been live."

He seemed shaken. "Bullshit."

"No, *we are live*, Loner," I said. "You shot Bobby Sewell in public, and told at least a few hundred people you've been dealing drugs to pay down gambling debts to the mob. They heard that you killed Sandy Palmer by accident and Will Palmer and Lowell Palmer on purpose, and now you're about to kill me. But there's no point, now. It's over."

"I taped it all first," Loner said. "I taped the whole damned show."

"Hear anything? I let the commercial play out and took us live, Loner. Bobby cut some of the telephone wires, but believe me, I can flat guarantee you somebody within earshot of this radio station has called the cops. Killing me won't change anything."

Providence arrived, as if rehearsed to intervene: the stair down below squeaked under someone's weight.

"Loner? Mr. McDowell?"

McDowell's eyes flickered away towards the stairs. I flipped backwards and kicked the swivel chair towards him. The crossbow went off and the arrow sank into the padded ceiling. The .357 slipped from McDowell's fingers and dropped into the sickening goo that had been Bobby Sewell's face. Loner reached, recoiled involuntarily, and

251

then reached down for it again, but by that time I had hit him from the side. He went back against the wall and clutched at me with his gloved hands, trying to push me off. He wanted to use his fists.

I kept my face pressed against that barrel chest and hammered his guts with everything I had. He held his stomach muscles tight and brought his arms down on my upper back, but I drove up and in with my legs and kept pounding. Finally he had to catch a breath, and it was then that a couple of punches to his diaphragm really hurt. He made a high, barking sound and tried to lower his hands to protect his ribcage. I kept my head in the way, hit him again, and managed to crack one rib on the upper right side; I heard it snap like a thin piece of firewood.

Loner moaned, raised his hands, and clawed for my eyes. I tried to turn away but lost my balance for a second. That broken rib should have stopped him, but it didn't. He got some kind of second wind and tried to knock me out.

His gloved fist came down on the side of my neck and everything went numb. My left knee gave. When I came down on all fours, my hand slipped into something wet and squishy with hard chunks in it. I figured it was Bobby Sewell's shattered skull and brain tissue, but didn't let myself look. I didn't want to know.

Loner leaned against the wall, clutching the shattered rib and wheezing for air. "Motherfucker," he said. He seemed amused. He spat on me, or at least I think he did, and then kicked me in the kidney. I anticipated the blow by a millisecond and started to roll away from him. The boot hurt anyway, caught me on the injured calf. The pain was blinding.

I rolled again, knowing I'd slowed him down some. My back struck the front of the wooden console. I looked back.

McDowell leaned forward at an odd, simian angle trying to protect that cracked rib. He was in big trouble. But then again, so was I.

He started towards me, long arms dangling. I forced myself back to my feet. My kidney was throbbing, my breath was wheezing like a leaky bicycle tire, and my head throbbed. I didn't figure the big man to have too many slick moves left, but kept my eyes on his belt buckle. The hips give a feint away. He stopped for some reason, maybe because I wasn't looking up. I saw his knees loosen a little, like he was preparing to charge, so I charged first.

I hit him low, like a linebacker tackles a running back, and drove him out into the stairwell. Loner clubbed me with his fist again, but I held on tight. I dug my fingers into McDowell's features, going for the nose and the eyes, hoping to blind him.

We tottered at the top of the stairs, equally matched and motionless, each straining against the other for any advantage. It went on for a long time, just deep grunting and sweat and muscular tension. Almost like arm wrestling. I had never cared about winning before, had never really known who was the stronger man, but now I knew. Loner McDowell was a powerful animal, and he was probably going to win.

"Mr. McDowell?" Jerry, at the foot of the stairs. "You okay up there?"

I think we were both startled, but Loner reacted to the voice more than I did. His muscles relaxed for a fraction of a second.

Take him out, boy, Danny Bell whispered. *No mercy.* I slipped my right hand away from Loner's eyes and viciously slammed the palm upwards into his nose. I meant to kill him, but the blow wasn't solid enough to drive bone into

253

brain. I did feel some cartilage give and heard a grunt of agony. I hissed with satisfaction and struck again, shattering the nose completely. McDowell cried out and then we both lost our balance. I went backwards into the wall, and while sliding down I kicked hard at McDowell's chest with all of my waning strength. I called out, quickly: "Jerry, get out of the way!"

Loner McDowell tumbled down the stairs, all rolling thumps and grunts. I heard the piercing crack of shattering glass and the sound of a great deal of water sloshing around.

Silence followed.

"Jerry?"

"Yeah. Yeah."

I half walked, half slid down the staircase, straining to keep upright. Jerry lay at the foot of the stairs, holding his bandaged waist. I knelt beside him. The wound was bleeding again, but he'd be okay.

"Where did he go?"

"Over me, then over there." Jerry pointed.

Loner McDowell had rolled down the stairs, slammed into Jerry's body at about knee level, and then sailed over the boy and into the larger tank. His big body lay face down, head surrounded by flopping tropical fish. He seemed unconscious. His legs weren't moving. I checked the wound in Jerry's side more carefully. I examined my own cuts and abrasions and tried to catch my breath. I hoped McDowell was out cold, for I had no fight left in me. After a few long moments, I limped over and found him dying.

"Loner?"

McDowell had broken his neck. He was paralyzed. The fish were still flopping beside him, but the light went out of his widened eyes as I leaned down to say his name. He had drowned slowly, his face under only a few inches of water, just like Sandy Palmer.

I don't remember much right after that. Somehow Jerry and I got ourselves together. We limped to the doorway like a couple of concentration camp survivors.

Outside in the night, it was cooler. We plopped down on the steps. After a time, a pair of two-toned vehicles arrived. There were three state troopers in one car; Glen Bass was alone in the other. The red and blue twirling lights made the wooden porch flicker like a strobe. I sat next to Jerry, one arm around my friend, weary legs extended. The troopers grilled us for few moments and then went inside to view the bodies. Bass stood rigid, his thumbs hooked in his belt. He seemed embarrassed. He studied the dirt.

"Callahan, I owe you an apology," Bass said. "You see, the truth is that Sandy confided in me about there being a drug lab somewhere around Dry Wells. I thought that if she knew about that body you saw Friday night she'd get scared and shut up, so I tried to keep it a secret. I trusted you'd back me up."

"I did."

"I know, but then Sandy had also told me that someone big in drugs was coming to town," Bass said. "I knew your history, and wondered if it was you. She must have meant that friend of Loner's, this Manuel guy who got hit. Sorry, but for a little while there, I really thought you might be on the wrong side of all this."

"I understand, Sheriff. Hell, I showed up and people started dying. To be honest, I didn't trust you either."

"Mick?"

I looked up. Annie parked her car and ran across the dusty street, crying. She hugged me. "I heard it all on the

255

radio," she said. "Are you hurt bad, or anything?"

I shrugged. "I'll live."

Annie kissed me, feverishly. "Thank God," she said. I did not kiss her back. She looked hurt.

"Sheriff Bass?"

The sheriff cleared his throat. "Yeah, kid?"

"You might want to put some cuffs on this girl."

Annie laughed, nervously. "What did you say?"

"I said he should put the cuffs on you."

Annie got to her feet. Bass was by her side in a flash. He gripped her bare arms just above the elbows and held on tight. "What the fuck are you talking about?" Annie said. Her voice went thin and shrill. She struggled against the sheriff's grip, but he held her fast.

"A murder," I said.

"What murder?" Bass said. "I don't get it."

"Sheriff, you probably heard everything that went out live over the air or you wouldn't be here," I said. "Loner flat admitted to a couple of murders, but all he said about Sandy Palmer was that he beat her up and ran away."

"Oh, come on," Annie muttered. She struggled for a moment and then went limp. She looked scared.

Bass was catching on. "Go on. I'm listening."

"So Doc told us Saturday that he thought there was water in her lungs, that Sandy probably drowned. He said that somebody probably held her head under water, just to make sure."

"Well it wasn't *me*, for Christ's sake!" Annie shrieked. "That's ridiculous. I told you, I wasn't even there."

I got to my feet. I looked down at her, and my voice went cold. "So you told me. But when I first saw you in the diner on Saturday, the knees of your jeans and your blouse were soaking wet."

"So? I was cleaning up."

"But your mop was out on the porch, and it was bone dry. I think you got wet kneeling in the stream over Sandy Palmer's body, holding her head underwater. And last night you said something about Sandy wearing a dress with sunflowers. That told me you *had* been in the park that day, but you were lying to me."

"Pretty thin," Bass said. He loosened his grip.

"Wait," I said. "And then last night Annie asked me if I had accused Bobby Sewell of *drowning* Sandy. Sheriff, you and Doc and I were the only three people who knew drowning was probably the actual cause of death, not the beating. Doc said he wanted to wait for the coroner to be sure, so I never told anyone about that theory. Did you?"

"Nope," Bass said. "I sure didn't."

"It was you, Annie," I said, slowly and evenly. "Talking to McDowell confirmed it. You saw Loner and Sandy arguing. Saw him punch her and watched her fall. You waited for him to leave, and then you held her head under water to make sure she would never compete with you again."

Annie spat in my face. "I told you those two Palmers were worthless. I hated them both. She was a slut, Callahan. I saw her shaking her ass for you. She was still teasing every man in the park, and her carrying her own fucking brother's child."

I wiped my cheek. "So you knew about the baby, about Sandy and Will. That must have really hurt."

"*Hurt?* Hell, yes! And you didn't even remember you'd ever fucked me, once you eyeballed that horny little bitch. Listen to me, Callahan. She got what she deserved."

"I think you'd better stop talking now," Bass said. "You have the right to remain silent."

He went on with the Miranda warning while Annie grew even more desperate. "But I didn't kill her," she said frantically. "I just made damned sure Loner did, that's all."

"Yeah," Jerry said. "You go and tell yourself that."

"She was going to die anyway!"

Bass cuffed her. Annie's eyes were wide and wild. I shook my head, sadly. "I hope they'll let you see a shrink. You have very severe Borderline Personality Disorder, Annie. Maybe a judge will cut you some slack for that, I don't know."

"Sheriff," Annie said desperately, "I didn't really kill her."

"Sorry, but it sounds like Murder One to me," Bass said.

"The hell you say!" Annie screamed. "You know when I said I killed your baby, Callahan? That was a lie. Shit, there never was any baby, and you know why? Because you're not man enough to make one!"

"That's enough." Bass yanked up on the cuffs. Annie moaned and the blood left her face. The sheriff led her away. I sat down next to Jerry again. He tugged his cap down over the burn scar and rolled his eyes.

"Damn, Mick," he said in a raspy voice. "Yet another satisfied woman?"

"I sure can pick them, can't I?"

"Fuck you, Callahan!" Annie Wynn shrieked. Her features were now contorted and ugly with rage. "You're just a has-been. You'll always be a has-been."

"Get in the car, ma'am," Bass said politely. "And you'd best calm down before you make things worse. You're in a heap of trouble already."

"Let me go, goddamn it!"

"Oh, lady, shut up." He shoved Annie into the back seat of the patrol car. She started crying. Bass slammed the door and locked it. I reached into my pants pocket for some wrinkled dollar bills and gave them to Jerry.

"Kid, I've changed my mind. I don't want the job."

Twenty-Six

It was a long night. I ended up being questioned four different times by the state police. Bass had called them; he'd been listening to the show and immediately radioed for help when the trouble started. Racing back towards Dry Wells, he'd finally learned the identity of Manuel, the dead man we'd found in the alley, and also that the deaths of Sandy and Will were both murders. He learned that Lowell Palmer lay dead back at the ranch because I mentioned that fact on the air.

Still, Bass was in hot water for quite a while. The state people were not happy. When he asked me to keep quiet, he'd been trying to avoid alarming Sandy Palmer, who had just begun to open up to him about the existence of a drug ring. He wanted to break a big case all by himself. Things blew up in his face when Sandy died. And old Doc Langdon was just trying to help out a friend.

They found the kid called Mex. He was still alive, and was sentenced to prison for a very long time. He didn't get the needle because only Loner and Bobby Sewell seemed directly implicated in the homicides. One strange thing: Donny Boy and Frisco were not in the gully where I'd left them. How they got away remains a mystery, since they were both injured and on foot, but this is not a perfect world.

I came to believe that what finally sent Loner McDowell over the edge was a combination of amphetamine psychosis, the disappearance of his partner Manuel, and the financial

259

disaster that represented, plus exposure to the incest in the Palmer family. Of course, his huge ego needed a way to rationalize killing everyone and keeping the drug money anyway. He could handle Sandy having other lovers, perhaps even carrying a child, but not if it was by her own brother . . . or father. Loner did some hard time, remember. In prison the lowest form of life is the child molester, or "tree jumper." I think he convinced himself he had the right, even the obligation, to kill Lowell Palmer and his son . . . which then conveniently allowed him to take enough cash to get the mob off his back.

I gave Jerry substantial credit with the police. That seemed like the least I could do. My version had him fighting valiantly with Loner and then shoving him back into that fish tank, thus probably saving my life. He heard that story so often he came to believe it. "Hacker" Jerry became a legitimate celebrity in Nevada, something he'd always wanted. He enjoyed the attention he got from the local ladies, and took to showing off his wounds, both real and imaginary, after a beer or two. But he never stopped thinking about our little savior Mary, or wondering why she failed to contact us. She never did, though we were both all over the airwaves and she had Hal's 800 listing. Me, I just figured her for relapsing on drugs, perhaps an overdose. Sad thought, but it happens.

The last I heard, Annie Wynn was remanded into psychiatric custody for an evaluation, but I am convinced she's technically sane. My guess is that she will get several years to life for her part in the death of Sandy Palmer.

The press descended on Dry Wells from as far away as Salt Lake and Reno and stayed for several days. By the time I'd given half a dozen statements and interviews and finished talking to the grand jury, the television opportunity in

L.A. was dead and gone. Darin Young now refuses to take my calls, but you know what? I don't give a damn. Ironically, I'm now a celebrity again anyway. There will be other jobs.

I sent the following e-mail to Hal:

> Thanks for your help in a messy situation. I guess evil has failed to triumph, at least in this instance, and that it is still possible for one man to make a difference. I finally understand that this is what you have been trying to pound into my thick skull for the last couple of years.
>
> Have a wonderful trip, friend, and stay in touch.
>
> Mick
>
> P.S. And by the way, I've never had it so good.

Epilogue

Two Months Later

It is mid-summer now.

There is a small radio station, located on the campus of a community college near Los Angeles. The red brick building sits back among the weeds behind a tall chain-link fence. It is dark. There is one used car in the parking lot. The porch light is on, and surrounded by moths. A scruffy old gray cat is sprawled on the steps, waiting patiently for dinner.

Despite the lateness of the hour, callers are backed up and holding. The phone rings constantly. As a commercial break comes to a close, the host slips a pair of black headphones onto his head and leans forward into the microphone. He is calm, at ease, and in his element.

"You're listening to KWTF FM, broadcasting from Northridge, California." He chooses a caller at random. "Hello, you're on the air live with Mick Callahan. How can I can help you?"

Acknowledgements

Readers familiar with the high desert country of north-eastern Nevada know that although there is a town called Wells, there is no such city as *Dry* Wells; this despite the fact that a *Star* Valley, the mountains surrounding it and the highways mentioned as leading to it all exist roughly as described. I have taken enormous liberties with geography. The town of Dry Wells and its inhabitants are all figments of my imagination. So are all of the various characters and events described in *Memorial Day*.

Thanks to editor/authors Kealan-Patrick Burke and Joe Donnelly, also to my friend Mr. John Boylan and his wife Jill; likewise Angela Dorio, Joan Bellefontaine, Lynwood Spinks, Joni Evans and Andy McNicol. Additionally to my brother Dwight Siebert and my sister Marsha Desiderio for their photographs and memories of Wells, Nevada. My list must also include Dory Kramer, the great Ed Gorman, Pat Wallace, Mary P. Smith and Jon Helfers.

My beloved grandfather, Henry Hallowell Cazier (an inductee into the Cowboy Hall of Fame in Oklahoma City) had a cattle ranch operating near the town of Wells, in the specific area of Nevada mentioned in this novel. I was named after Harry Cazier, was born on his birthday and fully adored him. He and his family built their ranch in the late 19th century and ran it successfully until Harry's death in the 1960s. I remember the high desert country surrounding Wells as being heartbreakingly beautiful. The people I knew there were uniformly kind and generous, and the many summers I spent there were among the happiest of my life.

Author Bio

Harry Shannon has written for magazines (*Cemetery Dance*, *Horror Garage*, *Gothic.net*) and several anthologies (*Brimstone Turnpike*, *The Night Has Teeth*, *Family Plots*, and *The Fear Within*.) His debut collection has become a collector's item. His first novel, *Night of the Beast*, is available from Medium Rare Books.com. *Night of the Werewolf* will debut at Horrorfind 2003.